Nights

of the

Velvet

Nights
⤚ *of the* ⤙
Velvet

A Conditional Dream...

Deepak Ranjan

PARTRIDGE
A Penguin Random House Company

Print information available on the last page.

To order additional copies of this book, contact
Partridge India
000 800 10062 62
orders.india@partridgepublishing.com

www.partridgepublishing.com/india

DEDICATED TO

My Darling Anjali & Papa

To my friend, who likes me the way I am
Ishq ki madhosi mein jo raha hai
Kaise batae woh kaisa nasha hai
Dil ko apne kho kar bhi dekho
Dil ki lagi mein kuch alag hi mazaa hai...

Friendship – a relation, which transfigures unknown to known. Someday you may stuck with a person who is all wrong; But you never feel when everything becomes right for you. You don't want to fight or argue; you just let it go!

"Under the same sky…, under one umbrella,
sharing the same thought
Sharing the up and downs of life…,
growing n letting one to grow…
Smiling n making one to smile…,
is what a FRIEND does, unconditionally…
But if that friend is a girl, then…
Whether here also 'Terms N Conditions' apply?"

PROLOGUE

After retiring for some time, I walked towards the beach; it was early dawn. Early morning sunrise was awesome to look at; the sunlight was adding colours in the water, reflecting and glittering all over the surface. Peace prevailed all over the place. I switched ON my mobile to capture the beauty and account of missed-calls popped up from Rajesh, Sanya, Neha and all others. I felt like calling Sanya first.

Sanya picked up the call and started shouting loudly, 'What happened, why you have switched-off your mobile, I tried many times, but…

'Tell me, how is she now…' I enquired.

'She is fine, no need to worry. By the way where are you…?' she enquired.

'In my world…' I replied plainly.

'Don't lie me, I called your roommate Sahil late last night, he told me you were not in the room', Sanya told.

'Don't know exactly where I am…, but yaa I am sure that I am there in my world', I replied.

'Coming to office?'

'No…, sick leave…I'll apply sick leave…', I murmured.

'Will you please elaborate…? If you don't mind… what happened to both of you…' she demanded.

I took a deep breath, closed my eyes for a while; all the memories of the past flashed through my mind, some blurred with time and shock and some as real as the sand below my feet…

You never know…

When 'TIME PASS' becomes your 'PAST' time…

Few hour back I was a different person and now it was someone else standing in a different world. A world where no one recognized me; all alone I was trying to befriend with myself…

I could hear the surreal sound of the sea, where tides were playing on the surface of the tranquil water. It looked as if they were staring at me. I wanted to divert my mind, but my inner conscience, reflecting in the clean water, seemed to speak volumes of the past.

I felt as if, along with Sanya over the call, the atmosphere also questioned me…

How and what all happened to me…?

How can I be so attached to someone, especially a girl…?

How everything got initiated…?

I closed my eyes, and words started flowing out of my mouth, with all emotions…

<u>ONE</u>

11 AM, 14th NOV 2012.

I was in deep sleep, dreaming of some irrelevant scene like running in a forest, afraid of something; chasing a beautiful girl unconsciously bla bla!

It happens mostly when someone is sleeping in morning time, thoughts running and smashing in one's mind feel so lively, so real. I couldn't realize where I was; be in my dreams or in my bed. The pillow was half displaced from its original position, and was near my neck. The silver plated chain with "OM" sign, hanging from my neck to the side of the bed, was shining due to the sunrays falling through the window. The door was wide open so sufficient light was there in the room. The thick blanket was pulled over to my chest and the bed-sheet over the bed was partially wrinkled due to my frequent movement in different angles. The laptop was half-open and kept in one of the corner of the bed, from the last night.

I was in those deep random thoughts of early day time. Suddenly some voices started banging on my ear-drums. Those voices were so faded that I couldn't figure out what those were all about. Slowly, the voices became louder and seemed to be crashing all my dreams with a tone of anger. A strong vibe ran through all my body and I became fully conscious, I blabbered.

"Oh Shit! Again it is too late in the morning to get up. Last night I promised myself that I will not repeat it...", the clock was ticking 11:30 AM. Voices became crystal clear to me. My mom was scolding me, 'I told you thousand times but you keep on torturing me. Why don't you wake up by 8 AM? Your papa always leaves for office, watching you sleeping and for that I get scolding from him', while keeping the laptop in its place.

I got off the bed and started searching my toothbrush and paste. My eyes were down with full of guilt. My mom had lowered her voice and told, "Beta I know you are still waiting for the joining date but for God sake don't spoil your schedule and health. I have prepared Aloo-poha for your breakfast, but now it's almost lunch time. Why you don't listen to me...?"

I was mute but listening everything properly and realizing the mistake. I was hurting my Mom knowingly but helplessly. I decided that I would not repeat this again, anyhow.

After half an hour I came out of the bathroom. My mom was inside the kitchen. A usual kitchen noise had filled the entire home.

I stepped into my room, opened my cupboard and took out my favourite blue-superman T-Shirt and jeans. I rubbed lotion cream over my body parts and combed my hair properly.

Finally with the 'Raja-Beta' looks, moved towards the kitchen as I was both hungry and curious about the dishes cooked. Mom was heating Allo-poha and preparing Badam Milk for me. I hugged her from her back. She smiled and said, 'you go to the drawing room, I will bring breakfast there.

By now love and pamper has taken over annoyance and anger. It is so true and real about all Moms that all mothers inherit the property from the same class "Motherhood", that they can never hold anger for long on their child. All mothers are blessed with this divine virtue, which is just priceless!

I was bit relaxed now when I stepped into the drawing room. I switched on the TV and sat on the sofa with TV remote in my hand. A video song was playing from the movie 'Tare Zameen Par', 'Main Kabhi batlata nahi… Par andhere se darta hu mein maa…'

Such a heart-touching song was this, so coherent to this moment. Really, I was not feeling myself different from the actor in that song 'Darsheel'.

I took out my mobile; saw four missed call and two SMS notifications. Missed call from my childhood friend Dev and one SMS from the customer care about prepaid offers. Sometime I feel so special that customer care people never miss a single day for sending offers and plan details to me…LOL!

But SMS from 'Dev' was really important and kind of a Boy's 'Gentle' reminder. Actually for that day we planned to go to our school. We really missed our school during graduation days and we all wanted to cherish our childhood memories. I was supposed to join them near my school by 11:00 am sharp, but couldn't make it because of my idiocy.

Before I could called back to Dev, suddenly door-bell rang. My mom yelled as TV volume was quite high, 'Open the door Sid'.

I got off the sofa and ran towards the door, 'Hey Siddharth! Dev here, Open the door'. I opened the door and asked him to come in. He was so furious with the eye widening expressions and curls over the forehead. I was so embarrassed that, I avoided eye contact with him.

Before he could have started scolding me, my saviour stepped into the drawing room. It was my mother, 'Kaun hai Beta; Oh Hey Dev! How are you? After a long time you came to our home… How are your parents?'

This series of greeting statements had diverted Dev, his anger and fury was diminished. All credit goes to my Mom. She unknowingly saved my ass.

"I am fine aunty! Everyone at my home is fine. My mom asked about you several times. Please visit our home whenever you find some time", Dev replied.

I was a bit relaxed but cautious as dark shadows of scolding had not completely vanished. My mom said, 'you two sit, I will bring the breakfast….' And she left for the kitchen.

Dev started, 'Do you have any idea how careless you are! You call yourself as "carefree-bird", but actually you have become a careless person. You have lost the basic social manners'.

I was brought down to normal as Dev was right with his argument. He was telling me all this in a low-tone and caring attitude. Dev was quite friendly by nature and also has an open-heart. He had always shown interest in my writings. I always try my best to help out my friends when they need me; and as I tried to do the same with him; his affection and care for me grew stronger. Sometimes I found him to do impressive stuffs like a very experienced and mature person; while other times he behaved like a complete fool. But the best thing about him was that he had no ego – if he was wrong, he would readily apologize without hesitation; which never made me remain mad at him for long! There have been incidents, which were enough evidence to prove that his love and care for me was truly genuine.

I had no option but to apologize.

"We have planned two-weeks ago for this 14ᵗʰ November, Children's Day to go to our school. We planned to meet old teachers and re-live those days again and yet you are spoiling this… And also Gayatri ma'am will be waiting for us… After school, we have to go to her house… It's Ok… It's not too late now; Avinandan and Nitesh will be waiting for us. Go to your room, change your dress and come back immediately".

Meanwhile my mom stepped in with a tray having two bowls of "Aloo-poha" and two glasses of Badam milk. Mom asked me and Dev to have breakfast and left towards the kitchen to finish other stuffs.

I took my black jacket, my DSLR and came out of my room, as rest was fine with the dress. We both finished the breakfast soon. I tied my shoes and said to mom, 'I am going to my school with Dev and other friends'. A usual response came from her side, 'OK, but come back soon… Don't make it late night and drive carefully'.

I spoke, "don't worry Mamma, Ok Bye!" and we both left.

When we reached in front of the school, we saw Nitesh standing there near the gate. The gate was closed and the gatekeeper was not allowing us to enter inside, as he must be strictly instructed not to allow any strangers and we were strangers for him. Then we thought of our wild old days plan... We then made our way through the backside broken boundary of the school, which was attached to the old banyan tree.

There we saw the stamp of time passed after passing from this alma mater, in the form of the green fungus on the school boundary; which was built in our time. The fungus made it a bit slippery, making hard to climb.

The one who was missing amongst us was Avinandan. Earlier my thought was that he was a self-centred guy. We could not stand each other, but eventually we became best of friends! What I understood with time, is that instead of finding out faults in others, we should try to inculcate the positive attitudes of the other person – as there is a saying that "No man in this world can proclaim himself to be perfect". With time, I found him to be a very ethical guy who excelled in academies as well. He was the kind of person who had the power to motivate others to take risks and make the person do things out of box.

I was expecting him with us, too. But he denied to come in the last moment, giving a stupid excuse that, "if anyone asks what are you doing, what should I reply, jobless... roaming without any destination...!"

We three were standing at a corner of the campus. Students were in their white uniform, in a queue, collecting sweets near the old banyan tree, where we used to play holding the strong hanging roots. Some old teachers of our time, were replaced by the new ones. They were helping in distributing sweets. I saw a smile in the face of the distributor, when each time she was putting the sweet on the hand of a student. Peon and ayahs were also engaged in packing the same for the staffs. In the background, children's day music was playing on the loud speaker, "Nanhe munne bachche teri muthi mein kya hain… muththi mein hai taqdeer hamari…". I was almost lost in my thoughts, just then I heard someone calling me, "Are Siddharth…!". We turned back to check, saw our class teacher Miss Ranjita Ratha standing in front of us, with a smile on her face. We three touched her feet, as a sign of respect to the legend of our schooldays. 'Ma'am Still you remember me…?' was the first question shot from my side. 'How can I forget the naughty child in you…? Who argued with me, whose name was always there on the top in the punishment list?' came as her reply.

Then she talked with Dev and Nitesh, asking what they were doing now. She talked with us for a while; a new staff member came and asked her something. She asked us to collect the sweets packets. Then she moved, talking with her perhaps it was about us, she was telling her that we were the ex-students of the school. With time the queue vanished. All students moved towards the school gate, and some towards the cycle stand to take the vehicles to their home. We were standing in front of the banyan tree, where those ayahs were packing the sweets. An old lady teacher with a square-shaped thick specs, was standing and guiding them. Dev greeted, "Suddha ma'am namaskar…". The old lady was surprised after hearing from him, her name. The thing is that she might have forgotten, but when she heard someone taking her name, she was trying to recall perhaps, who we were…!

'Do you remember Siddharth, who used to copy your signature and sign his homework copy on his own', Nitesh quipped.

'One day, we were disturbing the class, and you asked us to lean down in the hot sun. You came the class to check in the afternoon, to find us vanished from the place. Already we had crossed the boundaries of the school, climbing the old banyan tree's hanging root', Dev added.

She was trying to recall those incidents; her glasses along with her eyes were moving from down to up, covering our feet to head. She was trying to recall and finally she said, '2004 Batch pass outs…!'

"Yaa… this was the one more identity of ours, left out. In the history of the school, we will be remembered as the 2004 Batch pass outs…", I whispered to myself. She was our all-rounder teacher, sometimes she took our Odia class, sometimes drawing, HPER, GK, MED, etc… All the time, we prayed God to have the teacher as our invigilator, as wherever and whichever classroom she entered, luck followed in. She used to enter holding the exam papers and questions with a confidence that definitely the class will pass the examination, without any second thought.

A small smile came on her face, recognising us as the ex-student of the school. We greeted her, and she asked about us. We followed her to the staff room. She introduced us as the ex-students of the school, to the new staff. Some more old teachers, were also able to recognise us. No longer, we felt there, as strangers. The atmosphere was quite friendly and the moment was worth-living and worth capturing in my DSLR that I carried with me.

We stepped out of the school. Life inside the boundaries of that building was something different eight years back…, it was something special… We bid goodbye to Nitesh and moved.

On our way to Gayatri madam's house on Dev's bike, I was sitting pillion and we were discussing something important. As he tried to pay attention to what I was saying, suddenly the previous accident incident came flashing in my mind. That day also, we both were discussing and his mind got diverted and we both met with an accident. At that moment, I thought, I was going to breathe my last – I felt death so close to me. We both fell off his bike and were about to be crushed under the truck. I had closed…… He was bleeding profusely from his shoulder, and my hands were soaked in blood too. Though the accident happened due to carelessness for which I was to be held equally responsible, even in that situation, he apologized to me for the accident – I was touched, even though he was the one who was badly hurt and bled more… This, and a few other instances made us come closer to each other. I wished not to repeat the same so I turned silent till the time we reached her house. We parked the bike and stepped up to the first floor to meet her.

We found her with open arms and a cute smile standing near the door of her room, to welcome us…, 'Hello my Dear Children…How are you…?'

We were so thankful to see her love and affection for us that we stayed at her place for couple of hours. She prepared food for us, and then she showed her album, comprising old collection of school snaps. She was the one, who used to distribute sweets and snacks on her birthday to the whole school. She was the teacher who loved the children as her own. When we were about to leave, she advised us, 'If you have something in your heart to achieve, go for it... I am with you all. Fulfil your dreams, and once your dream comes true and you all are successful think about us...' which again made me to include her in the generation's updated teachers, who respect and understand the next generation. We then captured the moments in our camera, and left the place.

He stopped his bike through half-way, 'abe ruk ped mein paani dena aur apna pipe unload karna hai, nahi to phaatega mera...'(wait...! let's unload our pipes and give some water to the trees)

I joined him near the tree, attached to the wall and unloaded my pipe too.

'Abe tera pipe bahut slow hai, pressure nahi hai kya... Dekh mera pipe kitna tez hai be....'

Actually we used to compete while doing susu(urinating) also. We used to check whose susu stream goes farther, like we used to see in school, who runs faster in the race. We used to compete most of the times, may it be while riding a cycle or bike, may it be while exploring something crazy or number of times masturbating in a month, also while scoring marks in exams. The only competition that I lagged in was of having a girlfriend and his habit of consuming alcohol.

The day was over, and I felt really good and fresh when I shared the same with my mom and sister, in my laptop. My dad had already come from office by that time. He and my mom, added some more memories like – how I hesitated to enter the school, without a pack of joker chocolate I won't enter, tiffin should vary – sometimes little heart biscuits or ANYTIME Elaichi or Nice, uniform should be cleaned else no school and some other incidents too. We had our dinner and just then my dad once again enquired about the joining letter of the company that I was offered in the campus selection.

And as usual I replied, "till now no updates on the joining date…".

"Better you should try in some other companies, or you take some crash course which will be helpful to you… Wasting time unnecessarily won't help…", goes on like this the advice from him along with some comparisons and examples of his friend's daughter and son doing well and been established somewhere. All these were nothing new and I used to listen this at a regular interval from him.

He would keep on reminding me, but I never wanted to pressurize myself thinking about the career all the time, sometimes I felt doing the things in my way… The daily routine was like wake up late, eat breakfast followed by lunch, check your gmail for joining updates, roam with some of your friends, and before dad enter the home, come back and sit in front of the desktop, opening some presentations that were provided by the company as a common pre-training, irrespective of your domain. This continued for the rest three months, till the time I got the joining date to be March 11th 2013.

TWO

March 2013.

Bangalore, the fourth largest metropolitan area, is famous for the developed IT companies across the city. A number of people reach here daily with a hope to see their dreams come true. Even I came here to experience something like that. It took me a couple of weeks to explore the life style of the city. Everything was quite new to me. I don't even knew from where can I get a toothbrush or soap, then with time I get to know there are shopping malls, where everything is available, starting from toothbrush to groceries. General grocery stores were rarely seen.

None of my college friends were there to stay with me. I was suddenly burdened with a lot of tensions and responsibilities. Right from finding a place to stay till joining the company and of course clearing the exams – I knew my journey was not going to be smooth.

My life had become a struggle – every day I had to battle for maintaining 9.5 hours in office (training hours) and tolerate the nonsense in the place I was living in. I shared room with Sumit and Rajesh. Rajesh used slangs so frequently to convey himself, as if that was the only language, he had expertise on. Sumit was a guy who used his laptop, being placed upside down by its screen. When I saw it first time, I questioned myself 'If there was something wrong with that guy or with the Lappy?

I leaned over to look at the screen to figure out what exactly he was doing? But what I found out was quite disturbing. I expected some sort of valuable work being done there by putting a Lappy at so much stress, upside down. But he was on Facebook. So without a hesitation and without wasting one more second, a token of appreciation came out of irritation and I couldn't help myself saying, 'WTF...'.

Both differed a lot in character but shared similarities when it came to adjustment. I was the only odd one out, as this was my first experience of being away from the confines of my home. I had issues with the facilities that were provided in the PG, with the lifestyle of my roommates – they stayed up late in the night, while I was habitual of retiring early to bed. As they were two, and I was the only odd one out, I could not voice my issues. Only Rajesh sympathized with me – he tried his best to make me feel comfortable in his own ways. For me only, he used to study late night sitting on the staircase outside the room, so that I can sleep well, turning off the lights.

The training locations were different for all of us – It was Electronic City (EC) for Sumit distanced 13 kms from our PG, Rajesh's was near to our PG while mine was at Adugodi which was approximately 4 kms. The only time we got to interact with each other was the time each occupied the washroom in the morning or fighting for the TV in the evening after we returned.

So obviously, Rajesh was the last one to enter to the bathroom. Logically the first one should have been Sumit followed by me but that wasn't the case always. Because, Sumit wont wake up unless he has an alarm ringing into his ears. Literally, I had Zero months of internship outside of my home ever since I was born, so it was very uneasy in my part to cope with my roommates. Apart from all Rajesh was on an "ignore whatsoever mode", so a conflict was inevitable. One day I missed my bus and was late for the training. For which I had to take an Auto on share with two of my female colleagues Rupali and Supriya - which of course made me very uncomfortable. Inside I was fuming and it showed in my reactions – leading the tip of the iceberg of our friendship from breaking to create a chain of avalanche of misunderstanding, anger and bitterness to break the entire Glacier of our relationship.

With wrath, I was just waiting for the perfect spark that would fuel my emotions and my super lazy roomies were just about to provide me the golden opportunity. They woke up late, so I seized the opportunity and locked myself in the washroom for longer than usual…

Generally, when someone took longer time than usual, we teased him, asking him about the "feel-good" activity that he was indulged in; what made him look tired after he stepped out, whom was he fantasizing, and so on. I had to face the same that day. Rajesh started off, leaving no opportunity to talk all shit about me. The moment I stepped out of the wet floor of the washroom, wrapping the towel in my waist, along with Dettol skincare soap in my hand, I replied, "I will take as much time as I want. If you were to occupy the bathroom henceforth, you would have to wake up early before me".

"Please Sid, Don't be like this. Do come out soon. I'll have to go a long distance to EC which will take much time and I'll miss the 8.10 AM bus from Silkboard, and if I get late, I wouldn't make it to the Office in time by 8.45 AM…!" Sumit said in a Concerned plus irritated manner, while changing his grey colour flimsy towel.

"I'll come out when I am done, and you are basically no body to guide or instruct me about what to do and what not to" I replied carelessly. We had a few arguments and finally Sumit was about to occupy the washroom. Next one was Rajesh – sitting in his bed, and waiting for an opportunity to speak. My last statement to Sumit was -

"Don't bug my head, if you want to use the bathroom, sleep in time and wake up early, have your bath early and go to the training in time. So that you won't be late neither some motherfucker will be" I said harshly and quickly.

"Maa ki Aankh! Is that me? You inferring to me, Sid", Rajesh asked me.

"It's a generalized statement, anybody who is getting late here, it's for him", I replied while searching for my formals in the wardrobe.

"Well guess what; since you would not warn to yourself and you already did that to Sumit about getting late, I believe the word suggest none other than me the only remaining so called "mother.....", isn't it?" furiously he asked me.

"Don't go by my words, just try to comprehend what I want to say" I replied a little softly, trying to eschew a perfect class of intense wrangle.

He had an old reputation of winning almost all logical and illogical arguments with his friends since his school days. So, repeatedly he asked me the same -

"Well I only understand what I hear, and this time also I'll understand what you said and what you just said was, "So that you won't be late neither some else motherfucker will be". Kindly help me to discern besides Sumit who else is present here who you could have inferred as Mother... lover"?

Sumit was there standing right outside the attached bathroom listening to our conversation. Rajesh looked at him and shouted,

"And by the way, what are you looking for? You were the one getting late for the Training and now listening to our conversation as if it matters the most to you. Don't forget, I am in the queue after you, so be done with your work there ASAP. I don't want to be late just because you guys had some fucking problem last day and today someone, mind my words 'not an ass' wants to bring it back on others who have not suffered the same".

Sumit went inside the bathroom and locked the door without a word. I explained Rajesh hence after the entire scenario of the previous day, feeling that he would understand me. As usual, he likes giving suggestion and lectures as our grandparents do. So, was the situation, he replied me –"whatever happened was unfortunate but, this is not how we deal with things. I have been to hostels all my life and all I know is that, you will have to adjust". Then he made me listen to his long and well scripted track record of coping with friends and situation. But I was not in a mood to listen, I replied back saying,

"Well, I don't adjust with anything. I don't give a shit to anything. Either, you guys be ready and prepared on mentioned time or I'll have to repeat what I just did today. I can't always adjust with everything.

Firstly, I'll wake up early but will wait until the room is available, why?

Secondly, I do not like the disgusting food they are providing here as "Breakfast".

Thirdly, May be you don't know but I never had breakfast here in PG, because I just don't like the food in here, and how the hell am I supposed to have breakfast even there at training location if I am late and I certainly can't concentrate on training if I am not full on my stomach. So screw you and screw all, whoever tries to disrupt my regular scheduled and cause trouble to me".

"Excuse me Sid, Why the hell I would suffer for the childish and nonsense activities of you guys. I too don't give a shit about what you guys are up to but I don't like to be late either just because he is careless and you are childish", Rajesh replied.

It was not a pleasant day. By the end of that argument, nobody was ecstatic with each other. Everybody went to the Training without discussing about it further.

I walked to the nearby stop. As usual, people had already started running behind the crowded bus to catch one.

Bus started moving. I was looking outside the window. It feels irritating to see the Bangalore streets with heavy traffic & continuously moving vehicles.

After some time conductor came to me & asked about the tickets, "22 bucks".

I gave him 25 rupees. Instead of returning me remaining 3 rupees, he wrote the amount in the backside of the ticket & moved towards other passengers.

My estimated journey time was around 30 minutes. So, I turned back to my own day-dreamy thoughts. A bunch of plans & ideas were continuously jumbling inside my head. It seemed like they were too puzzled that even solutions to them would create a puzzle itself….Uff!. It is very true that whenever someone is alone, mostly quality ideas take birth.

Time passed by; I became cautious of my destination. The bus conductor passed by me, I showed him the ticket with the restful amount.

"*@$%!! II@*&%#$@##^^%$……………"

"Wohho…. What was that!", I said to myself. He continued to speak in his local language in a very disrespectful manner.

I replied, "I don't understand what are you saying?" For a moment I thought did I commit some crime just now? I had only asked about the remaining amount for the ticket and he was scolding like I was a beggar asking for conductor's personal money. After a long blabbering, he showed me two fingers and said, "2 bucks?"

I figured it out that if I give him 2 rupee he would return me 5 rupees, as restful amount was 3 rupee. I replied, "No, I don't have."

He was pretending that he does not have change. However, a clear & loud sound of coins was coming from his moneybag. Finally, he settled my ticket amount by returning me the changes. However, indeed I had a bitter experience.

In Bangalore, mostly bus conductor esp. BMTC one follow some common practices

First: Bus conductor can understand & speak in Hindi well but predominantly they never involve in Hindi conversation with passengers.

Second: If somebody asks for the remaining amount of his ticket fare; reply him so venomously that he can never dare to do the same.

and Third: It is never bad to earn something beyond the salary limits

This is a common experience of a common man in this city.

I reached the training centre. Stepping towards the lift, I saw some girls waiting for the lift to open-up. The doors expanded all of a sudden, 3-4 girls and me entered inside. The elevator's door was closed and once again expanded automatically; perhaps someone pressed the call button. We were on the same ground floor. All of a sudden, my eyes were wide open to see the person in front of me.

A girl was standing in front of the lift to get inside. No one among us was ready to give some space for her to get in. The partial-brown eyes, perfectly shaped eyeliner and eyebrows, stylish brown hair, a light pink colored lip balm placed on her lip, gave a contrasting beauty to her look. She was wearing a pink colored salwar suit, with pink colored sandals. What I can say is – in ethnic wear, she was looking not less than a fairy. My eyes didn't even blink for once, I felt as if I was dreaming and all of a sudden, she vanished from my view as the lift door got closed automatically.

<u>THREE</u>

I signed the attendance register, placed just outside of the training room and stepped inside. It was a huge room with more than 40 chairs placed row by row. My domain of expertise, unfortunately, had a greater count of girls than boys. Almost all rows were covered with girls and a few back seats were covered by some guys, those who belonged to the state. Before taking a random seat, every time I had to think where should I sit?

The situation was like all were strangers and you had to take the crash course mandatorily, without any choice of bunking it. Everyone was busy in their activities, gossiping and making friends with new people. I tried to engage myself – opening my notebooks and materials – going through it. Just then the trainer entered with a small introduction of herself – Hello everyone; this is Gulabi… your fluency trainer. When I saw her, I couldn't believe that the fairy-look girl who missed the lift few minutes back was standing in the room as a trainer.

As a formality, when a new trainer entered, we were asked to give the introduction and so was the case this time also. All trainees once again got a chance to remember the batch mates' name. Guys were interested to know the names and hobbies of girls in the batch, but I was eagerly waiting when the introduction will get over…

Within a couple of minutes, everyone was done with the introduction. Now it was the turn of "fairy" to give her proper introduction, so she started in her sweet voice…

I am sure all we boys were looking forward to listen – whether she was still single…

But unfortunately that was not the case. She added to her intro that she had been working in the organization as guest trainer for last five years and last year she got married to one of our senior manager Vishal.

Now everyone, especially boys remained silent for a couple of minute, since she had indirectly cleared everyone that – there was no chance.

She started noting down the pre-planned assignments in the white board, using a black coloured marker. Frequently and sweetly she was speaking in front of the class.

Hardly, I could concentrate on her words, and I believe so was the case with most of the guys. Even if she scolded, the sweetness in her voice would still inspire you to take the things in a positive sense. The whole day passed in doing certain tasks assigned by the trainer.

We three roomies returned in the evening. There was a sense of bitterness among us. Nobody preferred to talk to the other person. But as usual, Rajesh was good at making up with friends. So he felt like, it's a challenge for him to fix the problem we were having. Myself sitting in the right and Sumit in left corner, near the wall. The middle monkey was none other than, Rajesh.

"How was your training today?" Rajesh asked Sumit.

"It was good", he replied without any emotion.

"So, did you make it in time?" Rajesh asked further.

"Nope" the reply came straight.

He was very clever, he was talking to Sumit, at the same time, keeping an eye on me – he knew that I was listening to their conversation. He then repeated my dialogue –

"Sleep in time and wake up early, have your bath early and go to the training in time. So that neither you nor some "motherf****r" will be late".

That made me laugh. I looked at him and smiled. Then, he had to go further so he thought about some more points of discussion which he could have carried out, points with similar interest and bingo he found it, IPL. So he asked Sumit-

"Hey, Today there is a match between RCB and Mumbai Indians. I think it has already been started. Would you like to watch it?"

"Yes yes why not? I wanted to watch Gayle playing. Even I was planning to watch it live you know?", Sumit replied with interest.

And then they switched on the TV and started watching IPL in high volume. Watching in high volume gives you a stadium type sensation, a feeling as if watching it live. But it irritates the person, who is not watching, doing some other things. This thing happened to me and I reacted also as I was studying. This time, Rajesh asked to reduce the volume to avoid another conflict of interest. Sumit did that immediately.

Everyone was taking things easy. By the end of the day everything was at least looking quite ok.

Coming back to the training, I realized, I had to be friend with all, including girls, at least I had to maintain a formal relationship with them.

There are a lot of points that will help you to understand the reason behind my perception of the inability of guys and girls not being close friend…

- Understanding differs a lot; guys have a broader point of view.
- Want a lot of care and attention towards them, which generally guys lack in. Girls care about each and every small thing but a guy fails to do, for which a girl blame the guy.
- Clever and know how to tackle the situation smartly. As they have a good memory, they relate the situation nicely with the old ones and make you feel guilty.
- Their weakness is crying, they cry and make you feel guilty all the time.

I have seen most of my friends and their relationship status with their girlfriends. Initially, everything seems good and interesting, but as days pass by and you get to know each other better, then your life will no longer be a "bed of roses" anymore. It will all start with small fights for trivial issues, which will eventually become huge and serious and finally both of them will get so mad at each other that their cute love story will end up with a stupid "Break Up".

Subsequently, if you witness life in an extensive way, don't get attached to a girl as it will ever hurt you once they leave you alone.

This may not always be true; exceptions are always there, as we also believe – behind every successful man, there is a woman. Their love, affection and care for their guy are what makes a man successful.

However, that was the first time, where I found myself amidst so many girls. I felt uncomfortable – but I was left with little choice. When you find someone who hails from your hometown and speaks same language, you automatically get inclined to speak to them over others; even if they are girls. Among them, the most talkative girl was Neha. All the time, she used to enter the training room with three security guards Rupali, Supriya, Rosaline; her three close friends. If out of the four members; two came earlier, then first two rows were booked completely for their friends. Even being seated in the first row, Rupali had a habit of sleeping over her bag. She was caught by our trainer quite a many times for sleeping inside the class, but still she didn't hesitate to dream something big, even bigger than the classroom. Our trainer used to shout, 'someone is sleeping in classroom, guess…' Everyone would become serious and start looking to each other's left and right side to check who was the victim. But every time, she was the one. According to the trainer she was the one, who will be awarded as the best trainee of the batch. Though she slept in the classes, but she was doing well in studies and exams as the bonding between these girls was quite strong. Rosaline and Supriya used to maintain notes, and were quite studious. Rosaline was my classmate in my college, so from college I knew that she was sincere in her work. Neha had mixed attributes, good in studies, and other activities as well. They helped each other to get rid of all the difficulties.

Apart from that, Neha was elected as the Class Representative of our batch. She used to talk with each and every one. I saw her initiating talk with everyone; she was completely opposite to me in all sense. I got first impression of her as an over-smart, ultra - modern girl who liked to do friendship with everyone, make a remarkable presence in everyone's life. She used to collect contact numbers, mail ids of each trainee and if any information, issue is there; used to share with all. This showed her leadership qualities, which I lacked in. I talked with her hardly, as the only thing that bothered me was she was a girl.

The situation became worse, in the last phase of training, when the total count of students got divided into groups of two members each. Here, I was grouped with a Tamil girl, named Hrisha. She was very tall, brown in color, and was simple in look, so when the trainer declared the groups, everyone started clapping and making fun of me, as if I was getting engaged with her. Really pathetic!

Slowly I tried creating space for myself in such an atmosphere – but my partner was a bit foolish – She wanted me to allow her doing the tasks, even if she failed to complete the tasks in time. When all other groups used to submit the tasks in proper time, my group was the one left behind all the time. What I felt was that she knew the things, but she was not confident enough to complete the task in proper time.

Every other person sitting behind, used to tease the two characters sitting in the front bench and fighting everyday for small things like –

Hrisha: hey allow me to do yaar…

'Don't touch the mouse without my permission…' out of irritation, comes out from me.

Hrisha: Hey I'm a girl yaar, u can't be that much rude… I'll complain against you…

'Ok fine do it… if within 30 minutes you are not completing means, next time you won't ask me to allow you to do the task…'.

Another Tamil guy MMS used to put his ear on our matters: hey maachi, what's up…?

I used to think "what is the meaning of "maachi", its mosquito in our language, and why is he calling everyone that same thing…, is it like he feels he is the superior one in the whole batch and all others were mosquitoes in front of him?"

'Nothing yaar, just struggling to do….' casually I replied.

That guy gave a smile and told something in hindi, which Hrisha couldn't understand.

MMS – ladki to tumpe marti hai yaar, uski feelings ke saath mat khelo… woh bahut achi hai

Don't know whether this was his complement or satire, but hardly it mattered to me.

'What is this yaar, you are my partner, you should cooperate with me… everyone is making fun of us…' she told in a soft voice.

'Go to hell yaar, either do it else allow me to do… don't bug my head…' I replied.

Hrisha turned back when she felt like conveying something to her friend Geetha, so she did.

Hrisha – Gita akaa paaru entha arivillatha man enkitta ippaddi nadanthukuran, ennakku matthum sakti eruntha, entha man ha class la eruntha tukki potturuvean.

(See… how this idiot is behaving with me if I had power, I would have thrown him out of the class…)

They both talked in their regional language which I could not understand, but their facial expressions gave me a glimpse of non-sense, they were talking about me. When I asked Gita, she smiled and replied, 'nothing she is telling you are damn helping her a lot…..& she also wants to help you..!'.

Both of us fought, smiled but at the end, she would allow me to do the task, as there was a certain deadline to complete the job. Now given a very short interval of time, it was not possible in my part to complete, and the only person, who could save me from this scenario was none other than the class representative Neha; most of the time she helped me to complete the task in time. Gradually, her helping nature forced me to draw a positive impression on her, in my mind. Along with her, I was exposed to the three security guards as well.

I felt a sense of awkwardness, when Rupali and her group, used to talk idiocy about their figure, shape and size. I used to listen, but I had to keep my mouth shut as I was the only guy amidst all the girls. They used to talk about their personal matters among themselves, about the brand of inners, that they wear, and about certain stupid things that guys should not hear.

I was trying to manage a lot, but I was still hesitant and uncomfortable. The only thing I was trying to do was to act and behave as if everything was normal around me.

This continued for three long months until my training got over. In the last day of training, we prepared colorful Thanks Greeting cards for our team mates, wishing them a great achievement in the coming years. We learned this from our fairy trainer Gulabi. She was the one who taught us to be thankful to people, for supporting and helping you all these days. I was confused whom to give – Thanks note, just then I received one from Neha, now it was obvious that I had to give one to her. Next I got a couple of thanks notes from Rosaline, followed by Supriya, Rupali, Hrisha, and others. We wished good luck to everyone, and bid goodbye for the day.

I had experienced both enjoyable and terrible moments during these months. Among my friends who were in my training, Neha was different from others – she helped me out whenever I needed…

Training days were passing by and we roomies hardly had any time to spare for each other. Weekend was the only time, to be yourself, to sit silently and let your thoughts wander, and to be with my roomies, roaming and exploring the new world around us.

There were a lot of good and bad moments with Rajesh and my other roomies also.

Rajesh used to get some snacks for me after office hours; and sometimes he would ask me to get something for him. If someone asks the other person to get something, it implies that the person is trying to get close to the other; hence the person exercises his rights on the other without any hesitation. He is unique and stupid. I am innocent and conservative. But don't know how, everything went fine with passing time. Initially, we fought a lot over trivial issues like watching different programs at the same time, for the type of food served and several others. With time I felt he could be my good friend. Whenever he fell sick, I used to get worried and took care of him, tending to his needs; as if he was my little brother. I used to call him "Chhua"(small child). Even if he refused to take food, I ignored him and forcibly made him eat, even if in small quantities. We would fight for our share of the eggs that were broken or not properly boiled; for the mango pieces on the lunch table. All these instances made us come closer. We spent a lot of time together, roaming in Bangalore streets – from UB City mall to Bangalore palace and Adlabs.

We were naughty in several instances too. We disobeyed the security rules at Bangalore palace at secured zones; where we took snaps and videos. We even abused the security guard by hurling slangs at him. One of those idiots once tagged me in facebook, on the chest of a girl who was on the background of our picture that we had taken in KFC, Forum Mall. We also discovered that Rajesh and I shared similar interests in story writing and picture editing. We discussed a lot about our interests and kept pulling each other's legs every now and then.

Everything was fine till the time Rajesh left us for his project in Mumbai. It was the time, when our training got over. I was about to fly to my home town after 3 long months. Suddenly he had to leave and that too – the same day.

Neha did my flight ticket, and I had to leave my place before 9 AM, as the flight time was around 1 pm and it takes around 2 hours to reach the airport from my place. As per our planning, I had to join Neha at 8:30 in the morning. She asked me to help her carry some of her belongings, and I gave my word on it. However, just the day before I was supposed to meet her, I came to know about Rajesh moving to Mumbai on that particular Saturday. I felt very bad when I heard that Rajesh would be leaving me. I was not in a mood to leave him, as already he had cemented his place in my life, as a little brother. Rajesh's flight time was at 3 pm, but he wanted to spend time with me, so before the night he planned to join me in the morning itself. He planned to come with me to the airport from morning and wait there till 3pm. As it was the last time, we would have been together. This was the situation, which was not in my control. I was in a dilemma, unable to decide to prioritise between Neha and Rajesh. I wanted to handle the situation efficiently – but in the end, I messed it up all.

The night before he was about to leave for Mumbai, I was upset and so were my roommates – yet we refrained from talking about his departure the next morning as it would make us emotional. I was constantly getting calls from Neha, as we both had to fly to our hometown the same day. Our flight's departure was 90 minutes prior to that of Rajesh, to Mumbai. Neha told me that - she wished to go to Airport with me. I looked at Rajesh; he was not well, and was upset too, and Sumit tried to look out for buses to the airport.

It was Saturday morning, 22nd June 2013. While we left the PG with a heavy heart, I called Neha but she didn't answer. We got an auto at 8:30 am, and then tried reaching her once again, but my calls went unanswered yet again. Even the auto-driver was getting impatient and wanted us to leave – so we were left with little choice, but to leave for the bus stop. Sumit and I carried the bags for Rajesh as he was still unwell. The auto left past Neha's PG, and as ill luck would have it, she called me then. I told her that I had already left for the bus stop. She became furious and started yelling at me, not in a mood to listen. Even after we reached the bus stop and were waiting for her, she was still busy in getting dressed up. We were in a fix – we could not decide whether to wait for her until she arrived or leave for the airport. Finally, I made up my mind and called her. "Come to the bus stop, we all are waiting for you", I said. She bluntly refused on my face.

I looked at Rajesh standing with one of his bag and said, "Don't worry, let's take the bus to the airport. Some other girl will accompany Neha, so it won't be a problem. Besides, she will understand that we left early as you were sick". Finally after waiting for long, we left for the airport without her. After sometime she called me. "Where are you?". I replied, "I was waiting for you for long, but you didn't turn up, so we left". All hell broke loose after that. She screamed at me over the phone, saying "you made me cry, someday God will make you cry too".

We reached the Airport and while we were sitting there, Rajesh recalled reminiscence all the funny and memorable incidents that we had come across. Midnight hangout at the Juice center near our PG was one of them. We told Rajesh not to forget us and stay in touch.

He assured us that those valuable moments spent together, will never be forgotten. We knew - we would both be missing each other badly - but life is a bitch. The inevitable will happen…

In the meantime, Neha and her friend arrived. I had to bid farewell to Rajesh. He hugged me, and became emotional, "the World is round, so we will meet for sure, no matter which way we go". It was getting tough for me to bid goodbye to someone who cared for me and was affectionate towards me in the same way I did for him.

After me, Sumit would be accompanying Rajesh for another one hour. I went for security check up and finally I had to say good bye. I raised my hand to say bye to him but I really wished to stay with him for some more time. But that was not destined. So I had to bid farewell to him. I called him and wished him a safe journey; he wished me the same too. Fearing I would break down, I hung up. Finally I left Bangalore. In an hour I reached Hyderabad; from there I had my connecting flight to Bhubaneswar in another two hours. Neha was present with me, physically, but none of us spoke to each other – she was still mad at me for the incident in the morning, and I dared not make her scowl at me in public again. Neha and her friend, along-with me, had our lunch in Hyderabad.

The two of them were busy buying chocolates and other stuffs for their family, while I was seated in a chair in front of the shop, alone, and checked my mobile for any new notifications. Then my mobile beeped and I found a facebook notification from Sumit, where he uploaded a picture of the three of us sitting together at the Airport mentioning:

"Final few moments before Rajesh stepped out of B'lore n flew to Mumbai to excel his career in project. Well done buddy. Will be missing u badly. Already started feeling nostalgic. Best of Luck for ur bright future ahead n lastly will be meeting u soon"

And then I updated the same picture with three of us sitting together at the Airport mentioning:

A special time with my roommates at Bangalore Airport. Rajesh's common dialogue- 'Kaaso heichhi... chalo ma... '(Its awesome lets Rock) and Sumit's dialogue 'dhua karuchhhhhhh... (You guys are rocking)'. Really I wish the last time with him could have been much longer. We used to fight, used to argue, used to comment and make fun of each other, still we were with each other. I'll miss those days. May this relation of friendship reflect in our future also! Again Best of Luck Rajesh 4 yr new career".

These feelings for my friends made me overwhelmed. I looked up to check the timing of my next flight flashing on the big screen and I thought, "God, he had truly become a part of my life, and how much I would miss him when he was gone...".

We had made memories of lifetime during these short 3 months period. Later on I realized why people say we grow each day, we learn every day. I came to know, Life is not as simple as we think. You can't have a set of rules for your entire life long. You can't solely depend on your previous records that say, your ability at any given time to deal with any problem and defeating it has always been 100%. I was wrong, utterly wrong. I realized, one would always have to improvise to deal, learn and adapt in the changing environment. No one could walk the miles without breaking any sweat. It's the hard fact of the life. Few learn by luck and few like us learn by the hard way. Some idiots come and tell us the new rules of friendships. We sometimes find these people down the line of our path where they accidentally intersect our path and walk few miles, shares some moments and later on we realize that they were a hell of a Friend.

FOUR

"Good evening all! This is Rajeev, captain of this plane, along with my crew thank you for choosing Indigo airlines. We hope your journey will be pleasant with us. We will be reaching at Biju Patnaik Airport, Bhubaneswar within another 15 minutes. Weather is quite humid; temperature is 34 degree Celsius."

I reached at Biju Patnaik Airport, Bhubaneswar by 6:25 PM. I switched ON my mobile and walked towards the conveyer belt to pick up my luggage. Airport was not crowded; few people were wandering here and there. Mostly waiting benches were empty. I saw a group of people running towards Gate no.2; probably their flight was about to leave.

I collected my luggage from there and started moving towards exit. I dialled to my Mom's cell to tell them that I had reached and would reach at home within half an hour. I stepped out of the airport and booked a cab to my home.

Cab driver adjusted my luggage in boot space of the cab, and then we started. I was very excited. I was looking outside the window, streets, shops, traffics; everything was welcoming me with warmth. It felt so special. However, three month is not so long duration. Many people visit their hometown after 6-8 months and even after a year. But for me these three months were like punishment. I missed my home and town every moment very badly. Now it was so lively moment for me.

The cab reached at home. I paid to the driver and collected my luggage. I was standing at the door full of elation. Excitement was flowing through all my body. I pressed the doorbell.

My mother opened the door, expecting me and so she found the same. She hugged me tight and kissed my forehead. She was seeing me after three long months; her feelings at that time cannot be penned down.

A Mother never lives her own world; rather she lives the world of her child. She smiles, cries, worries, cares for her child. So, was my mom. She showed responsibility for all things that mattered to me, but was careless for herself, when she should take food, when she should take rest, how to take care of her own health etc. She was more of my darling than a mother. I shared everything with her, my deepest and darkest of secrets. I roamed with her, shopped, watched movies and enjoyed as much as I would have enjoyed with my girlfriend. At times, even my father could not convince her to do stuffs that I could. She means the world to me. My tone and respect for her is above everything else; as she is the only person who loves me the way I am.

'Did you face any problem... or the journey went fine...?' my Dad enquired.

I replied positively and touched everyone's feet, moved the luggage inside my room, and sat on the sofa. A low murmuring noise was filled in my house and continuously hitting on me. I didn't pay much attention towards it in the beginning. Suddenly, a sweet and soothing sound of 'pooja-bell' started coming up from nowhere. I was wandering that 'at this evening time who else is there in my house?'

'Is Aayi there…' I asked to my mother curiously.

'Yes! She reached today morning. She was willing to see you', Mom replied with a smiling face.

I became happy to hear this. My mother's mother travelled from her place Narsimpur, which is around 100 kms far from Bhubaneswar, to meet me. Truly speaking, I had not met her since last year. So I was eager to see her.

'If Siddharth has come?' my 'Aayi' asked in a low-tone and she came out of the pooja-ghar with a small plate filled with Cashew and sweets as 'Prasad'. She gave me a little from that and sat next to me.

'So how's Bangalore? Do you like the place and work?' she asked.

'It's lonely for me, but good at all; my training has completed so I took the leave and came to Bhubaneswar', I replied in a careful manner.

I switched on the TV and went to my room to open the luggage.

With my first salary, I had bought an idol of Krishna from the famous Iskon temple; as both I and my mom are devout devotees of Lord Krishna. When I opened my bag to show her, I found it broken. I became very upset. Suddenly I remembered Neha's words – "you made me cry, someday God will make you cry". I felt as if her curse had befallen on me and that made me furious. The next day when she called me to wish Good morning, I told her about the broken idol that made her upset as well.

My mom started making mouth-watering dishes every day. My daily routine for the next 10 days was – eat, sleep well, roam, shop and gossip. I own a cycle too – it was bought in my early school days. It still appears to be new, as I am very particular and take extra care of my belongings.

Roaming around the city in a cycle, without any planned work, visiting the old CD/DVD shops and talking with shopkeepers, eating road side "Dahi-Vada", excites me, as this was the life I led during my college days.

At home, I had so many people to look after me, to take care of me; while in Bangalore, I was all alone. At home, I had nothing to do, was not burdened with heavy responsibilities, no tensions, no deadlines to maintain; instead I had all the time in the world to do the things I wanted to do, in my own ways. No wonder, each and every moment spent here has been memorable to me. Time flies here, while at work I just kept counting my days….

Ten days flew past and once again, I came back to work. Then, me and Sumit along with some of our other friends, shifted from our PG to an apartment. Post training, we were in free pool – this was the real challenge that all of us faced, as bagging projects was an individual's responsibility. We had to maintain a duration of 9.5 hours in office (swipe-in and swipe-out) on a daily basis, contact some PMs and DMs, and do all sorts of other co-curricular activities, but work! After completion of 9.5 hours, everyone used to run away from office. Eventually, a few of our friends managed to get into some projects, while others were still giving me company – desperately trying to get into some project. Being tired of doing the same, for continuously 2 months, I was hopeless. Neha was with me, trying equally hard to get some project.

After the airport incident, her impression towards me was not the same as earlier. We hardly spoke to each other over the phone, but she always gave me hope; she always persuaded me to contact different people; hoping something might click. As goes the saying, "A Friend in need is a friend indeed" – she really proved to be one. She was the one, who inspired me and gave me confidence, when I felt I was losing.

After a few days, even she got through in some account, in a different location, and I was forlorn again. All I did was to continue roaming all alone in the campus for months. Though among the guys, MMS and Swami were there waiting for a project opportunity, they differed quite a lot from me. Swami – the studious and a confident guy, who believes in giving lecture and advice to all the people – if you stand in front of him, it seems you have to be cautious about what you are speaking. And MMS, the most daring person who hardly bothers to listen someone in the campus, he lives in his world – sometimes in dormitory and sometimes sitting outside the campus, smoking and busy in talking with the street shopkeepers about their bad and good. He easily adapts with the scenario – I mean he knows how to tackle the situation. The odd man among them was I, who thinks several times, before taking a step.

I tried to contact so many people, but it was all in vain. All they told me was, "sorry there are no requirements; we will get back to you once any suitable opportunity will be there in our projects". This was but a polite way to imply I was not fit for the projects here. This went on for a couple of months, and I was counting my days in free pool. And then the day came, when all hell broke loose. I lost all my patience and mailed them, asking whether or not I would be assigned to some project; and also sought for reasons if they thought of me, not eligible for it. I had put a few higher authorities in CC (carbon copy) too, as I thought this could be the only way to wake those people up from their slumber.

I was walking out of the campus, suddenly I saw Swami standing outside with a girl from our training batch. MMS was also there, it seemed they were discussing about project. I was too frustrated, I told them everything, all of them remained stunning for some times, 'Good, now don't think much, tomorrow something good will happen with you', MMS replied.

We had a small discussion and then Simran left in her daily cab. We were about to take a bus, just then MMS told he has created an account in some private CAB provider, and we can avail the facility. So, the cab came and we three moved out of the campus. While travelling Swami's lecture started again, for a couple of minutes MMS and me put our ears to it, then MMS told us about the actual Cab plan. After listening to him, we were surprized, he wanted us to join him in the red light area near Majestic. I and Swami, at a time denied to go there, but he started convincing us, saying once in a life time a man should experience something beyond life. And it's not bad to experience bad, rather it can provide a broad vision, according to him. We had already passed our places, and there is no direct bus to return back to our place.

'You both don't think much. You are fake mature adult, let's turn into a real man', MMS said in a hopeful but disgusted manner. He had already been to that place once with one of his close friend so he was portraying himself as a champion of that all.

I and Swami were drowned into the hurricane of thoughts. However, about MMS, I know him very well; he sounds like so brave and crazy but when it comes to the real, he is the one who is easily pissed, *saale ki fatti hai sabse pahle...*

But the fantasy sitting in the corner of our mind overcome the fear. The writer in me, was quite curious to know – how the place will be looking like, I have seen in movies, but till date I have not been inside, so maybe I will experience something new.

'Naye lagte ho babu! Jara sambhal kar' (you look like newbies, be careful), the cab driver warned us, maybe he was listening to our discussion all the while.

Now some different thoughts started jumping inside my head, 'should I stop here itself? What will happen if my parents will come to know? What will happen if some of my friends will see me there?

'By the age of 24, if you didn't lose your virginity you are a loser', MMS chuckled.

Cab stopped near an old building, Driver said, '575 rupees hogaya, apka account me 400 tha to aur 175 dena'.

We paid him and started moving sideways to streets. The place was crowdy. Mostly shops were open. Rickshaw pullers and beggars were seen here and there, just like Indian streets. No heavy vehicles around there, garbage stocked and pan-shop were up and running. I didn't encountered anything unusual.

We walked 200 meter along that street, from a distance I saw three sex-worker on the first floor of the building, and one of them was half nude with tons of make-up on the face. Another one wearing a 'gajra' (a flower chain used to tie in the hair) passed a flying kiss when we moved towards her. Swami avoided to eye-contact with them.

He was shit-scared and asked us to leave the place immediately, his face became dull and gloomy because of the inner haunts. We had not seen any policeman yet so a feeling of excitement and fear of police-raid made us a bit cautious.

Suddenly I felt someone putting hand on my back shoulder. I turned to check, a short height man wearing an extra-large shirt asked, 'Saab, yeh to kuch bhi nahi, asli maal toh humare paas hai, 700 rupee ek log ka'.

I was about to say, "NO" as I figured out he is a pimp and we are supposed to ignore them, but just then MMS's voice overlapped, 'pahle maal dekhenge uske baad hi kuch batayenge'.

We started following him, MMS had taken the lead, so begin asking some random question to the pimp. Swami was damn scared this time. His heart beat became faster than ever.

'No yaar! I would not go. You can continue and comeback soon. I will be waiting outside', Swami said in a low voice and left the place.

We gave money to the pimp. In return he gave us two tokens with room no. imprinted on it. He asked us to go to the second floor.

<u>FIVE</u>

There was a dirty and narrow staircase through which we had to go upside. It was full of pan-spits with puking smell, somehow we managed to reach at the second floor. Total four doors were there, attached to the corridor. One thing was strange, less count of people were seen, even if the building was too big in size.

"Why not much customers are there? Why so lonely here?", to my question MMS replied, "Buddy, the real fuck-points are least exposed and costs too much. This is the hidden treasure", pointing at the door.

I opened the lock and entered inside the room. Vibes of fantasies were running through all my body and mind.

'What the hell?', I saw something that has broken my dreams; my fantasies had been shattered into small pieces.

An old woman of age around 47-50 years was sitting on the bed. She was so ugly with wrinkles on the face. Her mouth was filled with pan-Gutkha, which she was continuously chewing. She was staring at me too venomously while listening to an old radio placed on her lap.

I didn't know how to react at that time. My body freezed completely. Then she yelled.

'What are you doing there boy, come near me….., I will give you a ride'.

I immediately shut the door and yelled by the pimp name.

MMS was not an exception there, same time he also came out of his room, scolding the pimp and the whore. We both were cheated badly. Hearing the loud voices, many other people came to our floor. Most of them were sluts and pimps.

MMS yelled, 'you suckers, he showed us different girls. Now you are telling us to fuck this old and stupid whores! Are you out of minds?'

I was standing quietly, mentally numb. Suddenly someone slapped MMS two-three times. We were shocked; she was the same woman who was sitting inside my allotted room.

"You bastard! What do you think of yourself? Here everything works like this only. But now we will show you the real thing! Beat 'em up…". She yelled.

The small crowd started beating us. MMS became very silent this time. They took out every valuable things from us - our mobiles, wallet, shoes, t-shirts. One of the pimp has snatched my wrist-watch. Tears rolled down the eyes of MMS. I was feeling so helpless.

We came down to the ground floor and ran towards the main street bare-footed. We both were in banyan and jeans.

Really it was a nightmare come true for the first time in our life. MMS started crying, I asked him to stop as other people will come to know and laugh at us.

Swami was sitting on a bench, enjoying a tea and watching the cricket match in TV. We moved towards him, making our face down. Maybe he understood what could have happened with us. He didn't ask much, rather he called the taxi driver and asked him to come to the place. We moved from that place, a bit relaxed inside the car, we were a bit comfortable, as being nude in your comfort zone, hardly matters. There is no such feeling of 'someone is seeing us', what impression they would be carrying. Me and MMS were silent, Swamiji was the one who was asking questions, and on guessing the scenario, answering his own questions too.

'Are yaar wallet bhi nahi hai humhare paas', I informed Swami. (Now wallet is not there with us, they have snatched it)

'kya Karen… with me 300 is there', Swami replied.

We asked the taxi driver to drop us somewhere near Shanti Nagar, as we don't have the money to travel to our destination. When we reached Shanti Nagar, we were standing on the left corner of the traffic road. Swami started calling some of his friends, to help us. But unfortunately their numbers were not reachable and we had to wait there just like that. People moving on the road, were watching us — probably thinking there was something wrong with us. Just then we heard someone calling by our name. A girl voice calling Swami by his name, we heard for the second time. Swami was confident enough to check who she was. But two of us were looking down, as we didn't want anyone to recognise us in this condition. The girl parked the cab near us, through the glass, she tilted her face and started talking with Swami. I had a glance of her look, maybe it was

Neha. I moved towards my left to avoid facing her. I couldn't hear what they were talking about, and then suddenly he moved towards us. It was Neha, he confirmed.

Now there was no other option for us to reach our room, but at the same time it was embarrassing for me to join her in the cab. She greeted us with a 'Hi'. I passed a foolish shameless smile, a bit cautious of my condition.

'It's OK, sometime happens...', she replied.

Now I doubted whether Swami revealed everything to her! But there was no way asking him in the cab. I felt very bad and embarrassed, promising myself never to listen to MMS and his ideas. For the first time, I was unable to look into her eyes. Being talkative, as usual, she was asking a number of questions, but hardly I answered, just I was in need of reaching my room, that's it.

We reached Silkboard, and I was the one to get off first. I walked towards my flat. All the while I was feeling bad as if my impression in front of a girl had gone down. I kept on thinking the same the whole night, till the time I got a call from Neha.

'Yaar, you behaved very differently today... what happened?' she enquired.

I was silent, what to say if someone knowingly asks you the same to repeat so that they can comment something.

'Thanks for your help once again today', I replied.

'Welcome, but that was not my question'.

'Swami told you everything, so there is no point cross-checking with me, right?', I asked.

'Even if he told me, it was not convincing. It seems something wrong happened with you. I saw you people were feeling something bad, something uneasy in my presence.

And one more thing, you three people were there, according to Swami his card is remained with null amount and you two had forgotten to take your wallet to office itself and as per him, the cab driver played with you people, making you travel in wrong direction and blamed you for not paying him in front of his taxi community. You people fought with those taxi drivers and it ends with - they tore your T-shirts and took your slippers. But what about Swami, nothing happened to him! Something is mismatching, I know you are a writer, you can cook up some better story line, but this time, it's not at all convincing yaar....', she told all that was told by Swami. Swami is a good storyteller no doubt, but a bad lair – if somewhere he has to tell a lie, easily he will caught off. So, was the situation!

'I am tired now, will you please allow me to sleep...?', I asked.

'Okies...', she replied and I disconnected the call. Anyhow, I escaped answering to her, but how to face her if some day she would ask me the same, standing in front of me. Just then, I recalled she might not get a scope to meet me, as she had to travel to some other location for her project. There was hardly any scope of meeting with her, and accidents like that were unlikely to happen. So, better stop thinking about the same. Just then a random thought came to my mind, about the office incident, about the bold step that I had taken. I started thinking about it.

I mustered a lot of courage to do what I did, as it could bring unpleasant consequences for me, it might not have worked out in my favor; this mail could have triggered my termination. I was prepared for the worst, but the fear was still there.

<u>SIX</u>

Fortunately, my nightmares did not materialize and finally the next day, I got a call from my manager who informed that he had a good opportunity for me in a project. I was relieved and stunned at the same time. It was surprising that he never got any opportunities for me in the past few months, but the moment I brought the higher authorities in picture, they had offer for me overnight!

Meanwhile, Neha too was tired of her manager's attitude towards her. So I suggested her to mail my project manager and apply for the same. She did that and made it into the same project with me, and finally we came close to each other once again.

Our account, project location, even our ODC, everything turned out to be the same. She was in an ebullient mood and with time, life was becoming smooth. But the fear was still there if she might question me about that evening's incident once again! If something might slip-down from Swami's mouth someday! Among the three, MMS was safe as he got placed in some other account, so he escaped from being questioned.

We underwent KT (Knowledge Transfer) together, had lunch together, took joint decisions, appeared for exams on the same dates and same time slots, argued and fought with each other, but always by each other's side, in times of need and otherwise.

We were a group of 7, namely Trupti, Swami, Neha, Simran, Vidya and Shyamily – all of us from the same training batch. All the girls except Neha, were in a different team in the same account. All of them belonged to a team, where the emphasis was more on learning than on other nonsensical stuffs. Whereas for Swami and me, it was the other way round.

In the first half, we had no other choice but to attend a mandatory "Datacom" training, organized by the great personality – Mr. Amarnath. He reminded me of those typical strict school teachers, who maintained discipline and expected the same from their students. He was one of those, who wanted everything on time, failing which he would make consequences unpleasant for those who defied him. We were once again students and were transported to a school environment; we hardly felt that we were professionals belonging to the corporate world. The second half of the day, we were corporate professionals again, transported back to the cubicle in our ODC; loaded with work that seemed endless. My mentors – Mona and Sweety, were supposed to help me learn stuffs and do the work efficiently. Mona was from my hometown, hence I thought I could be freer to her in expressing my doubts and ask questions without any hesitation, but eventually I was proved wrong. The other mentor, Sweety, looked sweet as her name suggested, but was extremely short tempered. Here I would introduce a very special and important character – Varsha, designated as the Project Lead (PL). She is seen mostly wearing designer net saris with thin embroidered border, which looks adorable on her fair slim body. She has curly noodle-shaped brown hair, with long earrings hanging from her ear. She looks so cute when she smiles from a distance, but nearer she approaches, firmer you start believing; that – beauty glitters with distance, a mirage it is.

Her daily schedule was to finish off her work by 6 pm in the evening and then come near to my cubicle, with either Mona or Sweety (or sometimes both) to ask for the updates. Mona and Sweety tried their best to help me, but it was difficult for me to multitask in a short span of time. They explained stuffs assuming I had a brief idea about it, but that was not the case. It was completely new for me, and I was finding it difficult to learn things without having a proper understanding about it. For instance, they used to tell the command for release download, but Varsha expected me to explain the command, why we were doing it in that way, to tell her the complete path, and all other technicalities. She wanted me to remember everything, which was impossible. She was experienced, knowledgeable but was not a "good guide". She wanted people to do the work efficiently, but never came up with solutions to make the work understandable and easy, particularly for people who were rookies like me. At 6 PM, all my stamina would give in, and exactly at that point of time, Varsha used to appear at my desk and fire questions one after the other.

I remained silent most of the time, as I never had satisfactory answers to all her endless questions. She shouted at me, and warned me to have the answers ready for her by next day.

Then she went near Swami, and repeated the same questions once again. And When we had all the answers ready for her questions, then she threw a different set to questions at us –

"What are the commands used for troubleshooting? Mug up the all the Test-cases and let me know what it's doing…, by end of tomorrow". She had a problem with everything; she would count your faults very easily, but would never utter a word of praise even if someone did something appreciative. I tried hard to collect all possible information from Mona and Sweety. Mona still agreed to help me most of the times, but whenever I asked for help from Sweety, she made a face and answered reluctantly. If I asked her about the debugging methods, she would shout at me – "how many times do I have to tell you, what did you do last time to get it passed – go and re-run it…"

For any test-case failure, the only solution she could provide was – "Re-Run". Some other days, it failed after re-run too. When I informed her of the same, she yelled at me yet again– "Go, Re-run…, it will be passed". This time I told her that I had already done that, still it failed. Then she would come up with another debugging trick – Reloading the device, even power cycle, if possible, and then give a try! While she would be telling me all this, all of a sudden, Varsha would appear to interfere – "What's up Sweety, what is he asking…?" Sweety would blurt out the entire story; and Varsha would then throw some new questions to me, always ready to show off her talent and embarrass me in front of everyone. I employed the trick that Sweety told me; fortunately this time too it worked fine and I was saved from further embarrassment.

While I was trying hard to cope up with the pressure in my project, Neha felt neglected. Of course the negligence was not intentional; it was my work which was not allowing me to give her time. We used to go for lunch and coffee breaks, and tried to leave for home together. But Varsha did not like it at all, so most of the times when I made up my mind to leave at around 6 pm with Neha, Simran and Swami, she would appear at my desk, to prevent me from leaving early. As a result, Neha had to leave for her PG all alone, at times. We had frequent fights over this, and I felt helpless as I was at the mercy of the cunning lady. Then I came up with a trick – I asked Neha to leave at her normal timing, and I would follow her after a few minutes. This worked for a few days, but Varsha outsmarted me this time too. The moment she spotted me walking towards the gate, she would call me from behind and start firing her nonsensical questions at me, eager to inquire about the day's update. I felt she had an internal "question bank" in her system, and every day in the evening, she looked for answers to all her stupid questions. She reminded me of the popular tele show, "Vikram Betal". Every time Vikram the king, carried Betal the ghost over his shoulder, he used to narrate a story on the condition that Vikram would not utter a word during the narration, else he would vanish away with the corpse. After he was done with the story, he would fire questions at him, forcing him to speak, but as Vikram refrained from speaking because of his promise, Betal made fun of him and threatened for his life; thus leaving Vikram with no choice but to answer him.

It was the same with me, she always had some stupid questions ready for me. The moment I answered those, she came up with some new ones; I felt her only goal in life was to embarrass me, and yell at me, saying – "What are you doing, whole day you were working, but you don't know the basics…". She was the deadly Betal behind me, who would leave her cubicle in the evening, to come over my shoulder and bug my head! That day too she did the same – "tell me cards present in the chassis…" I answered her few, to which she asked me to tell the variants of those cards…, and I failed to answer them. She ordered me to mug those up and give her the answers, only then would she allow me to leave for home. I was frustrated, but went back to my seat and called Neha to inform that I would be late, to which she reluctantly agreed. I was looking for the answers that she demanded, and tried mugging up those for the next 30 minutes, but I found it was impossible for me to remember them all - 20-25 cards along with the variants, and card type. I went near her and blurted out, "It's not possible to do it now".

Varsha replied – "Why, you are a recent college pass out, you should be able to memorize things quickly, or were you in the habit of carrying chits…?"

I wanted to hit her right away, but controlled my anger. I answered, irritated - "I can't do it now…" She called me near her desk, opened the notepad in her system where she wrote down all the card details. I was stunned, she didn't remember the details herself, but expected me to memorize everything and vomit the same whenever she wanted me to. Pathetic! Then she started –

"C'mon, I'll teach you how to memorize the things. She used to speak once, the next turn is mine. The thing is as if I should hear her and then vomit the same as many times she asks me the same.

Varsha: robert

Me: don't remember…

I remained silent, she answered, fe-1-port, now repeat…

Her big eyes bulged out, and with a sense of irritation, she screamed at me, "Sid, are you having short-term memory loss…?

Robert, Island, Adaman…Eth-10-port, fe-1-port, Robert, Adaman, Spinach…..." – Phew!

The drama lasted for more than 20 minutes, in different possible ways – as if I was a child in front of her and she wanted me to recite the poem. Then at the end, I asked her, politely – shall I leave now…?

She replied with a stupid smile – "Yup, you can, by tomorrow I want you to by-heart all the cards, got it? Now off you go…"

It was 10.00 pm, I was moving out of the campus, all alone; even Swamiji was not there. From morning 8:30 AM till evening 10:00 PM; I was harassed for more than 12 hours – never thought I would have to face all this. Recalling the incidents, being seated in a cab, I was all occupied. The road was too silent and the street lights were also not working properly. Hardly could I hear the sound of traffic, or anything else, I was quite silent, so was my mind. But suddenly barking dogs' sound reached my ears and my mind got diverted towards it. When I looked towards my right, through the glass of the cab, I could see a number of dogs following a scooter. Slowly my eyes reached the fat man with a woollen black-colored monkey cap, half-covered over his face, with a stripped half sleeves-sweater over his white shirt, riding the scooter. The situation and the man forced me to get off from my track and look at it. The unusual scenario was something unique and mind blowing to look at. The two legs of the man were over the handle of the scooter. And one big polythene wrapper designed as 'SPICY LOLYPOP', the brand name of the hotel mentioned on the wrapper, was hanging from the left handle of the scooter, smelling of some non-veg food inside, perhaps those dogs were following the person just because of the polythene was my first thought. Those dogs were trying to catch the polythene and the person was trying to ride his scooter speedily, just not to avoid getting late to his place, but to avoid the street dogs. I was continuously observing him, at that time I received a call; it was my mother. She called me to enquire whether I reached home, had dinner or not. I was talking with her, a bit diverted. Just then I heard something and looked out of the glass, and I saw the person lying over the road. I disconnected the call and asked the cab driver to stop there. I came out of the cab, just to check what happened. His polythene bag was opened-up and the pieces of chicken blocked some portion of the road for a while, until the time, those dogs had taken their share in their mouth. I could hear the person crying loudly asking for help. The help he demanded was not for his condition, but for the polythene bag that I got to know in the later point of time. He was too concerned about the chicken packed polythene bag. His scooter's front wheel was completely not in a position and he was fallen on the road. I came near him, and tried to handle him. Then I got to know that he was drunk and not in his proper sense.

I asked him to join me in the cab. While travelling, I found him too worried and tensed not for the scooter's condition, but because of the parcel. He told me –

What will I do now…??

'Don't worry about the scooter, you can get it repaired. Thank God, that you are safe.' I tried to console him.

'No, it's not the first time; my second hand scooter is used to meet with accidents, so it's not the matter of my concern. All that bother me is the leg pieces from SPICY LOLYPOP...'

'That was there in the polythene...! Don't worry we can buy somewhere in the next stop', I replied.

'No... she won't have it, she want the parcel from SPICY LOLYPOP hotel only, near electronic city and by this time, the shop must have been closed boss...', he replied.

'Oh..., then we definitely don't have a choice...'

'Yaa, you are right, I don't have a choice, but to listen harsh words from her. In relation, she is my wife. In general, husbands dominate their wife, but in my case, it's opposite...'

The cab driver burst out laughing all of a sudden, then the fat man, being seated beside me, shouted at him – 'Why are you laughing, mind your own business... Don't you know how to respect women, do you know her designation? She is the project Lead of a multinational company, so behave yourself...'

It seemed the person was too scared of her wife; at the same time, he respected his wife. The drama lasted for more than ten minutes, until the time I got off the cab, at my drop point. I paid the cab and asked him to drop the person to his home.

Back to my room fully tired, I cooked something, had my dinner, and slept just then.

The next morning, I was late for the training. The old head master of the training school – Amarnath called me and questioned – "Why are you late today?"

"I went late yesterday, I have to cook food for myself, if I sleep at 1 AM, then it's impossible for me to wake up at 7 AM; hence I am late… In my project, people expect me to stay till late, and here you expect me to come early; I am unable to balance efficiently", was my instant reply.

He then called Varsha to inquire. Varsha was very shrewd and cunning; she spoke in favor of senior officials when she conversed with them, while she called those same people names when she spoke to us. She would often remark – "Amar ko pagal kutte ne kata hai kya, uska training khatam nahi hota hai…, better stop going…, else wait I have to talk with Ram(our manager)". Swami and I became the scapegoats, as we could not refuse to attend the training, and also had to suffer in the ODC. No one understood our situation; a few sympathized but could not provide any solution, while for others we had become laughing stock. In this tragic phase of my life, I get in close contact with another interesting character – Simran, who used to roam with Swami, seemed to be his so called "half-girlfriend". She is the laziest girl I have met till date – physically present but mentally absent – a carefree girl who hardly bothered about anything. But she is confident enough to prove her points, whether she is wrong or right. She also had to attend the training, but could hardly work as she did not have a teammate and there was no one who could guide her for the protocol she was working on. Whenever Amarnath asked about her progress, her instant reply would be – "this protocol is completely new and I have no prior knowledge of it. Moreover no one is able to explain to me the concepts clearly; hence I will require more time than others to get the work done. If you can arrange for someone who could come and guide me, it would be great". Amarnath was very clever, but she outsmarted him and made him speechless most of the time, as Amar didn't have a solution to her problems. She inspired us to be cool and appear least bothered – "see, we are all employees, we don't really need to fear this old man or anyone for that matter. We have all the rights to question and irritate them. Unless we do this, these people will think twice before harassing you; otherwise no one will bother about your situation. You have to voice your opinion if you want to get things done in your ways."

Coming back to the incident, the news of my being late for training and complaining about the work hours reached Varsha's ears – courtesy, the cunning old man. Varsha called Swami and me to have a discussion; of course her favorites – Mona, Sweety and Pappu (Swami's mentor) were part of the drama too..

Varsha started – "When did you guys join this project?"

I answered – "since jan".

Varsha – "Tell me all that you have learnt till date…?"

She fired some stupid questions at us, one after the other, with the sole intention to prove that we were not serious about our work. As if that was not enough to satisfy her, she suddenly brought up Amarnath's topic.

Varsha – "Why is it that I get complaints about you guys?" Then she looked at me and asked, "What is your training time? Why you were late today?"

She was not ready to listen anything, whatever we spoke, she would cross counter it with her stupid arguments; always trying to prove that she was the only one who was right and others were fools. Pappu was also there, who spoke irrational things without understanding. I just can't stand him, he was never cooperative, instead he spoke bullshit behind our backs. All of them behaved as if we were two kids who did everything wrong, every time they were desperately trying to put us back on tracks. At the end of the discussion, Varsha asked us – What's your problem, tell…?.

I remained silent, as speaking something won't drill sense in the person, who was not willing to understand from our perspective.

Varsha asked once again – "Swami, what's your problem? Want to tell anything?"

"I am also trying to think, I am confused. Actually even I don't know what my problem is!"

Everyone bursts out laughing… I was giggling too.

After coming back from the so called discussion to which we didn't get any solution, Neha and Trupti were eagerly awaiting me to tell them about the drama. I heard Pappu narrating the same to his team-mates, making fun of me and Swami – "these two guys are considered to be kids which infuriates them, actually they don't know how to react". One day, he asked Swami about me and my relationship with Neha. He never had many friends, he hardly spoke to girls and was always interested in other people's affairs. All he excelled at was to dump his work on his teammates, and no one could object or refuse him as he was the Lead (TL). I left ODC at 6:30 PM with Neha; fortunately Varsha didn't notice me that day as she was engaged in a serious discussion with someone else. We took the bus, and I sat beside her, quiet and stressed out. To make me feel at ease, she brought up the topic of Ashima's brother's wedding.

Neha – "Are you coming with me to Asihma brother's marriage?"

"I don't know… I don't think it's possible for me to even exist in this project for long", I said, irritated.

"It's the same story everywhere", Neha replied. She wanted to continue but I stopped her midway.

"May be…, but I can't continue in this atmosphere. I can stretch my work for 9-10 hours, but I need a good atmosphere and people around me. I will be unable to deliver my best, if people come screaming at me every now and then, without any reason", I said, upset. She nodded, and held my hands and tried to pacify me and divert my disturbed mind. She put one of her earphone in my right ear, and another in her left ear. Though the music kept playing into our ears, we hardly paid attention to the lyrics; instead, we were engaged in a conversation. She wanted me to attend our colleague's brother's wedding with her. Her friends were reluctant to go as they felt it was unsafe for girls to travel all the way and attend the wedding, but she was desperate. Hence, she wanted me to give her company, but I was not interested. Travelling throughout the night, then share a room with her – the thought made me feel embarrassed.

Neha – "You and I can share a room, I don't have any problem…"

"I don't think I will be comfortable", I replied, awkwardly. Being all alone in a room with a girl – it was simply beyond my imagination.

"I won't do anything with you, I won't even touch you", she replied very cutely.

I looked at her, stunned and flushed, as this was supposed to be a guy's statement and not a girl's. She felt extremely comfortable with me, and was confident that no matter what, I would never harm or do anything to her that would tarnish her image. But I was helpless; I never liked attending functions where people didn't know me, and it becomes difficult on my part to maintain formalities in such situations. So I refused her, knowing fully well that she would lose her temper at that. She instantly texted Ashima, and informed that she would not be going as no one was ready to accompany her. Ashima started calling me, but I refused to answer her calls. Neha was annoyed with me, but she knew that her anger would not make me give in to certain situations; that I would stick to my words whether the other person likes it or not.

I slowly realized, she had grown fond of me. My philosophy – that guys and girls cannot be close friends, seemed to prove wrong for the first time; I felt they can be good friends, in fact they can become the best of friends. I gave life a chance to explore, to face what it had never come across before; to be flexible with girls. Within no time, we had become really close friends.

I bid her good bye, and left for my room. I got a call from the person associated with the channel; who had called to discuss about the program that I wanted to telecast on their channel. We were having a telephonic discussion, with the earpiece plugged in my ears and the phone was kept aside as I was multitasking. Neha's call was on waiting. I noticed but the discussion was more important than attending her call at that point of time. After the call ended, I was busy cooking food for the night. After dinner, I checked my mobile and found 5 miscalls from Neha. I suddenly remembered that I was supposed to call her back after the call with the channel person. The thought of calling her occurred to me, but it was 11 pm already and I didn't find the time convenient to call her. Before I retire to bed, I usually check my mails and messages. The moment I switched on mobile data, the messages sent by her in Whatsapp flashed –

"Sameer has not eaten anything today; his parents came to know everything...

Don't know what will happen to our relationship, situation is very tensed, don't know if all's gonna be well...

Quite tensed, need to talk to you..., please call me once you are done with your work.

Need your support, really broken..."

"She texted me at 8 PM, its 11PM now. What do I do...?" I wondered.

I felt very sorry for her, but felt helpless, as I would not have been of much help.

Neha's boyfriend Sameer can be portrayed very friendly and open-minded person, a believer in friendship and relations. He was not like other typical boyfriends who had issues with their girlfriends having a number of guys as her friend. My perception of him was that he was a modern guy, and he had great interest in all electronic gadgets and bikes. His parents were also well established and trendy.

Everything was going well with the two; don't know what happened all of a sudden. May be his parents overreacted at the situation..., and the poor guy went to bed on an empty stomach; his parents didn't bother calling him for dinner. Suddenly I thought about Neha; she was alone and expected me to be by her side so she could share her feelings, but I had completely forgotten to call her back. I felt guilty, but was helpless...

SEVEN

Sitting on my commode with brief down the bare legs, started texting, 'Good Morning'. Along with I added a smile symbol and sent it to Neha. I was doing multitasking, in my washroom. Same time I was typing in one hand and the other hand was busy in brushing my teeth. I forwarded the same to some of my friends too. A few messages popped up instantly. It was Neha's, who texted back without a good morning note:

"You don't have time for me, after office hours you behave as if we are strangers…"

"I was not in a good frame of mind, but you didn't bother to inquire…"

"How could you be so selfish yaar…?"

I closed the lid of the commode and texted, "Sorry, but I will talk about it in office", while flushing the toilet.

"Not required, I don't wish to tell u anymore", she replied, full of anger.

"At-least you can wish me morning, I am not that bad…." – I texted back, feeling guilty once again.

"Good Morning…" she texted and went offline. Even I got busy as I had to get ready for office.

When I entered the ODC, Varsha greeted me with a smile. "GOOD Morning", she said. I was surprised. Before her warmth could sink in, she suddenly came back to her original form and started asking me about the card details! It was then that I remembered that she wanted me to memorize the card details and their respective variants. I was almost going to blurt out, "Yes I do remember, in fact I have introduced a new card named "Mad Card", abbreviated as MC. It is Multi-variant, Type – PPA4, the latest one, yet to come. It can be inserted in any chassis, as it's the latest one with good memory usage capability. We were yet to check the same, will be updating the same to the team by EOD". But I controlled my anger and answered her politely, "I need some time…" to which she replied, "OK, I want you to memorize the things by EOD, and one more thing – shift to this place(the place just in front of her)".

She wanted me to shift to a cubicle exactly opposite her so she could shower her love on me even more! I came back and informed Neha about it, which made her furious. "Why, you should deny her, like I did to my mentor. Ohh… you also want the same, to move away from me…, fine then, do as u wish", she said, upset.

"Don't worry; I am not sure, when exactly I will have to shift…. As of now, relax. Please try to understand, just don't react like that early in the morning", I said, already pissed off with the morning events.

"Every time you come up with some bad news for me; I don't like it at all… You could have refused to shift there right away, couldn't you?" she shot back.

I don't want to argue with you, regarding this…, please can we speak about something else…? I asked her, trying to keep the irritation out of my voice.

"You started off, but you want me to divert away from it? Disgusting", she said.

"Leave it, now tell me about Sameer; what happened last night…" I asked her with a sense of concern.

"I won't tell you, it's personal…" she fired back.

"Then why the hell did you text me?" – I said, equally disgusted.

"I wanted to confide in to you, but I realized that would be wrong on my part", she answered in a soft tone.

"Sorry for the trouble. I was held up with other important work, so I could not take your call. After that it completely went out of my mind. But trust me that was not intentional"

"You know I have faith in you. I don't need any favors in return. All I want from you is some of your time; is that too much I am asking for from you?" She became emotional and spoke softly, and I feared she might break down at that very instant; that was the last thing I wanted to witness now.

"Of course you have the right to expect", I said, trying to calm her. "Put your ego and anger aside for a while. Look I accept my fault, so you should give me a chance to rectify my mistake…I am really sorry for whatever happened last night and I assure you I won't give you a chance to complain next time. Now please tell me about yesterday's incident", I pleaded.

Finally she began.

Neha – "Yesterday eve, he got drunk, before going back home. His mother was there, alone in the home, and Sameer got drunk so much that his mind and words were not under his control. He spilled out everything in front of his mom, and that reached his father's ears, when he returned from office. They came to know about me Sid.

Sid – "Don't worry; this had to happen someday..."

She was very disturbed and felt bad for Sameer. I tried to give her hope that everything would be fine with passing time. Then both of us got busy with our work. At lunch, she reminded me more than once to inform Rajesh to come for lunch.

Neha – "Call Rajesh, we will be late otherwise; ping him right away…"

"Have you gone crazy? Will Rajesh fly down all the way from Mumbai to have lunch with us?" I replied, astonished.

She started giggling – "Err, sorry. I was supposed to call Sahil for lunch". Then we started walking towards the cafeteria. Mid way, I got a call from the lyricist. I knew the call was important, and I had no other choice but to attend it. That meant Neha would have to wait until the call got over, and she was already famished. She got irritated and asked me to be done with the call ASAP. I was hungry too, but I could not call it off soon as I was in the middle of an important discussion. Finally her patience gave in and she screamed at me, "Nonsense, you just don't bother about anything. Can't you speak to people after lunch? How long am I supposed to wait for you? Enough, I am not waiting here for you for a second longer. I am leaving. Goodbye".

People walking around in the campus, kept staring at me, as they heard her yelling at me. I felt ashamed and embarrassed, but as I was in the midst of a call, I had to digest it all. She left suddenly, and I was forced to end the call hastily. I made my way in to the cafeteria and found her sitting in a corner, without food. I asked her to join me and we silently ate our food. Though I was brimming with anger, I kept my mouth shut, as one word out of my mouth and she will run back to her ODC without having food.

Sometimes being with a girl, makes you feel good, and sometimes it makes you feel disgusted. Strange! Isn't it?

We sat in front of the basketball court, and she started –

"I can't wait for you for hours on end, everyday", she said.

"I can't justify myself every time, but the call was really important for me", I shot back, irritated.

"Apart from me, everything else is important to you…"

"I don't know, but I am sure, I am not as good as you are expecting me to be…." was my reply.

"May be you are right, but I am not wrong either…"

"You cannot be right always. You cannot conclude about me without getting to know me properly…" I said, exasperated.

Neha – "Yes at times, I feel you are very complicated. You have a lot of attitude problem too…"

"So now, you are getting to know me better. With passing time you will only comment that you haven't seen a guy like me…" I replied confidently.

Neha – "I like you; I want you as my best friend…"

"Why…? I am not that good…" I said.

"I don't know, may be because I Iike your company…" came her reply.

"Give me a proper reason Neha…, do you really like spending time with me…?" I inquired, curious.

"Yes, of course. Don't you...? Do you consider me as your best friend?"

"Hmmmm... you are..." I replied.

"Then why do u differentiate between Rajesh, Dev, and me? Why do u prioritize them over me?" she became sad...

I hardly bothered about girls, in fact I tried my best to stay away from them as I feel if you can't handle them properly, life will become hell for sure. But after coming across a girl, who cares for me more than I do, who is beside me during good and bad times, made me change my concept that I had been holding on to for so long. Even with my faults, she discovered the positive attributes in me which others would have ignored. Though she had the habit of fighting over trivial issues, yet whether I am right or wrong, she happened to be the one who approached me with a "sorry" note. Though she is childish, she can efficiently handle if the situation is tense between us. She is very good at heart, but our nature differed a lot. So I used to keep reminding her that "don't expect wrong stuffs from a wrong guy like me".

Her reply to my statement was – "I am not expecting wrong stuffs from a wrong guy; you know how to care, how to love, and I find you different from others, which is why I like you. You know it all, you have emotions and feelings of love within you; but all that love and care are for others except me..."

"My attitude is different from others, I love to be with someone, who understands me and accepts me the way I am. I don't want to restrict myself from certain do's and don'ts. Instead of trying to bring changes in me, if you can handle me the way I am, the better for you."

Even after repeating the same stuffs over and over again, she had very good opinions for me. She was confident that I would never do anything wrong to her or harm her; but I did not trust myself as much as she did. "Though I respect girls, my stupid mind sometimes may become crazy and may attempt something stupid... - So don't trust me..., you shouldn't trust a guy like me...", I reminded her all the time.

"Don't give me suggestions, I can differentiate between good and bad... and whatever may be the situation, my trust for you will remain the same", her counter reply to my statement was instantaneous.

"Ok... then don't get hurt if someday I don't come up to your expectations..." I replied, smiling mischievously.

"You can't, I know you wouldn't...", she said, smiling back. We walked towards our ODC, with my tiffin box in her hand. Our lunch-time was over, and we had to go back to our respective cubicles, where we sat facing each other. While taking the steps to the ODC, she informed me, 'Tomorrow my niece's Annual Function is there, and she is playing the character of 'Rapunzel'. She will wear long golden hair, and according to the tale, Rapunzel was brought up by a wild witch. Everyday the witch used to lock Rapunzel in a tower in the middle of the woods, with neither stairs nor a door, to come out of the room. In the evening the witch would return back, standing beneath the tower and call loud – 'Rapunzel, Rapunzel, let down your hairs, so that I may climb the golden stair'. Rapunzel would help her to climb with her long golden hairs, and get into the room through the window. One day a prince comes to give her freedom from the wicked woman. This is the story to be played by a couple of her classmates, the central character will be played by Tupu, my niece.'

She was very excited, even more than her niece and she asked me to join her. I did not give her a proper word that I will join her, I just nodded my head, giving her a positive hope that I may join. After all the stupid fights and heated discussions, once again we got busy with our work till the time we left for home.

Returning to my flat, I saw my roommates watching TV in the common room. There was a bulletin running on some child rape case. I ignored and came back to my room, as I never bothered to waste my time, in watching news or reading newspapers, as apart from that I have many things to do. I considered it as wastage of time.

EIGHT

I was in a hibernate mode, lying on my bed half-naked. The alarm of my mobile near the bedside had already started irritating me saying that I should get-up, having some important work for the day. But, eyes closed, and lying on the bed, I was conscious that it was Saturday, and no one should disturb me. I leaned across the bed to get the phone, so that I can make it sleep with me for a while. I switched off and slept.

When I got off the bed, it was 10:30AM. I could recall that I was supposed to join Neha in some Annual Function of her niece, as she was about to perform the character of Rapunzel in the play.

Instantly I called her to check whether she was still waiting or she has already left for the school. She didn't pick up my call; I messaged her and got myself ready to join her. Though it was already late but, it's better to be late than never. I took a bus to the place of the private school. There was a heavy rush and the traffic was also thick on the road. Being seated in the bus, I tried calling her. After a couple of trials, fortunately she picked up, 'Where are you…?' I was not able to listen to her; all I could hear was the voice of the crowd and vehicles over the phone.

'I am unable to hear you…' I told her, but she was also unable to hear, all I could manage to collate was, 'I am standing with her in front of the school gate…'

'I'm on the way to the school, will see you soon, bye', I disconnected the call. When I got off the bus, in front of the school, I saw a huge crowd near the school gate. From a distance, it looked like a distribution of different colors here and there, covering the road. Slowly, I crossed the road to come near the front gate of the school. I was looking for Neha, in the crowd. Then I noticed, some small children were standing in their fancy dresses. Guardians were standing and discussing something serious. The environment gave me a clue that it's not because of the annual day celebration, the gathering was there for something else…

I observed the crowd, the countless personal vehicles parked on the road, police commissioner's special vehicle, countable number of security guards in their respective uniforms, and the media people, reporters with pen and notepad in their hands. The big media companies, with the help of their high definition cameras, were engaged in capturing the scenario and the reaction of the crowd. The respective representatives of the channels were holding the wireless microphones to capture the bites.

Some were shouting and howling, 'we demand safety and justice…', while some were throwing stones and showing their violence against the incident that might have happened there. All this gave a clear picture that something bad had happened, with the people and they were engaged in a place to fight for their rights. Once again, thought ran in my mind, 'why in front of a particular school? Is school a good place to have such things happen, definitely 'No', that means it's obvious that the incident or the revolt of the crowd was somewhat related to the school'. Gradually I came to know that maximum percentage of the crowd, were parents, accompanied by small children. Rest of the crowd, was made by the localities staying nearby. Before trying to know the details of the incident, I stepped forward, making my way out of the crowd to search Neha and her niece. From a distance, I saw Neha standing with Tupu, her backside touching the boundary of the school.

They were quite disturbed, that reflected clearly in their facial expressions, though both of them managed throwing a fake smile to me.

'Sorry, I got off late from bed today, but I called you a number of times… Only once you picked up my call that too your voice was breaking…' I replied.

'Yaa… sorry for that, but I missed it, in this huge crowd, it was not possible for me to check whether…', before she could complete I started, 'it's quite understandable, so no issue…'

Neha introduced her niece to me, and it ended up with a formal handshake with the small kid.

She was looking very cute in the pink-rose blossom dress with sparkling beads near her neck. A silver-plated star was there in her hand. The duplicate golden long hairs touching the bare ground, and flower painted over her small fair hand add to her beauty. A small star on the forehead completed her fairy look. The only thing that I discovered missing was the smile. The charm of a princess was missing in her facial expressions. Perhaps it was because of the heavy crowd, in front of her.

'It seems something is wrong there…, I heard some people demanding justice… but…' I told Neha

'You must have missed the recent news, that's why…' she replied.

'You informed me yesterday about the Annual Function, so I was aware of…' I replied.

'Annual Function was there, but it got cancelled due to a mishap…that happened yesterday. And the rape news spread throughout the city yesterday night itself…', when she told me that, I was able to recall that some news regarding child rape was there in yesterday's bulletin, while I entered my room, some of my roommates were sitting in front of the TV, watching the same.

But I was not aware of the details, as I ignored watching the same; Neha narrated me about the incident…

'School's health and physical trainer, has raped a six-year old girl of the school. According to the news, her mother says, "after coming from school, usually, she'd ask for lunch. Yesterday, she went to her bedroom and slept. When I called her for lunch, she silently came and ate very little". The mother noticed that her daughter went to the bathroom frequently. The small girl complained of stomachache, and said trainer did something to her, for which the scratch marks seen on her body… When the family took her to the hospital, the doctors confirmed that someone had sexually assaulted her, which was obviously the trainer. Now the child is in the hospital.'

'And as of now, everyone questioning about the safety of the kids and for this incident, the Annual Function that was about to take place today, has been cancelled', is what I could conclude.

'Sis... I want to see her... she is one of my classmates. Can you please take me to the hospital, where she is admitted?' Tupu demanded.

A big 'NO' came straight away from Neha; I was surprised why Neha denied.

Neha held my hand and asked me to move a bit away from the child, and then she whispered in my ear, 'she is a small kid, and she shouldn't be entitled to such bad face of the society at this tender age'.

I got the point. Then, spoke to her niece, 'Beta... we shouldn't disturb her right now... Once she recovers, I will take you to her..., Ok...?'

'Okies... and what about my fancy dress play..., it won't take place naa...? she asked.

'Most probably the school may plan to re-schedule the program. Don't worry... someday definitely everyone will clap for you... You are looking like an angel beta..., so cute...' with a smile I tried to flush that topic off her mind.

She smiled back with a cute thank you.

Just then, I heard something louder. When I turned my body and looked towards the entrance of the school, I saw the gate of the school was sliding to the right; the security guard opened the school gate. And two men, moved out from the premises of the school. Just then, I saw all media persons and crowd took their position in front of them. I wondered of what happened...!

Was that person belong to the school, was he the chairperson, or the person belonging to the management of the school who came forward to represent the school...!

After a while, the questions from the media representative cleared my doubts, 'Sir… do you believe, the school is going to give your child, a proper justice…? Or you want media to help you come up with the solution…'

People started discussing; he was the father of the victim and the other persons beside him, maybe some of their relatives. They were trying to avoid the situation, but constantly media questions were thrown one after the other…, some logical and some illogical, some quite personal and some emotional too…

The person, perceived to be the victim's father, was crying aloud, without speaking a word. Expressions of some of the parents showed their fear and share of pain in the incident.

Every one of us, prays for good to our relatives and near ones. Even if something bad happens accidentally, we try to keep it confined just to the concerned parties. Every one of us feels that the personal things should not be staged in front of others…

Now as the news had already spreaded, he was quite broken and helpless…

Whom to tell…? And what to tell…?

It maybe a news for the crowd, standing next to the person, it maybe a special footage for the big media companies, who targets on the TRP of their programs, by giving minor and major updates…But it's the biggest loss for the victim's family; it's a big insult, questioning the safety of the future citizens of the country…

I could listen, the person standing next to the father of the victim, shouting at the media persons, 'Do you know, in what mental condition this person is…? What type of reply do you demand?' Everyone stopped gossiping for a moment, kept on staring at the person.

'Go and ask your conscience if someday the same thing happens with your near and dear ones, would you like to put your thoughts in front of the public…?' the counter questions of the person must have embarrassed the media, still they were shameless enough to continue standing there. Even if the guardian of the victim, were trying to move a step forward, they were following them from all around.

With no time, the issue took a bigger shape. The media persons were continuously giving live updates to their respective channels, standing there in the hot sun. Humidity was too high in the atmosphere, and the sun's intense heat was at the top level. Some were looking like they were taking sunbath in the hot sun, clothes being drenched due to excessive sweating all over the body. The crowd appeared reddish with anger and concern mixed depressions. As if, the city was crying along with the victim's family. The emotions of parents for their children were remarkably painful. They were questioning about the security of the future…

'Trainers and staffs should have a character certificate, rather than acquiring an educational certificate…then only they should be allowed to be a part of the educational institute…, It's really a barefaced incident, and it shouldn't be overlooked…' one of the parents spoke in front of the media.

Some were raising their hands and shouting in front of the cameras, 'the school should promise justice to the victim. We won't leave like this; we are with you Sir…'

Some parents trying to give hope to the victim's guardian, but it was not enough to give them moral support.

The father of the victim was quite broken, he wanted to hide his face and run away from the crowd, but the media representatives and news reporters, started flashing over his face, one after the other. For them, the father was no way lesser than a celebrity, and the emotions of the father were no way lesser than the performance of actor like Amitabh Bachchan. Mean while, it came into light that a small child, out of anger had thrown a big stone, targeting the lenses of the camera that one of the media representatives was holding. The media representative was about to show his irritations and anger over the child, but with no time he was pulled out of the crowd and thrown away from the crowd.

Shouting and howling, gossiping and roaring all around the atmosphere, has already started questioning the city… Bangalore was seen with angry protests over the incident. The traffic police tried to control the increasing crowd near the school by diverting them. This was not the first case reported in the city, three such cases already came in news this year and no account of how many may have gone unreported to avoid the shame and pain faced by the victim and the family. Seams nothing matters in these fast running metro cities…

Still the father of the victim was standing in the hot sun. I felt sorry for the pain and agony felt by the victims and their families due to the prejudice and the hostile nature of the society for all such incidents. The feeling of guilty of being a helpless father to his poor child must have been breaking him… No one was trying to give him a space, to move… I felt very bad and shocked. I stepped forward, pushing the crowd from my two extreme sides. When I grasped the person's hand, he stared at me with all his emotions.

'Uncle, we should move now…, the more you stay here, the more you will get feeling of helplessness and guilt, you will get depressed…' I told this to the person standing next to the father. I tried making a small space for them to move out of the crowd, and finally they moved. I observed, the media persons were still following them, from behind till the time they were disappeared completely from the place. Once family of the victim was gone, the media moved their equipment towards the school gate once again to capture the crowd and their stories…

If someone would have asked me, "Is the Annual Celebration still going on?" I might have replied…

'Yes! It is a celebration of violence, prejudice and hostility towards women from so called MARD, a celebration to fight for the upcoming disaster in the path of the innocent lives…'

The discrimination has already been there since a decade or two, with an alarming number of female foeticide conducted secretly in hospitals, and now it's the rape and violence against women that raises questions – how safe a girl is in our society. It's not only a particular age, where they feel unsecured, now the thing is like, as we mention in our marriage profiles, 'Age – No bar…'. The culprit, the rapist profile is just like that, he can rape or commit crime, anywhere, and everywhere, regardless of the situation, or person involved, may it be a child…

The in-human activities of the media representatives were also quite questionable, instead of giving a moral support to the victim and her family; they demand a good bulletin for their TRPs…

Asking questions to the victim or her family should be restricted to some limit; it shouldn't morally depress a person from inside. It should not hamper a person's reputation, and it should not break the person, emotionally in any means. However, the in-humane questions of the reporters make the person cry in front of the public. It's really pathetic...!

People in today's world, have stopped thinking logically from a humanity point of view. There are different shades of life, but we don't feel comfortable to disclose those in front of all. There are people who believe in nudity and are shameless, they can roam in a small piece of clothes covering their groins and on the other hand there are people, who believe in covering their whole body with clothes. So, it depends on one's mentality how and in what way they can represent themselves, we can't force someone... to disclose something, especially when it comes to family and emotions... Each one of us has a family and we should respect it...

Back to my room, I checked the online newspapers regarding the child rape case to get the proper information and found the things that Neha had already informed me. Along with it, a couple of similar rape incidents were there. Additional information regarding the particular incident was something like this – 'a charge-sheet was filed in the case of rape of a six-year-old girl in the school and actions will be taken soon'. When I saw that the family hailed from Odisha, I got shock down the spine.

Felt very bad, and felt like the victim should get justice. Then, I felt like creating a page in facebook, asking people to support the victim. I did so, and just before going to sleep when I checked, I received more than hundreds of people voting and demanding for justice. The page included many safety measures that can be taken in practice to avoid happening of those kinds of incidents. The guidelines included installation of CCTV cameras in schools and GPS in school buses. The staff members up to class seven should be female only. The male attendants should be ignored from being employed in a primary school. Police guidelines should be followed strictly; failure of which should entitle cancellation of the license of the school. Sex-education and guidelines about people behavior should be clearly discussed as a part of the curriculum. Children should not be allowed to move out of the school premise, without a proper guardian's sign over the register, before taking the child from the school premises. The child should be open enough to discuss the pros and cons of the school, in front of everyone and that should be positively accepted by the management. The meeting comprising parents-teacher get-together should involve the students also, to raise their voice against violence, if any. There should be a mentor for each standard, who can point out the problems, issues and take actions on the same.

I closed my eyes and prayed God to give strength to the family.

NINE

That day, from morning itself too much of traffic was there. Being seated near the window, I looked out of the window to check the traffic – a long queue of vehicles was there. Then I heard the conductor of the bus asking everyone to get off the bus. When I got off the bus, I saw people sitting on the road, with some posters for justice. People were discussing it's because of the rape case of the school girl, that took place two days back. Police, securities were all over the place to check on any unexpected happening to take its shape, in anyway. As in all strikes, an unpleasant thing always happens… Some crazy people always involve in such type of activities, sometimes they do so for the good of the society, and sometimes they do so, under the pressure of political parties. Their main objective is to do something in order to get the recognition and show up their leadership qualities. The case is like this – they will shout, they will speak big words of concern and responsibilities for the society, and get themselves captured in the main headlines of the newspaper and media. That's it…!

The place where we got off the bus was two kilometres from my workplace. I walked to my office, having no option to book a vehicle. People were walking beside me, to their respective offices, discussing about the case. It appeared that the news was all over the region now...

As soon as I entered the ODC, I wished Neha – "Morning" to which she didn't reply. Then I noticed, she had the earphones plugged into her ears and was happily chatting with someone. When I moved my face towards her, she unplugged the earphone and smiled, minimizing the chat box, holding the mouse on her right hand. She stared at me for a while. When I asked her, 'what are looking at...?' she replied, 'you and your humanity, though you don't bother caring my emotions..., but I have seen yesterday your concern for others. A special respect from my heart for you was born yesterday. And you know, Tupu was too impressed by your activities'.

'Ok..., anything else... by the way is she fine now...? I mean was she able to overcome that...' I asked her.

'No... we stopped discussing in front of her about all that, but I am sure she is still behaving in a different way, maybe she would take some time to recover. Yesterday she told my cousin that, she didn't want to go to school..., to which my brother said, "as long as you don't feel like going to school, you mayn't. We will not force you to..." in order to reduce the child's mental pressure. Maybe she is thinking that she is not safe.'

'Hmm... it's obvious that she might think in that way, but we as a guardian should make sure that she overcomes from the incident, right...', I suggested to which she agreed. Then I moved to my seat, in order to start my work for the day.

After a while, I found her smiling and giggling to herself. I was disturbed once again, I asked her, 'what happened...' She did not respond to my words. I stood up to check what she was doing. Then I observed she was listening some song, earphones plugged into her ear, along with chatting with Rajesh – her enemy. It was surprising for me, as I knew she was furious at him regarding the airport incident that happened the last time we decided to go home, and he was leaving for Mumbai. Suddenly she turned around and saw me. Instantly she minimized the chat box.

"You were talking with Chhua(Rajesh – my child)...?

That means, you were chatting with him at that time also, so you minimized the chat box all of a sudden, when I wished you morning...", I enquired.

"Hmm..." she nodded her head.

"Show me the conversation..." I demanded.

"Nope, I can't... it's personal..." she replied.

"Personal! That too between you and Rajesh...! Don't fool me, show me right now..." I was stubborn.

I forcibly checked her system's chat box, it was written –

"Thanks for understanding me..." Rajesh wrote.

"No problem. You are most welcome..." was Neha's reply.

I wondered how the hell that was possible. Rajesh and Neha gelling well together, that too all of a sudden; I could not believe what my eyes witnessed. I became very curious and asked her to tell me what exactly those two spoke but she refused to open her mouth. Frustrated, I pinged Rajesh to tell me what exactly happened.

"I promised you that I will settle everything between Neha and me, and I have kept my word. Now stop worrying and be happy…Don't ask me how I did all this; I will not teach you the trick to flirt with girls…" he chuckled.

I felt something fishy, as I knew Neha avoided speaking to people whom she didn't know enough, and Rajesh would have been the last person on earth to whom she would speak, as she hated him all this while. I just so wanted her to tell me everything, but she refused, enjoying the fact that I was anxious to know. I had to wait for the right moment, and that came soon too. She kept her mobile at the desk and went to her mentor to discuss something about the project. My curiosity got the better of me and I took her phone and started checking her mails and WhatsApp messages. I noticed a mail from Rajesh in her Gmail account. It read -

Hi Di…,

This is your enemy Rajesh. I wanted to share some incidents with you, so I asked Sid bhai to give me your mail id. Please read it when you have time.

One day while watching IPL, Sid wanted to watch a Hindi serial that he watched regularly. It was a nail-biting match as the last over was left to go and it had become very exciting. Co-incidentally, the serial that Sid watched probably had a turning point in it, and he was equally eager to watch it. As Sumit and I were interested in watching IPL and he was the only one who wanted to watch the serial, we voiced him down. I even went to the extent of putting forward an absurd logic, "As the Constitution of India allows us to form government with two-thirds majority, and the same rule will apply in our case".

"You guys watch IPL every day; did I ever object to that? You watch it on high volume; still I have never said anything to you two. One day I want to watch something of my choice for a few minutes, and it becomes a huge issue for you both", he yelled at us furiously.

Sid's argument was quite compelling as he truly never objected to what we watched. We watch IPL every day and it would not have been a big deal if we happily passed over the remote to him; but we were stubborn and it was difficult to make us understand. The match was nearing its end and the excitement just got quadrupled; we were just not ready to part with the remote, no matter what. As soon as the match got over, we handed over the remote to him, but unfortunately his serial was already over by then. I could sense that he was very upset. After the match, we retired to bed. It was then that he started playing on his laptop in full volume.

At first I thought he might be checking if the speaker was functioning properly or so. But when Sumit asked him to lower the volume, Sid erupted like a volcano. "As you guys didn't let me watch the serial of my choice, and yourselves watched the IPL on high volume, I am going to do the same."

While reading Rajesh's note, I was able to recall those conversations that were still afresh, and that brought a smile on my face. I didn't know when Neha came back and sat next to me, intently going through the mail although she had read it the previous night. The mail continued...

Rajesh wrote -

Listening to him, I woke up and sat on my bed. I said to myself WTF!

"Listen Sid, if you continue to behave in the same way, you will never achieve anything in life. I can adjust with you, and I won't complain about your behavior too, but tell me honestly; do you want to give yourself this life? ", I blurted it all out, angry and furious at his stupidity.

"Yes, I want this kind of life. Whoever messes with me, will get the same piece of shit back", he said with the same indignation and stubbornness.

Finally I lost all my patience and I promised to myself that I will make his life hell. The feelings to take revenge overpowered my goodness. But of the blue something strange happened when Sumit said,

"Listen Sid, We know you wanted to watch the serial but you can watch that tomorrow too as these serials show the previous days' episode for a few minutes. So you can be a little cool in dealing with us, as we all have to attend the training tomorrow", while surfing the internet.

"Same thing goes to you too; even you can watch the highlights tomorrow. It will also be telecasted tomorrow before the new match begins. Isn't it? " Irritation still evident in his voice.

Both were logically correct from their perspective but what made me calm down was Sumit's response. The guy whom I thought of as careless and irresponsible made me realize my position as a good human being by his calmness and non-revenge attitude. I always took pride in the fact that I am very good at adjustments and also provide solutions to other's issues. But my pride was shattered by the sweet and calm delivery of words by Sumit. I was the one who had experienced life outside the comforts of my home, who claimed to be experienced in all these affairs, but I felt all the experiences were in vain as I lost my temper and thought ill of the guy who had never experienced life outside his home. It was obvious that he would be wrong at times, but instead of taking revenge on him, I should try to teach him the ways of life. I felt I was no different from him; he was naive, but I should have acted mature. I looked at both of them and suddenly they appeared innocent and childish. I developed respect for Sumit all of a sudden, while the anger for Sid vanished in thin air. Hence I politely asked him once again to lower the volume, though now it didn't matter to me anymore. It was past 12 am, I tried to sleep with the music still playing loud; Sid had not lowered the volume. The next morning there were no fights for the washroom. Sid was an early goer to bed, while Sumit and I stayed awake till late in the night. Sid was having issues with that, but he did not complain because of the last night's incident. Having realized that he was having difficulties in sleeping, I took my book and notepad, walked outside the room, switched on the corridor lights and sat on the stairs to study. After sometime, Sid came out of the room and assured that it was ok with him if I studied inside the room. But I refrained from going inside and assured him back that I was comfortable in the corridor too. He looked at me, smiled and wished good night and went inside the room. I knew he was trying to change. There are different ways to make someone realize their mistakes but the method that has a direct effect on the heart works better than ways that mess up their minds. I gradually developed a liking for the two; they were just doing what they thought was right, which was not wrong, and I was trying to make them understand through simple ways possible.

During the last days of my training, I fell sick and was quite disturbed as I got a project in Mumbai where I didn't wish to go. But life is a bitch; it will offer you stuffs that you don't want... I started neglecting my health. Life had saved the final set of cards that was destined for me. Sid and Sumit started acting like my guardians; they forced me to have food and fruits on time, whether I liked it or not. Amidst all this, I could sense their love and affection for me that replaced the anger and hatred they had for me in the initial days. Sumit, who skipped his lunch and dinner just to avoid going out, went out the other night just to get some medicine and electrolytes for me. It was difficult to bring food for two from the ground floor to the third floor (where our room was), but Sid managed to get it for both of us. That reminded me of my days at home when I fell ill and parents took care of me in a similar way; I was touched. The adversities of life unfold who are true to us. I didn't thank them in person, but deep down only I knew how much I was thankful and grateful to them for all that they did for me.

The three of us were emotional the day I was to leave for Mumbai, and as nothing was pre-planned properly, everything got messed up. Neither of us was wrong; just that Sid was not able to handle the situation, and that was unintentional. Hope you will understand me and change your negative impression of me.

Thanks,
Rajesh

The mail had an impact on her. Although she still was not ready to accept him completely, yet to some extent she was cool with him. The hatred was there no more.

There were incidents where she used to cross check both of us; she tried finding out if we spoke ill of her or hurled slangs at each other while conversing. She used my system when I was not at my seat, and logged in to the communicator to chat with Rajesh, most of the time. She fooled him almost every time. Rajesh chatted with her without any inhibitions, as he was of the impression that it was me who was at the other end. When I got to know about it, I cautioned him to be careful, as Neha was using my id to chat with him, and he should not blabber anything that might sound offensive to Neha, or to a girl for that matter.

Rajesh was informed earlier. The following day as usual Neha logged in to my communicator and typed him a message –

Sid: "Gm".

Rajesh – "Are you Sid or Neha?"

Sid: Sid here.

"Gm…, if you are Sid, then scold me using slangs…" Rajesh typed, to confirm whether it was me or Neha.

"stupid…, idiot…", she typed.

"Sid never uses these as slangs…, it seems you are Neha, right…?" Rajesh inquired.

"No Chua, it's me, your Sid…" she typed.

"Tell me something crude, need to confirm…" Rajesh.

"F.A.", she replied.

"Playing with me, ***hole…" Rajesh.

"Love you Chua…", she replied, and it was similar to the way I spoke; I lovingly referred to Rajesh as "Chua".

Now, Rajesh was convinced, he replied to her in the same style like he did to me when I typed all these.

She was smiling mischievously. When I came back to my seat, I found her using my system.

"With whom were you chatting...?" I asked.

"It was Rajesh..., I fooled him yet again...", she chuckled.

"You still hell bent on taking revenge on that poor guy, is it...?", I asked, trying to bring irritation in my voice.

"Yaa... he fooled me on the day he was leaving for Mumbai, and I am going to take my revenge on him. Honestly, I was just checking if you people hurled slangs at each other while chatting or not...", she replied.

"He knows very well how to flirt with girls; he is not of my kind... Don't think of him as innocent, he will type stuffs beyond your imagination", I warned her.

"He did that already, that's what I wanted to check, and I could do that using your id only. Oh yes, even you know the art to flirt with girls...when we fight over some issues, you behave very sweetly with other girls, while you ignored me completely", she replied, trying to sound upset.

"I don't even look at their faces while talking..." the words spat out of my mouth instantly.

"Yaa... I know, you don't look at their faces, instead something else interests you....", she shot back.

I understood what she implied and as I knew it was useless to drag the conversation on, I ignored and opened the chat box.

When I checked the conversation, I felt flushed. Rajesh had typed all idiocy, full of slangs and abuses, oblivious of the fact that it was Neha whom he was chatting with. I dared never use any abusive words in Neha's presence, but Rajesh had done it, though that was unintentional. I felt she would have a negative impression of him yet again, which he tried to get off her with great difficulty.

"You shouldn't have done this…" I argued with her.

"Why…, can't I talk to him?" she asked.

"You can, but not in this way, fooling people using my name… It's bad Neha, to cross-check someone like this. He was innocent all the way, and ended up typing shit, thinking that it was me who was chatting with him. Of course I know it would create a negative impression on you…, which is actually not true. He is naughty with me, this is how we guys talk, and by no means was it meant for you". I explained to her, and she nodded her head..

"I don't consider someone to be bad, if he/she uses slangs while talking…, even I use…", Neha said mischievously.

"What…?" I was surprised.

"Yaa, I use slangs most of the time, and don't over-react, I am sure you do it too.", she replied casually.

I smiled and asked, "Tell me the slangs that you generally use…"

"First do it yourself, then I will follow", came her reply.

"I don't use any", I replied, trying to sound innocent.

"Don't act as if you don't know anything. The conversation is a proof that you guys use slangs while chatting. What do you have to tell about it, Mr. Siddharth?" she shot back.

"Ok, you are free to think what you wish to, but I have work to do now. I will land myself into trouble if that MC demands an update about the work from me", I said, relieved I could divert the topic for the moment. She left towards her cubicle while I got busy with my work that seemed endless.

I was about to leave for the day, when Varsha came near me and once again started questioning me about all the card details.

She started – Spinach

I - eth-N-port

She – Island….

Neha was waiting for me and she saw Varsha screaming at me when I was unable to answer all her questions. Neha felt sorry for me. She walked out of the ODC and decided to wait until I was over with MC's question and answer round. She usually chided me like a kid and everyone enjoyed the entertainment that began every day after 6 pm in the evening. Suddenly my phone started vibrating and I noticed Neha was calling. I suddenly remembered she was still waiting for me outside. Varsha understood I wanted to leave. "Whoever it is, inform her that you are not leaving now", she replied adamantly, knowing fully well that it was Neha who was waiting. I wanted to hit her right away, but I controlled my emotions. "Let me leave for today…, tomorrow you can ask me if you have any more questions in mind", I said, trying to maintain my calm and composure.

"No, I won't leave you like this… it's only 6:30 dear, I am usually staying back till late in the office. I have observed many a times that as soon as the clock strikes 6, you people vanish from the ODC. One takes the initiative to go out and wait until the other one follows up. You don't come here to play, your work is not just "dot-slash"; you have many more important things to do. You waste my energy and time on a daily basis. I even asked you to shift in the cubicle opposite mine, but you still haven't got the time to accomplish that too. Just because of you, going near to your cubicle and coming back to my seat for 'n' number of times in a day made me shred a few kgs!"

Amidst all the dialogues she delivered, the last statement made me giggle. But I kept a straight face.

"I didn't ask you to come near me…, I have already sent you the updates", I replied, controlling my laughter.

"Just sending the updates and running away, doesn't solve my purpose. Itni jaldi ghar jaake kya karte ho..." she was inquisitive.

"I come at 8:30 am, and now its past 6:30 pm. If I start now, it will take me close to an hour to reach home. I need to prepare food for myself too", once again updating her with my routine facts.

"Don't irritate me Siddharth, don't give those lame excuses…, it' been more than a month now, I don't expect this from you; you need to be more responsible towards your work", she replied indignantly.

"I will try my best…", I assured her, pleading to her in my mind to put an end to her torture for the day.

"Ok, you may go now, and also try to shift in the cubicle opposite mine ASAP", she said.

I nodded my head. "I'll take care of that…". Having said that I finally managed to come out of the ODC and breathe some fresh air. By the time I came out, Neha had left. I walked out of the campus all alone, feeling exhausted and drained out…

I was sitting in the bus, all alone, resting my head against the window pane. My phone started vibrating in my right pocket. It was Dev, one of my close friends. I received the call.

"Darling, what's up...?", to which I replied, "on my way back home from office yaar, just too tired...".

"I am coming over to Bangalore. We will have fun, and together we will celebrate your birthday...", his voice full of excitement.

"Are you sure you are coming for me or you have some other plans...", I inquired.

"I will be here for three days' time, out of which 2 days I shall spend with my girlfriend and one day I shall dedicate to you my love", he replied.

I – "All you will do is dump your bag in the room, be with your gf the entire day and the only time I get to spend with you is at night, right...?"

"Yup, most probably, but we will see to it. But most importantly I would love to celebrate your birthday yaar..., and also I shall share the bed with you", Dev said mischievously.

"So...?" I asked.

"So, I can do naughty stuffs to you. See the entire day I shall be with my gf but I am dedicating the night to you. You should understand how much I love you and prioritize you over everyone else, including my gf", Dev blabbered.

I – "Nonsense, I don't want to spend time with you at night. Instead you can plan to spend the night with your gf".

"Nope I want to be with you at night...", he insisted.

"Ok, as you wish..., by the way, what exactly are your plans?

"There is no such planning, she would be buying a new scooty for herself, so she wants me to accompany her. As I had not met you for the long time, so I planned to come over for the weekend so we could get to spend some time too…", Dev replied.

"Oh, do inform me, if you plan something. Else we can plan for a short trip to some good place", I said.

"Yaa, I'll let you know…, this time I will introduce you to my girlfriend, you also call Neha…", he replied.

"I don't think she would be comfortable with all of us. If I end up giving you more attention, then she might feel neglected. And I want to avoid that", I replied.

"Don't worry, nothing will happen. I will be there, and I will make sure everything goes well. Infact I would have a word with Neha about your birthday celebrations", Dev said, excited.

I spoke to him for almost half an hour, all the while discussing our plans. I felt a lot relaxed and happy after a hard day at work, and I was eagerly awaiting his arrival.

TEN

19th March, 2014 mid-night.

"Darling, Wish you a happy birthday"… Dev wished me.

Neha – "Happy Birthday to you"…

All my family, friends, and roommates wished me one by one. I felt special, thanking God for the wonderful people I had around me. We were supposed to go on a team outing the following morning. We went to a very good resort. Everyone wished me for my birthday, and I distributed the sweets amongst all post lunch. Most of my team mates were busy in games and other activities, while I was engaged in taking snaps from my priced DSLR. Neha was sitting idle in a corner, waiting for me to spend some quality time with her. But I was busy with my camera, so didn't really give a thought to the option; instead I called her over to pose so I could take her pics too. She refused and I didn't press her further, thinking she was uninterested, but that was not the case. She looked excited in the morning, but gradually as the day passed, her temperament changed from bad to worse. She was boiling with anger, but was unable to vent her frustration in everyone's presence. Finally we left the resort and came back to office, from where everyone would go back home. It was then when she suddenly questioned:

"Shall we wait for Ram, or we three will leave by bus? It's already 8 PM, and she is getting late."

The third one was Trupti. As per our plans, we were supposed to leave in Ram's car, which was on the way, and he would need another half an hour to reach there.

"Since it's already late, we can afford to wait for another thirty minutes or so. Besides, if we catch the bus now, we will be real late by the time we reach home, and we have to walk quite some distance too. Its better we wait a little longer here", I suggested.

Neha – "You may choose to wait, but I am leaving with Trupti right away. Her husband and family members will be worried for her, but you won't understand all this".

I – "Ask her to leave then, there's no point asking me", I replied irritably.

She – "I never thought you could turn out to be so selfish. How can you ask her to leave alone? You always choose the option that suits you, caring a damn about others and their choice"

I – "When you guys have already decided on an alternative, then I don't see the reason to ask me what to do and what not to. I was not a part of the alternate option that you people thought of; if you just want me to accompany, then tell me that clearly".

She – "Why will I have to take the initiative to feed you just about anything? Can't you for once stop being selfish and think about the wellbeing of others?"

"Please don't talk bullshit. And for God's sake stop putting the blame on my shoulders", I was irritated too.

"Go to hell, I am leaving with her...", she was fuming.

As she walked away, I asked her – "Should I join...?"

"You don't have to", she replied and walked away.

I saw Trupti got inside a bus all alone, from a distance, and came near Neha.

"C'mon, the bus might leave now. We should go with her", I suggested.

She – "No, I will go alone in the next bus".

Finally the bus left and Trupti bade goodbye to us. Neha continued her argument with me.

I – Listen, do you want to come with me or not?

She – "No"...

I – "Please don't irritate me anymore; lets go"...

"No means "NO", I won't come with you"...

I asked her repeatedly but she refused. Irritated, I started walking away from her. Just then, she shouted –

"Finally you left me, I could not have expected anything better from you"

I turned back and came near her, held her hands and gently asked her to come, but she continue in the same pissed off tone–

"I won't come with a selfish fellow like you. The entire day I saw you busy with everyone. You just don't bother about me, nor do you have any respect for my feelings. I hate such people. Just go away from me, I don't have any more expectations from you. Every time I give in my best to you, but in return, all I get is negligence and disappointment"..., she replied.

"I have told you already..." I wanted to continue but she stopped me midway.

She – "I know what you want to tell; I should not expect wrong things from a wrong guy. The truth is you are not wrong; you are selfish."

"Fine I am bad and selfish too. Do you have anything else to say?" I was on the verge of breaking down.

She didn't reply, I continued – "Please leave me alone..."

At that moment Ram arrived and we got into his car. He dropped us at our stop, and left.

I bid her goodbye. Just when I started walking away from her, she caught hold of my hand. I could not control my emotions and tears started rolling down my cheeks. "Please leave me alone, let me go", my voice choked as I spoke. She continued to hold my hand in hers and asked me to accompany her till the next stop. I walked with her, crying all the way. I was in a terribly bad mood.

"Sorry, I hurt you on your birthday...", she said in an apologetic tone.

"I will never forget this day. This is perhaps the best gift I have ever received on my birthday. You have told stuffs about me that I could never imagine of...", I managed to speak through my choked voice.

She held my hand tightly– "Really sorry, please forgive me. I didn't mean all that I said, just that I was extremely pissed off."

"Please leave it and let me go, I don't want to disturb you", I replied.

She ignored what I said and forcibly took me to CCD. Then she asked me to eat something, but I refused...

She – "Please swear on me, you have to eat something. I know I hurt you and I am truly apologetic for that."

"I don't want to eat", I replied.

She ignored me yet again and forcibly ordered a sandwich and coffee for me. Then she said, "It was your birthday and I thought of spending some quality time with you, but you seemed to be so busy with others. You approached me for snaps only after you took everyone else's. I felt very neglected and ignored so I eventually lost my temper at you."

I understood, whatever she might blabber, however much she shouts at me, at the end of the day there was only one conclusion to it – that she loved me, she cared for me, so all she demanded in return was a little love and affection. I always questioned myself as to how she could love and care for me to that extent. But she has always been that way; I have seen the concern she has for her friends a number of times. After knowing all this, it's difficult to blame her for the way she behaves. She is very immature and short tempered, but the goodness in her heart overpowers everything else..

28th March 2014

It was Friday evening. I was shopping groceries for the weekend. Neha was there with me, as directly after office hours, we went to the market. We were busy checking out soaps, detergent and other essential items for my home when she suddenly got a call. After she was done with the call, she came and told me that it was Dev.

"Dev had called. He wants us to join him tomorrow", Neha informed.

"Well, I don't think we should go", was my reply.

"He is expecting you to be with him. He needs both you and his girlfriend. Try to understand his situation. I think we should definitely go", instantly came her reply.

"My friends mean the world to me. But I don't think I will be comfortable in Chandini's presence. I am not to blame Dev if Chandini receives more attention from him, but I know I shall feel hurt. I may be wrong in my approach, but I will not be able to accept his negligence. Anyways I will catch up with him in the evening at my place. I want him to spend some quality time with his gf, to enjoy with her, which definitely is not feasible in my presence", I tried to explain Neha while crossing the road from the market place.

"Yes... sometimes we need to do stuffs against our wishes to please others", Neha replied.

"Maybe, but I am still not sure. You can try convincing him that we can't go; he won't pay heed to my words. I hope he listens to you", I replied.

"I'll try my best. Bye for now, catch you later. See you" She left for her PG.

I came back to my room, changed and was getting freshened up when I received a message from Dev –

"Darling I boarded the bus just now. I shall reach there by 6 am, meet with my gf and then come over to your place".

"Sure. Happy journey", I replied back. Then I got engaged in other work. By the time I cooked food and had dinner with my roomie, it was past 10.30 pm. Just when I was going to retire for the day, Neha called me –

"Dev called me. I tried explaining him everything, but he is just not ready to listen to me. He assured me that he would effectively handle everything".

Finally I gave in and the four of us met each other at the pre-planned destination - Iskon.

29th March 2014:

Dev was very comfortable with Neha, till the time his girlfriend was not there. There was a formal introduction of us and then it all began. We planned to have lunch in McD. I was supposed to treat them for my birthday, but I did not have enough cash and they were not accepting any cards. So Dev had to pay the bills. We chose a four seater table, where Neha and I were seated opposite Dev and Chandini. All the while we were concentrating only on one thing – having lunch. We hardly spoke to each other; probably none of us felt at ease with each other. Dev and Chandini were busy conversing in some regional language that we didn't understand, and that made me and Neha feel even more awkward. Finally to my relief, lunch was over.

Dev – "Sid, just 5 minutes…" (Requesting to provide them privacy for some time).

I smiled and freed him from the so-called formality-constraints. I felt as if they needed some space, so I walked away with Neha to the first floor, checking for fiction books in Landmark. Suddenly Neha reached for my hand and I followed her to the next store. There was a heavy rush of people in the Sari shop. The store was crowded with families shopping for ethnic wears. A small argument for exchange of dress materials, leads to a small fight, Neha described it, showing her finger towards the fat person, who was standing in front of the exchange counter. I was not in mood to check all this, as I was in my thoughts. I was about to move, just then something I heard, for which I moved a step backward to check the person standing there. I subdued my other senses and tried listening to the matter, the person was shouting with anger – Do you know, with whom are you talking to…This is Asit Kumar. And this saree, I am asking you to exchange is for my wife, who is working in a MNC as a Project Lead.

'Sorry sir, we care and respect each of our customers equally…, but we can't go beyond the rule. It's already more than 7 days from the purchase, and it's not possible in our part to…', the cashier was trying to explain him the scenario but he was not ready to bear the insult of his wife and repeatedly he was telling, 'We were not sitting here without any work. I own a computer business and she is the Project Lead, under her more than hundred employee work. Do you think for this stupid job, we need to take special leave…?' Just then, his wife came forward and she tried to handle the scenario. I was shocked now…, looking at the fat man. I recalled it was that person, whom I met a month back on the road, late night carrying chicken for his wife, in a second hand old scooter. Next to him, when we both saw his wife, holding his hands tightly and trying to pull him back, we were shocked for the second time. It was unbelievable – it was Varsha, our Project Lead. I saw Varsha handling the situation. I asked Neha to join me to the next store, and we both moved out of the place. I told Neha everything of the previous incident when I met the man quite a long back and we both laughed a lot.

'Really it's unbelievable…' she said.

'Good pair… but it seems Varsha behaves the same way in her home too… That person was not concerned about money, but the concern was for his wife's demand. He wants to fulfill her demand all the time, sometimes the demand of Chicken lolypop from Spicy Lolypop restaurant and sometimes for something else… Don't understand how someone can bear with her…'

'But I don't understand why people make a big issue out of a very small thing… It's their fault, they should not come for exchange after seven days, right…?' she told.

'Sometimes we don't want to make issues, but our atmosphere forces us, maybe because of Varsha he is behaving like that…'

'Leave it…, now you should take my snaps, today I am going to change my profile pic on fb…'

She asked me to take snaps, while moving in the corridor of the mall.

Then we took snaps, enjoyed with small children who were sitting next to their parents. We tried our best to give them the time they needed to be with each other, while we endeavored different things for our own time pass.

I occupied myself in unconventional stuffs. I had always considered Dev as my brother, and always wanted his happiness. This was the reason I gave him the space he needed with his gf, but deep down in my heart I wished I could get to be with him. Though I did not utter a word about it to Neha, she somehow knew that I was not ok at all.

Neha – "What the hell is this?"

I – "What…?"

"He is your best friend, right?", Neha started off…

To avoid discussing with her, I tried to divert the topic. I told her to sit next to a small child so I could take her snaps. Once it was done, she trailed off again…

"I haven't seen another friend like him. Why did he do that to you? You just don't deserve all that. I had heard a lot about him and hence was eager to meet him, but I am disappointed…", Neha said, annoyed.

"I don't want to discuss about it, please…", I replied.

"I cancelled all my appointments. I didn't even visit my brother as I wanted to come with you. Am I a fool?", she questioned.

"This was the very reason why I wanted to refrain from coming there. But you were adamant", I felt irritated..

"I understand your point…, but it never occurred to me that he would behave in such a weird manner. None of my friends behave so uncanny in their bf/gf's presence. He was literally pleading me to come over with you, so I had to forcibly convince you. His image on me was completely different until I met him. I am surprised people can turn out to be selfish to this extent…", she sounded upset..

"Leave it, we should not expect anything from anyone", I replied back.

"Yes, maybe you are right.", she nodded her head in agreement.

'Love' should know how to love someone, without any terms and conditions. Love shouldn't construct a boundary for your loved ones. Rather it should award freedom and it should facilitate your loved ones to go ahead in their life efficiently. It should encourage your loved ones to walk safely, to smile openly and to make others feel comfortable and happy with you. At the end, all I want is to see him happy…

"Prioritizing his girlfriend was not wrong, but ignoring your friend completely is. It's his fault that he was not efficient in handling the situation", she was fuming again.

"Can we please get over this? You are with me now, and that matters to me now. So please let's not ruin our moods and explore the other areas here", I tried to divert the topic.

We were taking snaps outside, and from a distance, I could see both of them standing and talking; they smiled and waved when they saw us. Finally I indicated them to come over. We posed for a few snaps and then decided to leave. We took a bus. As four consecutive seats were not available, so Dev and Chandini sat in the front row, while we chose the back row. I could see Dev was very happy with his girlfriend and the same was I; but I felt ignored at the same time.

"Sid please, swear on me, don't be upset".

I tried to smile, wanted to behave as if everything was fine, but it was all in vain..

We got off the bus; Neha gave a hint to Dev that I was upset..

As per the planning, Dev had to stop here to buy Chandini's scooty from the showroom nearby.

Dev and his girlfriend bid goodbye to both of us. Dev added – "I shall have dinner with you at night. See you soon. Bye for now".

I walked with Neha; she was holding my hand, to make me feel comfortable.

"Tough situations will make you differentiate between the good and the bad. Don't worry, I am there for you, and will always be...", Neha tried to pacify me.

We spoke for some time, and then bade goodbye to each other. It was past six in the evening.

I walked inside our room. It was empty. My roommate Sumit had gone to his hometown. I closed the door, switched off the lights, and lied down. All the memories came flashing in my mind, right from the school days till today. Just then I received a text message. It was Dev.

"I'll reach in another 30 mins. Don't cook anything. Once m back we both can prepare food 2gether. Wait until then☺". I didn't reply.

Then Neha called me, I received.

"Are you ok…?", she inquired.

"Hmmm", I said softly.

"What's going on in your mind…?", she asked.

"Nothing at all", I tried to sound casual.

"Sid! Even if you don't want to tell me, I will get to know", she replied.

"Leave it… What are you doing?", I asked.

"Nothing as such. My mom called and blasted at me as I didn't go to visit my brother", she replied casually.

"I am really sorry for all the trouble. The whole day was a waste for you. You could have instead visited your brother's place", I said in an apologetic tone.

"Hey please don't feel that way. It was not your fault. Besides, you were with me, so I don't care a damn about others. What still surprises me is that he begged me to come over with you so he could treat us this way…", Neha said, her voice full of anger..

"I am really sorry about that", was all that I could say.

"Please don't be. You were not at fault. It's already past 9, please go and have something", she told me in a concerned voice.

"He texted me to wait for him, he wants to help me in cooking", I replied.

"But how long are you going to wait? I don't think he will be back soon. Anyways do as you feel ", came her reply.

I hung up and stood near the balcony; looking at the sky, the stars. The sky was wondrous to behold that evening; I felt deserted. As if, everyone left me standing in the lonesome city. The sky seemed to be quite stable, while the city quite unstable. Similarly I appeared stable outwardly, but my mind wasn't. Sometimes loneliness affects you from inside. It questions whether you were wrong that made people around you desert you in this busy world! The turmoil in my mind was in full force when suddenly I got a call from my mom.

"What are you doing, son…?", she enquired.

"Nothing much, standing in the balcony now…", I replied casually.

"Dev is there with you?", she enquired.

"No, he went to meet his friends. He said he will be back soon".

"It's already 10 pm now, call him and ask where he is. He is new to the city. Before he lands into some trouble, ask him to come back soon. It's not good to stay out for long in an unknown city", my mom said in a worried tone.

"Don't worry, I will call him in a few minutes", I assured her.

"Where did you roam all day? Where did you all had lunch?" she enquired. She sounded very happy, and the last thing certainly I would never want to ruin her mood by telling her about the day's events. I told her everything…, in a way that made her feel that I had enjoyed a lot.

"Ok, it seems you are very happy my son…That's why you didn't even bother to call me even once today", she tried to sound upset.

"Mom, I can never forget you, whatever be the circumstances. Love you maa", I replied guiltily...

"Yeah, I know that. When you are with your buddies, you forget everything around you. Even when you are speaking over the phone, I am able to understand your feelings, without even getting to look at you", she said.

"How?", I inquired.

"You sound very cheerful and jolly when you are happy. When you are morose, you speak less, plus the excitement in your voice is missing", she explained.

"You are right maa. I outsmarted you with my acting skills today. I am far from being happy, but I lied to you. Forgive me mom...I am not ok, not at all...", I whispered to myself, looking at the sky.

"Ok, it's already 10:30 pm now. Call him and ask him to be back soon and inform me once he does", she said. "Ok sure, bye for now", I said and hung up. I was waiting for him. I called him at 11 PM. He didn't receive my call but texted me – "will reach home soon, don't worry"

I came back to my bed and dozed off for some time. Suddenly I woke up and found it was already past 12, and he had still not arrived. I thought of preparing food, but I was in a dilemma. I was unsure if he still did not have food outside, and if he did, then it would be waste if I prepare food for the two of us. He didn't even take my call, probably he was on his way – all these thoughts crossed my mind. Finally I decided to wait until he was back. I lied down once again with all the lights switched off, except for a dim night bulb. My mobile rested on my chest. Once again at 12:30 am, I tried reaching him but he didn't respond. In the second attempt, he picked up and said, "I am on my way. I will call you once I reach". I was very hungry too, but didn't feel like having anything. Around 1, my mom called again.

"Is he back?", she inquired.

"No…, don't worry. He will be here in another few minutes", I tried to sound normal.

"Arey, do you realize how late it is? What is he up to?", she questioned angrily.

"What can I do if he is not back on time? He is not a spoon-fed child. I can advise him to come back early but I cannot force him…", I replied, my voice harsh..

"I am worried here beta. I am not able to sleep. It's so late", my mom sounded worried.

"Please go off to bed mom. Don't worry he will be back soon. Bye, good night and take care", I wished her and disconnected the phone. I was surprised to see my mom so worried for him!

I was very upset. I felt hungry but was too devastated to have something. Somehow even I was concerned for him as it was really late in the night and the city was not known to him too. I looked at my mobile; it was 1:10 am. I closed my eyes for a while. I was drained out, mentally more than physically. I didn't realize when I dozed off with the phone in my hand. Suddenly I felt the phone vibrating in my hand, and then I realized that I had dozed off. Dev was calling. I woke up with a jerk and attended his call.

"I am standing in front of your door…", he said in a low voice.

I ran towards the door. He entered, exhausted. Meanwhile I checked my cell phone and I found 15 missed calls from his number. Don't know why but somehow I felt guilty about it.

"Sorry yaar, don't know when I dozed off...my phone was on vibration, so didn't realize all the more", I said apologetically.

"How long could you wait...it's ok", he replied.

"Have you had dinner...?", I asked.

"Yes, she forced me to dine with her, I couldn't refuse. Hope you will understand me...", came Dev's reply.

"Ok if you don't need anything else, shall I go off to sleep?", I asked him.

"Nope, I don't need anything. You can go off to bed", he said.

I wished him "Good night", took a mouthful of water and retired to bed.

He wished me back, changed into his pyjamas and slept on the bed next to mine. Finally I went to bed with an empty stomach.

<u>ELEVEN</u>

The time when I opened up my eyes, lying in the bed, I could feel the warm of the dark yellowish haze coming through the transparent glasses of my door. All the previous memories of last night came in a flash, I closed my eyes once again to thank God for giving me one more chance to live, one more day to explore.

Just then, I received Neha's call. She wished me morning and I too wished her back.

"How long did you wait for him yesterday?" Neha was inquisitive.

"He turned up around 1.40 am. I dozed off in the meantime", I replied.

"I knew he would be late and I warned you beforehand, didn't I? And when did you have your dinner?", she questioned again.

I remained silent for a while, didn't know what to say…

"You skipped your dinner…, Am I right…?" she demanded to know.

"No… I had my dinner", I almost whispered to her softly.

"Alone…? Or with him…?" her questions seemed endless.

"I told you he reached at around 1.40 am, so it was expected he would dine with his gf and be back", I answered.

"You cannot have your dinner all alone; it's too good to be true. C'mon tell me the truth", she demanded.

Her question was answered by my silence. She understood that I had slept on an empty stomach.

"Never mind, have your breakfast right away. I will speak to you after that", she said.

"I am confused if you are ordering me like my Lead Varsha or requesting me as a friend?", I asked innocently.

"Yes it's an order. Fifteen minutes are all you have to finish off your breakfast. I am going to call you soon after", she sounded scary.

I agreed. Meanwhile I got a call from my college friend Sarada, asking me to come over. I was not in a pleasant mood, but the very thought of sitting in the room all by myself, made me feel uneasy. Hence I decided to pay them a visit, hoping that would refresh my mind. Dev already had had his bath by then. I got freshened up and asked him to drop me over to my friends' place. He agreed and said apologetically, "Sorry I am unable to give you time"

I cut him short. "It's ok", I said. "Can we leave now?"

"Ya sure, come", said Dev.

We both started off and he dropped me on the way and left. I was meeting the college bunch after three long years and they were super excited to find me there. They welcomed me with a gesture of warmth and ordered drinks and all junk food that we loved to have. My mind that was so disturbed since last day suddenly brightened up. Their love and gesture towards me made me feel happy from within. I was with them throughout the day; didn't realize how time flied. They didn't want me to leave, but my concern for Dev made me bid them Goodbye. I sat in the bus, and as I was reliving the moments I captured in my camera, my phone started ringing. It was Dev.

"Darling, what's up…?"

"On my way back", I replied.

"What are your plans for dinner tonight?" he inquired.

"Nothing decided yet", came out my reply.

"Let's do something special today. I shall reach within half an hour. It's 7 pm now. 7.30 pm sharp and you will find me at your place", he said assuring.

"Ok. Bye", I replied.

I called one of my roommates, Sahil. He was in some mall, purchasing some stuff for another roomie's birthday celebration. I joined him there. He had already made the purchases; I just increased the quantity of paneer and chicken as Dev wanted to have dinner with me.

I waited for him till 9 pm. Sahil and my other roommates asked me to lend them a hand in cooking. As I was preparing the curry, Sahil, who stood beside me, inquired, "At what time will Dev arrive?"

"He went to meet his girlfriend, so he might be late I presume", I replied.

"Hmmmm", he smiled and left the kitchen. It was already 10.30 pm by then, and I dialled his number. His phone rang and he picked up instantly.

"Hello…where are you?" I asked.

"I need some more time yaar. I am discussing something important. Will let you know", he replied in an irritable voice.

"Fine", I said and hung up.

Just then, one of my best friends called me. It was Avinandan.

Avi – "Hey Sid, how are you?"

I – "All fine. What's up with you?"

Avi – "Ok… I have two good news. Just could not resist to share with you, so called you right away."

I – "Yes tell me. I am all ears."

Avi – "I got placed in RBI, at the post of manager."

"Wow! Heartfelt congratulations dear. What is the other one?" I was eager to know.

"Getting engaged at the end of next month…, and of course you have to come", he sounds excited.

"Now that's news to me. Awesome yaar. Congratulations once again", I replied. I was really happy for him.

"You are the only one amongst my friends whom I have informed. People get jealous when you talk of your success, so I didn't bother informing anyone else", he said.

"No problem. I was confident of your success and finally it materialized", I replied.

"Yes. Only few believed in me, and you were one among them. I had been through a real tough time, but all your wishes and my hard work paid off well. Feeling quite relaxed and contented", he said with a sigh of relief.

"Hmmm. All my best wishes for your new job and new life. Oh yes! Are you getting engaged to the same girl you dated since college?" I inquired.

"Of course! Do you doubt that?" he pretended to sound angry. I laughed aloud.

"Nope, nothing like that. Just wanted to make sure. Generally people are not fortunate enough to get married to people of their choice. But you are lucky", I told him.

"Hmmm. That I am", he giggled. "You will have to come to attend; I am not going to buy any of your excuses", he replied with a tone of warning.

"I'll give it my best try, but I cannot assure you. Last month I had been to my hometown and I am left with no more leaves", I replied.

"But I will expect you…, Please do come", he pleaded.

"Of course dear. Even I want to be a part of your happiness. I don't need a formal invitation from you; neither you have to plead me. I really wish to be with my best friend on his special day; I had been awaiting this for long", I said. I felt nostalgic.

I spoke to him for a while. I felt good.

It was 11PM by then, and my roommates called me for dinner.

Sahil – "Hey Sid, will you join us for dinner or wait for your friend…?"

Before I could answer, another roomies jumped in – "We expect you to come and dine with us, so please come along. Prioritizing a friend doesn't mean you will neglect the others; even we exist in your life…"

Left with little choice, I decided to have dinner with them, literally hoping that Dev would reach soon and join us too. I had already put his share of chicken and paneer aside. Post dinner, we cut the cake as a part of our roomie's birthday celebrations. There was no sign of Dev yet. After the cake cutting ceremony, everyone retired to bed at around 1 am. I was waiting for him to come.

Dev's text arrived– "Don't worry, m on the way. Will reach in thirty minutes".

I waited for him; he finally arrived after 2 am. As soon as he entered, I asked him to change and have food. He removed the covers off the plates, looked at the dish and said, "I am not feeling good. Let it be here, I will have it in the morning".

"Don't sleep on an empty stomach, please have something…"

'I already had. We were discussing about our future plans. Her parents are not ready to accept me, and she was crying over it. She wanted to skip food, so I forcefully made her dine with me", Dev justified.

"What about me? You promised to have food with me. I cooked all this especially for you", I whispered to myself. I understood now that between a friend and a girl-friend, the latter gets the priority.

I realized, I would have gone to bed on an empty stomach yet again had I not joined my roomies for dinner. Finally I drifted off to sleep.

The next morning he was supposed to leave. He woke up early. By the time I woke up, he already had had his bath. I sat up on my bed, depressed as he was about to leave. I offered him the amount he paid for the lunch in McD.

"There's no need for this", Dev refused to accept.

"I was supposed to pay for it; it was my treat, remember?" I argued.

"It's no big deal. You can treat me some other time", he replied.

"No, I want you to accept this…, please…", I insisted.

Dev – "What is this Sid? Where does this "money" come between you and me?"

"I was to give the treat, so it's obvious that I should pay", I shot back.

"There is no difference, whether you pay or I pay", he replied.

"There is difference", I continued to argue.

"Can't I pay for my friend? Don't I have that right, Sid…?" he said.

"Why will you pay for Neha? Look there's no point arguing, please accept it", I told him forcefully.

"Oh, in that case, I will only take back the amount that was due on her", he replied, to which I didn't argue. I quietly gave him the amount and engaged myself in some work.

Finally he got ready to leave. As per his plan, he would meet his girlfriend, spend the entire day with her and finally leave for his place in the evening. Because of that he had to bid me goodbye in the morning itself. Before leaving the room, he asked –

"Will you come with me till the gate….?"

"Yup. Sure", I replied.

We took the lift and reached the ground floor, where his scooty was parked. Before starting, he hugged me and said – "sorry yaar, please forgive me…"

I tried to smile, "It's OK, no problem…"

He took the scooty out of the gate and was about to start. Suddenly everything appeared smudged, just then he turned back. All the feelings that were bottled up all these days could hardly contain themselves anymore. He came near me and held my hands. "Sorry yaar. I know I was unable to give you proper time. I tried my best to balance, but it didn't work out. You know how much I love her, and the moment I am with her, I forget everything else. It was a tough time for me, and I can't explain it to you right now. Forgive me if possible…"

"I understood yaar. Please don't justify. Leave now else you will be late".

He started his scooty and looked at my face.

Dev – "I can't leave you like this yaar, feeling very guilty"

"Please! Now you are getting late. I will be all right. Goodbye and take care", I desperately wanted him to leave.

"Are you sure you are ok? Please don't lie…" Dev insisted.

"Yes I am fine. Please leave", I almost begged him to leave.

Finally Dev bade me goodbye and left. I was returning to my room, just then Neha called me.

"What are you doing…?"

Me – "just sitting…"

Neha – "And Dev…?"

Me – "Left…"

Neha – "Have you had your breakfast?"

Me – "Not yet"

Neha – "Please have something"….

Me – "Don't feel like"…

"You seriously want to skip food because of him? Whether he had dinner with you or his girlfriend last night?" she inquired.

"He came after 2 am, so…" I tried to defend him!

"I knew it. Stop thinking about him", she said angrily.

I yelled out, "Do I deserve all this?"

"Not at all! Don't worry, he will definitely realize his mistake someday. Now stop bothering about him and for God's sake, fill your stomach", she pleaded to me.

Finally around 2 pm, I ate something and went off to sleep.

Around 8 pm in the evening, his text arrived– "M on my way, about to leave Bangalore in another thirty minutes".

I called him to wish a safe journey. He didn't pick my call. In the second attempt, his girlfriend attended.

"Hello. Sid, he is driving now. Will text you once he will reach…" she said.

"Ok, wish him a happy journey. Bye…" I replied, before I hung up.

Around 10.30 pm, he texted, "Crossed Electronic city now".

"Happy journey…" I replied.

"Had your dinner?" he asked.

"Yes. What about you?"

"Yes. Feeling really tired".

"Ok. Take rest…"

"As soon as I reach, I will give u a call".

"Bye. Good night".

He wished me back. I switched off my cell phone and went off to sleep. The next day, I reached office on my usual time. I called her, staying outside the campus gate,'

"What's up?" I asked.

Neha – "Nothing much, have to check one script, and submit by EOD".

'I am waiting outside the campus gate, Come, for breakfast...' I said while waiting outside office gate. She came out without delay.

She asked me, 'Are you ok now...?'

"Yes, I am..." I replied casually.

"Please don't recall whatever had happened. I am always there for you", she held my hands and patted gently.

We walked to the nearest tiffin stall. The atmosphere seemed a bit polluted, but people were crowded in front of the stall. The stall offers tea, and all types of snacks, along with sandwich and bada-pav. We ordered corn sandwich and some chips, along with two regular cup of tea. I started munching on the snacks. She was looking at the person with cigarette.

I asked her, 'Do you like that guy...'

'I like the way he is smoking...' suddenly pulling my hand, notoriously she pleaded with childish expressions on her face, 'Let's try one...'

'What...?'

'Cigarette...' with craze, she shouted.

'Are you crazy...? I don't even know how to hold it... Being a girl, you shouldn't try all this nonsense..., what people will think about you...' I told.

'Who cares..., let them... Just I am waiting for you to say 'yes', that's it...' she replied offering me a bite of sandwich.

I saw the person smoking was constantly looking at her, may be because he heard our conversation.

'No way! I am not going to say you 'yes', don't create any scene, the villain is looking at you... Eat quickly, we will move… Else I may lose my temper, and a big scene will be created unnecessarily', I warned her.

She held my hand, and shared with me her plate. She received a call from Sameer. He wanted to enquire about the downloads that Neha was to give him.

"It's done, but how do I give you. It is around 80 GB", she asked Sameer.

She spoke to him for a while and then looked at me.

She – "Hey…, I need your hard disk. Can you give it to me for a week?" She wanted to transfer the 80 GB data in the hard disk from her system so she could give it to him.

"I could have given but…" I became silent.

"So you don't want to give, right? Fine I don't need your help", she said.

I paid for the tiffin, and finally we moved towards the campus.

"How can I tell you that my hard disk is half-consumed by a wide collection of all HD-videos where we get Warning/Disclaimer as 18+ Adult Content", I whispered to myself.

"Please listen to me. There's no space left in the hard disk…" I trailed off, but she stopped me midway.

"Whatever I ask for from you, all I get is a big "NO" in return. Just leave it. I hate you", she was hyper again.

I tried to make her understand. She was short tempered; any trivial issue ignited her. Finally she will settle down in return of another demand that has to be fulfilled. She asked me to kiss her then.

"What? Me? I don't… don't know how to", I stammered.

"That's not my problem. You made me angry and now you have to pay for it. Now don't act and kiss me", she demanded.

It was the very first time I was about to kiss someone. I kissed her on the back of her hand, and she closed her eyes. We were almost near the gate, when I looked at the guard he gave me a stupid smile, seems he has seen me kissing her. Suddenly we walked to our ODC. For a few seconds I was silent. Sitting in my cubicle, I wondered – "What did I just do?!"

Just then, I received a message in WhatsApp. Neha snatched the phone from my hand to check. It was Dev.

"Reached around 6.30 in the morning. In office now. What's up?" he texted.

She was furious at him. "Stupid fellow. Now he has all the time in the world to talk to you".

I snatched the phone back from her and texted him back – "I am in office too".

Dev – "Hmmm. Will talk to you once I am back to my room in the evening".

Neha snatched my phone again and typed – "No need…, do I really deserve all that you did to me?"

I was grateful all this was happening over the phone. I dreaded the thought of Dev facing Neha at this point of time. She would have probably gobbled him up!

Dev – "No. Really sorry for that… I know I was a little selfish, I chose her over you every time. But trust me, I was helpless. Even if I wanted to be with you, the situation was not in my favour".

I took the mobile from her hand and replied – "Please, I don't need any explanations. I have some work; will catch up with you later".

I switched off my mobile data and looked at Neha.

Neha — "Don't answer his calls. I don't want him to disturb you unnecessarily".

"I wanted to avoid all this. That is the reason I wanted to refrain from going there", I said.

"Leave about that day. Twice he kept you waiting for dinner; he filled his stomach on time but didn't bother to ask you for once whether you had your food or not. What kind of a friend is he? I could never imagine he would turn out to be like this, as I always heard good about him. How could he be so selfish; inviting us over and behaving weird, conversing in an alien language as if we were not expected to be there. His attitude and behaviour really pissed me off."

I remembered, she was the one who forced me to go there, that day, and today she was asking me not to speak to him anymore. With time our perception for others change, to their behaviour and attitude. From what she had heard about him from me, she thought of him to be a good guy, but that incident left a negative impression of him on her mind.

I worked for the rest of the day. After I came back home in the evening, he called me. No sooner did I receive his call, he started to explain his weird behaviour that I witnessed couple of days back. I was not in a mood to listen to his explanations.

"Do I deserve the kind of behaviour you exhibited, not just in my presence but in others' presence too? I really felt ashamed. This is the reason I wanted to decline your invitation right from the beginning. I was confident this was inevitable. Anyways let's get past over this, but don't expect me to forgive you for all that you did. I just don't want to be a part of your life anymore", I exploded; all my bottled up feelings finally gave vent to him.

"Sorry yaar, please try to understand me. I won't be able to force you to be in my life, but I definitely want you to be there…" he said, stunned by my outrage.

"Don't lie, I have witnessed and heard a lot from you", I said, angrily.

"Ok, if you have decided on something, I can't force you", he replied.

"It's ok. Can I hang up?" I asked warily.

"Please yaar don't do this to me, I really don't want to lose you…" he pleaded.

"Please don't create a scene. I had misconceptions about it, but now everything is transparent to me. So let's just finish this off here…" I said, disgusted.

"Enough now! Don't behave like a girl. Girls behave like this as they are possessive. Chandini behaves in a similar manner, and that's acceptable as she is my girlfriend and she has the right to expect from me. I don't expect the same from you", he yelled.

"So now you are drawing comparisons between me and your girlfriend? Well she expects everything from you, someday you two might make a family. I am just a friend to you, and all I wanted from you was a little love and care that you had for me all these years. My mistake, I expected you to still be the same. I am surprised you had the audacity to compare me with your gf. What exactly do you think you are? I have always thought of you as my brother, and look how mean and cheap you turned out to be. Your gf labelled me a "sautan", and now you are speaking in her language. Fine, just go to hell and don't bother talking to me anymore", I burst at him.

I disconnected, without giving him a chance to speak further.

I started changing into my pyjamas and was getting freshened up when he constantly kept calling me. I just didn't bother to answer him. He texted – "I don't mean all that… it just came out of my mouth at the heat of the moment…"

I was way too pissed off, but I managed to scribble back, "It's ok. Be happy with your life. Good night".

My concept changed. I understood that day, why people used to say – friends are friends till they don't have a girlfriend. People in a relationship tend to emphasize on expressing their best behaviour so they can make it work. The "girlfriend" becomes the cynosure of their life, with whom they like to spend time.

That day, before retiring to bed, I tried to recall whatever happened till date. I wanted to ascertain if I was wrong somewhere, someday. The day, before sleeping; I recalled everything… in-order to crosscheck that - whether I was wrong at any point of time! Then I realized – it's not mandatory that the way you perceive life will be the same in which others envision it. I admire Buddha's teachings –

a) The very beginning is like the sun which emerges from the clouds, or like a mirror which, when rubbed, regains its original purity and clarity.

b) Long is the night to him who is awake; long is a mile to him who is tired; long is life to the foolish who do not know the true law. Hate never yet dispelled hate. Only love dispels hate. This is the law.

c)   Attachment leads to suffering.

d)   The Way is not in the sky; the Way is in the heart. See how you love.

All these statements have a true impact in our relations…

I got answers to my questions, and thanked God for the day, before going off to bed…

<u>TWELVE</u>

"Every artist undresses his subject, whether human or still life. It is his business to find essences in surfaces, and what more attractive and challenging surface than the skin around a soul?"

- Richard Corliss

Few days later...
12:30 PM Day time...

I was seated in my room, busy going through the presentation prepared by Neha. I was dressed in a half sleeve vest teamed with black shorts. Neha was seated facing me. She had come in casuals. It took me a few minutes to re-check the ppt; and all the while she was being impatient to speak to me. She had arrived in my flat for the first time to discuss work. She was lazing around, holding one magazine in her hand and flipping through the pages; hardly bothering to go through the contents but carefully examining the coloured pictures that popped up in most of the pages! Suddenly, she tapped on my shoulder to get my attention. She leaned closer, almost near to my shoulders. A little more close and she would have brushed against my face.

I tried to distance myself a little. "Don't get so close. People will have a wrong impression of you if they find us in this situation. And even if the guy is equally at fault, it's always the girl who is to be blamed", I chided her.

Neha– "So what? Are you talking about your roomies? I just don't care"

"I know, you wouldn't give a damn but you have to take care of all these details. Don't forget that you are a girl", I tried to explain.

"It would be nice, if I were a guy. I could have been a lot closer to you, I could have shared each and everything with you. But as a girl, I have a lot of limitations", she sighed.

"You can still do that. I don't have any issues", I said.

"I cannot be very open with the opposite sex", came her instant reply.

"That's your perception. My thinking is different. I don't think being open to the opposite sex is a big deal at all", I replied.

"Then kiss me", she said, out of the blue.

"I…I won't… people will see us…" I stammered.

She moved closer to me. "Kiss me", she whispered into my ears.

I looked at her and smiled. Just then I could feel the softness of her lips on my cheeks. I closed my eyes and moved backward.

She smiled and said, "I did it. It's your turn now".

I nodded and touched my lip with my finger and pressed the same on her cheek. "I only know how to kiss in this manner", I gave my explanation. "Now please be seated, today I want you to witness my artistic skills. I am going to sketch something surprising", I said in an excited voice. "Really? Can you sketch?" she asked, amazed. I smiled and took a pencil and an eraser from my bag. I asked Neha to show me a picture of a nude couple. She searched God-knows-what and found none. I took the mobile and typed in the Google search bar – "images for nude couple". A few images showed up, and I picked one out of them. In that the girl held the guy in her arms and both were undressed. The moment I showed the picture to her, she exclaimed, "Oh my God! Chhiii, it's so bad…" "You cannot define good or bad in art. It's all about the way you look at things around you", I replied.

I knew I could not sketch a woman, in all her natural inner beauty. I may have the perfect skill, but putting something in pen and paper, is interesting, unique, nothing less than a challenge. It gives you good vibes when you know you are successful in your attempts. After a long time, I was trying to sketch something and this was different from the sketches I had done all through. I was a little skeptical as I had not tried my hand in drawing sketches for a pretty long time, and I feared I might not come up to the expectations. It was a challenge for me as this would prove my skills as an artist.

An artist derives his inspiration from his audience, his admirers. It was the same with me. But unfortunately, no one really showed interest in my art after my school days were over. Rather they felt it was a waste of time, so they wanted me to put in more efforts in studies than in art. People fail to understand the real essence of creativity. Life is not just about studies and clearing exams. It's actually one's hobby that defines an individual. The overall development of a human is possible only when he excels in every field he wants to try his hands on. Gradually my love for painting got replaced with writing scripts. Studies apart, this had become an inseparable part of my life. Elders at home had issues again – they wanted me to devote time on all this only on vacations. What they failed to understand was that a creative person can never restrict himself/herself within a particular timeframe. I was no longer a school-going boy. The writer in me revolted – I started to voice my likes and dislikes. Slowly elders at home felt my passion for writing and allowed me to pursue my hobby...

That day I was in a quite good mood, and after a long time wanted to try my hand in sketching. I wanted to be left alone in the room so I could properly focus on my sketch, and she agreed. She left the room, and engaged herself in telephonic conversation with her friends so she could kill time. In the meantime I started sketching the girl's hair. I was trying to give proper dark linings, and gradually my pencil sketched her hair, followed by her head, her shoulder and then to her attractive parts. I stopped there and began with the guy. After I was done with his shoulders and arms, I focused on the girl again. I was to draw the girl's curves then. The girl's arm was close to the guy's, and her round firm breasts were half exposed and half covered up by the guy's arm and the rounded butt was also quite sensuous to look at. I had always fantasized about girls and their curves and as I was putting my art on paper, I felt as if I was actually holding her in my arms. The girl's lip was locked with the guy's and her right hand was near the guy's hair. Then I concentrated on her butt. I tried to give it a proper round shape. Her bared legs were entwined with the guy's. Most of her body parts were covered by the guy. They were nude, but it didn't seem vulgar to me as an artist. Nudity is an art, there is a saying over this –

"What spirit is so empty and blind, that it can't recognize the fact that the foot is nobler than the shoe and skin more beautiful than the garment with which it is clothed." So it's not bad to figure out something labelled as "nude". In fact, even to depict a clothed structure, one need to fully-visualize the concept of what is underneath.

There was a sense of romance, the feeling of being two bodies and one soul. I imagined that her body was pressed against mine, her soft curves brushing against my body. She put her hands around my arm and I pulled her towards me, kissing her soft and deep. Love was in the air. I was in a state of eternal bliss as I imagined and sketched, when suddenly she called out my name and broke my reverie.

"Sid, are you done? I just can't wait any longer", she sounded curious and excited.

"Just a few more minutes and I'll be done. A few more detailing is left; it will give a realistic feeling to the sketch", I replied back.

Finally after sometime I was done. I came out of my room, called her and handed over the paper to her. Shocked as hell; she looked at me, closed her eyes and exclaimed "Oh my God!" She ran away with the sketch towards the balcony as she was hesitant to scan the sketch in my presence. I smiled at her and sat with my laptop. I could see she was carefully examining it. Finally after a few minutes she came back.

"It's just awesome! I can't believe you did this…" she said softly. She was really amazed.

"I only tried my best to put my emotions on paper."

She kept staring at me.

"What are you looking at…?" I asked.

"I still can't believe you did this", she said again.

"There are a few fine details that are still missing in this sketch. I shall try one more someday which will depict finer details of the body structure and the romance too", I said and winked at her.

"Ok. Enough. Lock your system right away. I am famished; can you prepare something?" she asked.

"Nope. Sahil and Viren are there", I said.

"How can you be so ridiculous? You didn't bother to offer me anything; and now when I am asking you, you are refusing on my face!" she said angrily.

"Wait. Let me see", I said and closed my laptop and walked out of the room. Only Sahil was there; Viren went out for shopping. I asked Sahil if he wanted me to prepare food for him too.

"I already had. Others will have lunch in the mall itself. You guys only prepare for yourselves", Sahil replied.

I walked inside my room and smiled.

"What happened?" Neha enquired.

"Nothing, get yourself ready to help me in the kitchen", I replied.

"But I don't know how to cook yaar", she replied ruefully.

"I will teach you. C'mon let's go", I replied.

She was ready, so we went out of the room. I took some potatoes and an onion and started chopping them with knife. She observed and asked me to allow her, doing the next one. I handed over the knife to her so she could chop the next potato. She put in her efforts but I noticed she would take a decade to complete; instead I instructed her to place the vessel on the induction oven and pour oil into it. I resumed back to chopping potatoes and suddenly asked her, "Do you want to take that paper and show it to your roommates?"

"Yes, I liked it a lot. And you sketched it for me. So it belongs to me and I am going to take it with me", she said.

"Oh nice. I will make some more for you like I said, with better detailing!" I said mischievously.

"There's no need for that. You have already proved yourself", she said.

"So what? I will do a few more. I was not trying to prove myself to you; just wanted to revive my olden days and ensure I could still sketch even though I don't do it regularly. And I am happy I did a decent job. I am glad I did something different from the regular monotonous routine work", I said, truly satisfied with my work.

"Hmm…, you are right. However, try something good. Don't do these stupid things. Do some good and meaningful sketch", she chided.

"What is bad about it, are you a child?" Are you not aware of all this, then what's wrong to put it on paper? See, I like this, so I will do this. Don't act or behave as if you don't know anything and also don't have any impressions about me being innocent. As you have become a close friend of mine now, we can open up and freely talk to each other without feeling embarrassed. This sketch is nothing. I can even sketch my wife while she is intimate with me and send it to you!" I said mischievously.

"I will break your head Sid. Just don't talk shit. I see you have become a gone case. Having come to Bangalore and staying with your "great" roommates, you are becoming naughtier day by day".

"Shhh… don't shout, Sahil is here", I whispered.

"During college days, you were quite innocent. But you are not the same Sid I know. Nowadays you use slangs, sketch nude pictures and hardly listen to anyone – you have changed a lot", Neha said, annoyed.

"Change is nature's rule. Each day, we people try to learn from our surroundings…" I was trying to be philosophical.

"Ok Ok… it's enough now, don't give lectures…" Neha said curtly.

"What is your problem Neha? Even if I say something good, you are not ready to listen", I said, angry at her attitude.

"Ok. I have understood. I will not say anything, and you too keep shut", Neha said in a pissed off tone.

"Fine, but the thing is I can't pretend to be what I am not, anymore. I am generally reserved and try to put on a decent behaviour with people until I get close to them. People who are close to me will define me best. Until I knew you well, I had put on a behaviour that any girl would want in a guy – reserved, decent and well mannered. Even I am like any other normal guy; I become crazy at times, watch porn and do weird stuffs. As we have become close friends now, I don't think I need to continue being pretentious. I am pretty transparent with all my close friends, so I am trying to be the same with you too. I am only sharing my thought process, my feelings – it being bad or good is immaterial. And of course it should not imply to you that I am a bad guy and have evil intentions and also I shall never ever cross my limits", I explained to her.

"You don't need to mention that. I am confident about you. All I am telling you is to avoid watching all this on the Internet", she sighed.

"Watching something crazy is not bad as long as it isn't reflected in your activities, right?" I asked her. I was almost done with my potatoes chopping.

"Yes. But I know you will not listen to me; instead you'll come up with some stupid explanation in your favour", she mocked me.

Her expression made me smile. "Let's start cooking. Wait, bring one pen and paper, and note it down", I told her.

"There's no need for that. I have a good memory", she winked at me.

"Great. A few potatoes, a medium sized onion, ½ tsp mustard oil, ¼ tsp turmeric powder, ½ tsp red chilli powder, ½ tsp garam masala powder, and salt are all the ingredients we need", I told her

"First heat oil in a pan, and crackle the mustard seeds", she beamed.

"Followed by adding the chopped onions and frying it till it turns golden brown", I continued as I cooked. She was standing beside me, observing me intently.

"Now we will add the chopped potatoes, salt, turmeric and all the other spices. We have to sauté it for some time and keep checking in intervals to ensure it's cooked properly", I was explaining to her. Finally I asked her to get me some water. She passed me a bottle.

"It's quite easy yaar…, I remember the steps…" she beamed and started murmuring the steps, keeping a count with her fingers like a child. In the meantime, I received the parcel of Parathas that I ordered online before Neha arrived. The quantity was not enough as while ordering, I didn't know she was coming, so we shared with whatever we had. While she went to wash her hand, I transferred the contents from the food packet on one plate. Also, I brought in whatever little food that I had prepared.

By the time she came back, I had already started gorging on my food like a monster, who had not eaten for days!

'Chi…chi…!', Neha exclaimed.

'I am not going to eat in that plate; let me get a new one'.

I looked at my plate, and felt disgusted – no sane person would have chosen to share the food from my plate that I had effortlessly messed up. She got a new plate from the kitchen and I tried to serve her food in the plate, carefully parting the food with my spoon from the sides of my plate.

'You shouldn't make your plate dirty as you eat, it doesn't look good', Neha said as she took a bite from her plate. She seemed to be very happy and contented. Post lunch I transferred the modified ppt in a pen drive and asked her to leave to which she replied innocently – "Feeling sleepy yaar, want to take rest for some time".

"C'mon now, you can take rest in your PG. There are certain rules and regulations in our apartment. Girls are not even allowed; and I have already broken that rule. You've got to leave soon, else you will make me land into trouble", I said in a worried tone.

"Rules are meant to be broken. I will be by your side; just don't worry", she replied casually.

"Shit! This was supposed to be my statement and not yours!" I said, stunned by her carefree attitude. How could she be so naive!

"I don't have a problem in staying with you", Neha replied.

"Even I don't have", Sahil called out from his room and giggled. I understood he overheard us. I wanted to hit him on his head right away!

"Please yaar, leave now, else people will start talking about us", I pleaded to her.

"Ok ok! Don't worry, I will anyways leave now. I was just pulling your leg. And I am not even dying to sleep with you", she made a face, snatched the pen drive from my hand and started walking away briskly.

"Wait", I called out. "I will drop you to your PG", I said.

We took the lift and reached the ground floor. 'Hey! Awesome yaar...!', she exclaimed. I was delighted as I thought she was praising me for my culinary skills. But I was proved wrong, when she finished it off with 'Audi... my favorite'.

Audi! Her favorite car! The car inevitably brings a smile on her face. She seemed normal again! Thank Audi! Thank God!

"Thanks for the food dear, it was awesome. You should cook for me at least once a week", she demanded. I nodded my head.

It was 4:30 pm and we were walking towards the bus stop. In the bus, she generally sits beside me, preferring the window seat. That day too, she did the usual thing. There was heavy rush and we were lucky to bag two seats for us. Neha was watching someone intently. My eyes followed her and found she was looking at a guy, who was intentionally standing very close to a girl sitting in the aisle seat and kept pushing her.

"This is the very reason why I always prefer the window seat. Look at that guy, he is constantly pressing his body against hers. I don't understand how people can be so desperate!" she said, annoyed.

"Am I also included in your so-called despos' list…?" I asked.

"Not at all. Whenever I see people doing that, I feel disgusted. I feel like hitting them in their balls", she said angrily.

"Omg! My body is also brushing against your arms at this very moment… Will you hit there, me too?" I asked her.

I tried to distance myself from her a little, to my left, when she grasped my hands tightly and said, "No. Of course I don't mean you. You are different from others…"

"How?" I asked innocently.

"I know you very well. Your attitude is different. You know, you are hatke… I am pretty comfortable with you. I will never hit you. You are lovable", she said sweetly.

"Oye… don't flirt with me. People are looking at us", I scolded her.

"Huh? Now that should be my statement. Not that I care though", she said in a carefree manner.

She smiled and came closer to me. Her lips were almost close to my face; she was doing that intentionally. Just when I was about to tell her something, the conductor arrived to collect the tickets. Suddenly she moved aside and sat straight. As I was paying for the tickets, I received a message from Dev on WhatsApp. We checked together. It was written:

If possible, please forgive me for my mistake…

If someday God gives me a chance to prove you that I can do anything for you, I will be thankful to Him….

Love you so much…

Miss you Darling…

All of a sudden, my mood changed. I remained silent for a while; it was more than two weeks and we still didn't speak to each other.

When you are in the habit of sharing every little secret, every little incident in your life with someone, and suddenly you stop speaking to that person, you will feel that something is missing in your life. You will be hurt, and you will want to get back to normal with that person. It's difficult to convince your heart to stop loving and caring for someone, even when you know the other person does not bother. Neha read my mind; she understood how I felt and held my hand to comfort me.

"I know that you are missing him now", she said.

"No, I am not. Why should I?", I asked more to myself than to her.

"Don't lie to me, I know you very well… I have seen your love for him. We are very similar in nature, even you get emotional and talk idiocy at times, but the truth is that you still miss him in your life", she said.

"Yes, I do", I almost whispered.

"I know you can't throw him out of your life. Call him and speak to him. It will make you feel a lot better", she said.

I remained silent; determined not to call him at any cost. I felt quite heavy; there was a lot of traffic that day, so we were getting late as well. She checked her watch and then popped her head outside the window to look at the traffic.

Finally, we reached her stop. After seeing her off there I returned to my apartment. I changed into my pyjamas and took a short nap. The nap ended with sunrays falling over my face from west window of my apartment. I got ready to prepare my food. My mom called me and asked me the usual questions, "How is your health? Did you have something beta? How is your work going on?" etc. I spoke to her for some time. I was planning to go to my hometown the following week. She was eagerly waiting to welcome me.

Finally the day came. It was Friday. I was supposed to catch the train by 7:30 pm, so I left the ODC at sharp 3:30pm. A couple of days back, Neha and I fought over a small issue. I was so pissed off with her that I asked her to maintain distance with me. The issue was very petty; I can't even define it as an issue. Two days back before the argument, I prepared lunch for office. We were undergoing training related to our domain during those days. In the first half, we had to attend that. Post lunch we would come back to the ODC to work. That day Neha attended training only for an hour as she had an urgent work in the ODC, but I had to be present in the training room as I was going to give a presentation on my topic. Meanwhile inside the training room, Simran inquired what I had brought for lunch. I told her I was carrying parathas and sabzi. She wanted to taste so I offered her, my tiffin box. That was my mistake – I offered her, my tiffin to taste! I still can't believe she fought with me over this. She had a lot of questions in mind, and I shot back at her.

"What do you think you are? What are you blaming me for?

Don't treat me as your boyfriend; I can't please you every time. You are free to think whatever you want, I just don't care."

We were looking into our plates while eating, to avoid any eye contact.

Finally, she interrupted the silence between us. "I know you don't care, but you can talk to me at least. I feel miserable when you are silent. Forget whatever happened and speak something".

"I need some time to recover, leave me alone. I don't want to talk to you now". I was really hurt by her behaviour. I accompanied her to lunch, but hardly spoke to her. It continued for the next two days. Finally on Friday when I was about to leave the ODC to catch the train, I asked her, "Are you going to miss me? Or would you be happy that I won't be there to irritate you for the next few days". She was silent. I tried to convince her to speak, but she was adamant. She didn't utter a word.

"Ok, so you don't want to speak to me? Fine, so be it. Be happy. Have a great life", I said and bid her goodbye.

Finally she responded – "Happy journey…, take care". I briskly walked out of the ODC.

I, my bag and my roommate were ready in no time as we were running out of time. We just managed to reach station on time and started looking for the train number for which our tickets were booked. I could not resist smile at the corner of my mouth, out of the mixed feeling of "going home" and "missing her". I wanted to text her, so I switched on the mobile data, and just as I was about to type a message, a few messages popped up. It was Neha.

I miss u dear. Don't forget me. Have a safe journey. Love u.

I felt good. She texted me before I planned to do. I replied back, "Miss u and love u too. In the train now, bored like hell. Did anyone inquire about me in the ODC?"

"No", came her reply. I felt relaxed. Just then I saw the lady sitting in my front seat, leaning towards the window and was half covered with a maroon shawl... Captivated with her aura, I was bit nervous; her body language looked very confident and professional. I guessed her to be in her early thirties. I couldn't help but to take a sneak peak in to her. Co-incidentally she also glanced at me lowering the book a little. There was a temporary eye contact and exchange of smiles. "Hello, how are you doing today sir?" she said in a soft voice. I was a little surprised but greeted her good evening with a smile. My roommate and I conversed for some time. Finally we had dinner and slept on our respective berths. After 26 hours of struggle in the train, finally I reached Bhubaneswar. My family was excited to see me after quite a few months. Needless to say, I was enjoying all the pampering and attention that I received from everyone. Only 3 days were wasted in Hanuman Puja that was arranged by my parents. They hired him because my mom had a bad dream about me and she believed that praying to lord Hanuman would make me free from all kind of evil shades.

I told Neha, the whole story - how entire day they tortured me. For this drama they have ordered 108 bananas which according to them would have been eaten by Lord Hanuman itself at night and how exactly those bananas got vanished, the following day. Actually he used to consume those in the name God and in the following morning, he used to say – Hanuman is satisfied with you my child… he has taken those bananas. Nothing bad will happen to you from now. Listening to this, Neha bursts out laughing. Days flew by and my holidays were nearing their end. Finally the day came when I had to leave for Bangalore yet again. Everyone was gloomy at home, no one had the heart to bid me goodbye. I felt terrible, but I had little choice. I parted with their blessings and advice to take care of myself, have food on time, to be patient at office, etc. No matter how old I grow, I will never be a grown up for them. Back at work place, no one cares to ask if I had food on time, or inquire about my health or to share my good and bad times. This is a part of life; you have to accept certain things not by choice but by compulsion. Returning back from my hometown was the toughest job of all, but then there's a famous saying – tough situations don't exist for a long time, but tough people do. This gave me hope and kept me going on. Finally, I reached airport. Dad had accompanied me. We both stood silently for some time, unsure what to speak as both of us were emotional. The announcement was made and it was time for me to bid him a final goodbye. I touched his feet to seek his blessings and found my way towards the security counter. All my father said was, "Fly safe. Do inform once you reach". I turned, smiled at him and after the check-in, I made my way towards the boarding gate…

<u>THIRTEEN</u>

Holding pencil, my right hand was ready for action on the paper. I saw the image of Elina for a couple of minutes, and then started with all my concentration. While doing the sketch, I was in my imagination world; my girl is standing in front of me, comfortable with me undressed. As I was trying to give shades to the sketch, a sense of humour ignited in my mind.

I closed my eyes, and thought of her real beauty that I have been across in the train journey, it was still fresh.

In the sketch she was standing beside me. My neck, my face was closer to hers. Her skin was so soft and sweet, I was feeling like kissing her. Though I was acting as if innocent; but being nude with someone, especially with a girl, you can't resist, no matter how innocent you are. She was not reluctant; she was happy and safe with me.

Her round sexy butt was touching the lower part of my body. Her left hand was near my waist and the other hand over my shoulder, extended to my neck. She was with her complete beauty; everything was very clear and transparent. Not even a piece of cloth was there in between our bodies. I touched her lower part passionately a bit, and then I felt like touching her butt, which was hiding my lower part. At the time of kissing her bare shoulder, face; our lower(bottom) parts rub against each other and I could have hardly noticed my straight extended part was semi-erected and grown up harder against her round sexy butt. My mind, my body was full of desire. Maybe I have reached the perfect height of emotions and love. My eyes moved faster, at the same time my pencil moved down her neck, over her breasts. My pencil, my fingers were kissing her pointed part and giving her breasts, a perfect round shape. I felt her, in my imagination and my shorts were about to get wet with fluid of emotions. It was a crazy moment, I could not resist. For a moment, I vanished from the place to my washroom, and after a couple of minutes returned back to the place to complete the same.

I took a snapshot of the sketch and sent it to Elina, in order to update her. Just then I got a call from Elina.

"Ya Elina... how are you doing? And did you like my sketch" I asked anxiously.

"I am fine… Yes, I liked it; it's really nice, a very bold and beautiful sketch", she said very pleasantly. "Thank you Elina, It means a lot to me" I said politely.

She- "I believe you can still make few changes to make it even better."

I – "Yes Elina, Sure why not, I am open to your suggestions and would really appreciate that"

"Sid, in the picture the lady is standing without wearing any dress. That's fine, the picture is as I said undoubtedly good and magnificently expressing the beauty and shyness of the lady but I was more interested in giving it a sensual touch. For example, if you can make her hairs open and wet and then make her wear a wet transparent Saree. The Saree from which every details of her body can be properly shaded, it would give the same feeling. In addition to it, you can make the guy hugging her with an intense feeling. Standing together with love will certainly hit the heart of your Audience by giving a steamy feeling to their desire. By the way I am really impressed that you have sketched my face so accurately. It means, (she paused) you really have a very fine imagination. Just one question, do I really look that much attractive in real, the way you have sketched me?" She asked in a friendly tone with a light smile.

I was really moved by her professional approach to it. I realized that only a true artist can understand the reality behind an art. While most people will find it merely nude and obscene, an artist will look beyond its content representation, exploring the flavour of the emotion with which it's been sketched.

So holding a smile I replied back, "You look more than just beautiful, you look fabulous", before disconnecting the call.

The day I met her in the train I was reluctant to speak to a confident and professional lady like her, since I was not habituated to that. Elina was the one who started the conversation asking me about myself, my native place and my schooling. While she came to know that I was from Bhubaneswar and a DAV pass out student her interest just doubled. She told that she was also from Orissa and was going to Bhubaneswar only. Above that she said, she had already been to my School, besides she knew the drawing teacher of DAV who had been very supportive to her. That caught my attention. I could have glimpse of the book she was holding, it was a sketch book. She was holding a pencil. I saw few images were sketched there. Then I came to realize she must have been associated with paintings otherwise why would someone will sketch on a train journey. It just made sense why she knew my drawing teacher. Listening to her about my teacher all my emotions started flowing restlessly like the mountain water flows down.

How strange it was right? One single motivation can bring back stunning memories of the past. Otherwise who would have thought that the boring journey would turn out to be so exciting? Who would have thought that the achievement that I once considered went unnoticed, was actually a discussion topic on passion. I think destiny has its own way to show us the path at its convenient time.

I was lost in her thought for some time, and then I looked back at the sketch.

I found the erotica of it turning me on to give the artistic touch to the sketch in a perfect way. However, as everything was in my imagination and a mere sketch, I was unable to do all that it persisted on. The guy's lower extended part was half covered up by the girl's round butt, but was clearly visible. It should be in a proper shape, so I tried many times, erasing the same. Then at the end, I did it. In addition, the boy's hand was just behind the girl's butt. In romance, very natural it is; your hand would discover every part of your opposite sex-partner.

These parts are quiet sensitive to pressure and vibration, and my body was very well responding to it. My sketch, almost done, the pair was too cute to look at in their original form. The person's muscles were also good to look at, and the most remarkable part was the lower ones, placed between the legs, for both of them. It was a sketch but if on examining it, it would give one the feelings of doing many crazy things. I shared the same in whatsApp to Elina. Then I slept as it was around 3 AM. I was all alone in the room.

Monday morning, I was back at my workplace after the vacation. Varsha welcomed me back and reminded me to shift to the cubicle opposite her cubicle. I had managed to escape all these days, but I knew I could not continue it for long; she would not rest in peace until her wish was fulfilled. Finally I shifted to the new cubicle by delighting Varsha and upsetting Neha! I too was unhappy but I had no other choice.

In tea time, I showed her the sketch, with a sense of hesitation. Don't know how she would react. As usual, she asked to leave her alone, as she could not check it in my presence. I left her alone for some time, and then she came back and shared her comment over the sketch – Sketch is good one, but your mind has gone polluted. What else is there to hide in that sketch…, I hate you and your sketch.

'Really sorry, I can't help you out. I did it for someone, not for you… You already have one boyfriend, so don't behave innocent…'

She reacted to my statement, 'Sid, mind your words carefully and tell me how is it related to Sameer…?'

'You should tell me, what all you people used to talk, used to share…?'

"What the hell, we don't discuss all these stupid things, he will kill me if I talk with him all this", She replied.

'That means, he don't know anything, he won't do anything with you after marriage, he don't see adult x-rated videos…?' I enquired.

'Neither he nor I am interested in such things…'

'But I am interested in all such things…, so I would do…' I replied.

'Fine! Let's not fight over such petty issues'.

"If you feel I am bad, so be it. I can't change myself for anyone", I made a face and remarked.

"Yes, I know that. Even if you are wrong, your ego prevents you from apologizing to me. But Sameer – he forgives me even if I am wrong and is always so supportive", she said with a sullen face.

"Stop comparing me with your boyfriend. After all I am just a friend – how do you expect me to behave like Sameer?" I lost my temper.

"I am not a fool to expect from you. I have been hurt enough and by the way who told you anything regarding him being my BF? ", She said even more furiously.

"Excuse me!! You mean to say he is not?" I asked with a shock.

"Have you ever heard from any of our friends that I have a boyfriend?"

"No, But that day you said that you were unsure of what would happen to your relationship with Sameer just because his parents came to know about both of you, the day when he was drunk and vomited everything in front of his mother which ultimately reached to his father. And besides help me to clarify what would you have referred to as "relationship" between you and him?" I asked her rudely reminding her of the past incident.

"I don't want to discuss a single word about him to you, knowing that your heart isn't half of what his heart is made of. So leave this matter here only. You are that friend of mine, who doesn't have time to call me back for even for 5 minutes even after knowing that I am hurt and need support. On which ground/rights are you asking me the details of my relationship with him?" she shot back.

"Leave me then, I don't want you in my life. I am bad and I can't behave as your Sameer. I can't behave innocent, and if you think I am an egoist, yes I am. I just don't care what people think of me; I will do the things I want to do in my own ways and I don't think I need to justify myself to anyone", I told her rudely.

"I know you are indifferent towards me, but I still care for you. No one is perfect. We should accept people the way they are. I don't try to find faults in you, please understand me", she was almost pleading.

"Please don't do mercy on me…, leave me alone"

"Ok, if your happiness lies in me leaving you alone, so be it", she wanted to say something more, but before she could do that, I left her place in fury. After coming back to my seat, I was pondering over what happened, and finally after sometime I pinged her on messenger –

'Sorry, I should not have been so open with you. I know I should have restricted myself. I accept my fault. But you have to agree that you were at fault too. You expected me to be like your Sameer…'

'I am sorry about it', came her reply.

It's ok if you tell me something, but you drew comparisons between Sameer and me that made me lose my temper. Dev did the same, remember? Just because I don't have one, I am treated like this…, I replied.

Leave it, I will not argue with you.

'Ok fine, don't talk with me. I want to be left alone', I was losing my temper again.

Is this your final decision?

I replied with a Yes…

Soon after I went for lunch, not bothering to inform her. Later I got to know that she skipped her lunch, crying. I felt bad, but the ego in me restrained me from going near her. I got busy with my work and finally around 5 pm, I made up my mind to reach her. In the midway, one of my colleagues, Sita, called me over to her cubicle. She was talking about some funny incident; I could not help but burst out laughing. Just then, I saw from a distance that Neha was observing me intently from her place. I ran over to her place, and tried to break the ice.

"Yes?" I said, "Do you want to tell me something?"

"No. I don't want to spoil your mood. You seem to be comfortable with others. Am I just another option for a friend to you Sid?" she asked, her voice as low as a whisper.

"Absolutely not. I always prioritize you among all other friends", I said, shocked at her allegation on me.

"Please don't lie. It was evident from your behaviour today. If you would have really considered me to be a good friend, you would have asked me for lunch", she argued.

"I wanted to, but my ego didn't allow me to. I apologize for that. Please come and have something now", I said sheepishly.

Just then, Simran came near us and told us to join for tea. Swami too agreed with Simran.

Simran – "Let's go for tea"

Neha – "Not today, don't feel like"

Simran – "C'mon yaar, no drama now. Jaldi chalo(be quick, let's go…)"

Simran forced her to come, and finally all four of us walked out of the ODC.

She and Swami were discussing some official issues while they were preparing tea for themselves in the pantry. Both of us walked into the pantry after sometime and took a sip of water. As Simran was preparing her tea, she suddenly asked Neha, "You don't want to have tea?"

"No, right now I don't want to have. You guys prepare for yourselves and come out, I am waiting", she said.

Simran then offered me, "What about you Sid? Shall I prepare for you?" Even before I could reply, she started making tea for me too. Neha heard it all and left the place all of a sudden. After a few minutes, we came out and looked for her, but she was nowhere in sight. Simran called her to ask where she was. Neha picked up and informed that she had some urgent work to do, so she left suddenly. I understood that Neha was lying to her; the pangs of jealousy were hitting her hard. After sometime we all came back to our respective cubicles. As soon as I logged into my system, a message popped up. It was from Rajesh. It said –

"Sid Bhai, please don't do this to her, Don't be so rude to her…"

"You don't know anything, so it's better…" I replied.

Rajesh – she told me everything, she was crying…

'What can I do, I also need space yaar… I also deserve a little freedom; I can't live like that…, in a cage'.

Rajesh – Yaa, I understand, I asked her to let you do certain things as you wish. If Sid bro does something in his way, he gives his 100%, and if you force him to do the things, he may not give his cent-percentage. She agreed with me. She is accepting that it's her mistake. If someone accepts the mistake, then we shouldn't be that rude… After all, she loves you; she was requesting me, as if you are her only destination, without you she can't live…

I – But I know, the very moment, I'll get attached to her; she will once again start all the nonsense.

Rajesh – See! Loving someone is not bad, but at the same time, we shouldn't be so possessive. We should allow living his/her life… If that person is happy in his/her life, only then he/she can love us, that I tried to convey her and I assume she understood…

It took me only a few nanoseconds to understand that she was pissed off as Simran offered to prepare tea for me. I went over to her cubicle around 6 pm. I was standing near to her, but couldn't muster the courage to speak. Suddenly she said, "I am leaving now".

"Alone?" I asked, my voice barely a whisper.

She nodded. "It's already six. You were right, I should not have expected you to be a good friend of mine. I don't want to see your face again. I am going to ask Ram to release me from this project".

"Don't mess-up your professional life because of your personal issues. You don't have to sacrifice for me", was all I could say at that situation.

"I don't need your suggestion", she said.

'Excuse me! I just want you to inform that that sketch was for a lady named Elina, whom I met in last train journey'.

'Who is she...?' she questioned.

'He he... Now you saw my face, right...?' I chuckled.

With anger, she walked away without asking me to accompany her or bidding me goodbye.

I stood there silently for some time and finally after sometime I came back to my cubicle. I was disturbed. Just then, Varsha appeared from nowhere and began firing questions at me. She was accompanied by Sweety, so she could enjoy the humiliation I was to go through. I was in a disturbed frame of mind and I ended up giving a couple of incorrect answers. That triggered her temper and started yelling at me. She asked me to recheck the details for which I gave wrong answers and I did the same; still she was far from satisfaction.

Varsha – "Tell me what each member works on? You have been here for quite some time, you should know this." She always had excuses to make me stay back late. I didn't know about it in details, and I could not look up to someone for help as most of them had already left office by then. It was more than 10 hours, and I was still rotting in office…

"I want you to answer me, only then I will allow you to leave. Only coming to office and leaving on time won't help you. You need to be aware of certain basic stuff", she said again.

"I will let you know on Monday. As of now I want to leave", I sighed.

"I don't see you doing any fruitful work. If this is how it is going to continue, I have no choice but to ask Ram to release you from the project. I don't want you in my team anymore. Don't show me your face Monday onwards."

My patience was giving in. I was frustrated too. "Fine, so be it', I said angrily.

"It's ok with you? You sure?" she was shocked at my reaction.

"Yes", I said and left her gaping at me. I walked out of the ODC. I had had enough. Finally after reaching home, I texted Neha –

'You have good news. You didn't want to see me anymore in the ODC. God has fulfilled your wishes. I had a fight with Varsha today, and she doesn't want me to come to office. I will inform Ram and ask him to officially release me from the project. Be happy. Bye.'

She panicked and texted me back –

'No I can't be happy without you. Please don't take decisions in a hurry.'

'I don't need your advice. I felt like informing you, so I did', I replied back irritably.

She got worried and called me, but I didn't pick up her call. She was trying my number continuously and on her tenth attempt, I finally took her call.

"What happened? Please tell me what happened, I want to know", she pleaded to me.

"I don't wish to tell you. Your wishes have come true, so don't bother. You don't have to see me anymore"

"I am really sorry for all that I said. You know I didn't mean all that. Please put your ego aside for some time and tell me what exactly happened", she said softly.

"Nothing. I am just not in a mood to tell you anything. I have had enough. I can't take all this anymore. I will inform Ram about it", I said.

She understood that I was extremely pissed off. She tried to support me, make me feel positive, but it didn't work. Finally I hung up. The very next moment I texted Varsha –

I won't come from Monday.

'Inform the same to Ram', she texted me back.

'I won't. It's you who said that. So you should inform him about it'. She still wanted me to directly discuss with Ram. I just mailed him, mentioning every little difficulties and unwanted humiliation that I had to go through. That night, before I retired to bed, she called me and asked again, "Please tell me what happened? Did you have your dinner?"

"Yes", I replied curtly.

"Will you tell me now, what happened?" she asked me.

"Why should I tell you? I am not your boyfriend and neither am I liable to keep you updated on everything", I said, my tone full of sarcasm.

"I don't understand why people show so much of attitude in spite of being at fault themselves"

"Look I am exhausted and I need rest. Will you allow me some peace time?" I was getting rough.

"Fine. Sorry to disturb you. Don't worry; I am always there for you". Having said that, she disconnected the call.

I felt guilty about my behaviour to her. Though she loses her temper very frequently, yet her concern for me overpowers every other feeling.

Good night, I texted her in WhatsApp.

"Good night. Love you", she replied back in an instant.

I switched off my phone, and tried to sleep. I had weekend to relax. I was worried about Monday as I was apprehensive of my Lead's reaction. I was in a fix, unable to decide if I had put my job at stake, by undertaking such a huge risk. My colleagues were not that supportive, and I feared the worst.

The weekend felt unusually long. Finally Monday arrived. I was very pissed off at Varsha, and I decided not to work for the entire day. Ram called me for a discussion regarding the mail I had sent him, and he provided me a solution to it. I was happy that my issue was looked into, but after a couple of days I realized no one told me anything about my work. Just then I realized Varsha's importance; though she behaved weird, yet she was the one who wanted me to work smartly and efficiently, who wanted me to learn and grow. With all these thoughts haunting me, I finally decided to ping her one fine morning.

Good morning, I typed.

Good Morning Sir, came her reply.

Please don't respond like this, I want to speak to you, I replied.

Fine. I am a little busy right now. Will let you know once I am free. Is that fine with you?

Yes, fine with me. After that I came over to Neha's cubicle only to find her resting her head on her bag and sobbing like a child.

"What's wrong? Why are you crying?" I inquired.

"My relationship with Sameer will not work out. It's been a week since my parents have come to know about it and they have been looking for an alliance ever since".

"You didn't inform me about it", I said.

"We were busy fighting with each other over the last week. Moreover you were worried about office stuffs. How could I come and tell you my problems? I just don't know what to do. Our parents are dead against us.

She was weeping incessantly and I was unable to understand why their parents were against their relationship. I wanted to ask questions, but remained silent on seeing her plight.

Then I asked her to come out of the ODC so that she could be free with me. We sat on a bench, I held both her hands and asked her politely, 'Neha, you can share your thoughts with me. I won't let you down this time'.

But she said it was a little complicated and she didn't know how I would perceive it. I assured her that I always had a great respect for her caring and loving attitude even when I had been angry. I was not certainly going to break that belief even if some rough images would come across during the talk. She then started off…"We don't belong to the same caste. He is two years junior to me and….and…", she was crying and was stammering. I kept quiet for some times, holding her hand firmly without caring about the people walking past us and asked her and…?

I then knew that the answer to the entire problem might have lied in this single 'AND' that she is unable to share. I tried to guess but I could not imagine of anything watching her crying in front of me, inside the campus like a broken little soul from inside.

Then she opened her heart, 'Sid; do you remember why our Annual day during M.Tech was called off on the 2nd day?'

"No, Not exactly", I expressed nodding my head. She then continued, "Two boys from our college had a terrible accident near the Campus main gate. Where the one who was sitting on the back side of the bike died on the spot, the other one was not that lucky either. He is also dying every moment in his life".

Tears were flowing down from her eyes through her cheeks. Anyone would show sympathy to her and help her get over the situation but I wanted her to vent out all the pain, every moment that she had treasured in some hidden corner of her heart. So I asked with a concerned and low voice…"Why, what happened to the other?"

"He got his legs broken and head was also severely damaged", she put it straight. Saying this she stopped crying gradually. Her eyes were like dreaming something. It looked as if she was losing herself in some dreamland of the past memory. Memories that were hurting her good enough to turn her in to some cold stone heart. She wasn't even looking at me then. At that time I got a call from Swami. Neha looked at me but I disconnected it as receiving that call would have meant like I was not prioritizing her matter. I knew that if anything urgent regarding work, Swami would definitely whatsapp me. I requested her to continue.

"It was the 2nd day. I was practicing my song that the group was to present before the Audience that evening. When my father arrived exhausted late in the morning, I asked him if everything was ok. What we heard from him, I and mom both got shocked. He explained that, one student from our college died last night in a road accident near that college and the other one is seriously injured, breaking one bone from the leg which was replaced by the metals and still has not got his sense back. He also cleared that even if he comes back to life it would be very difficult on his part to keep walking for a long time. He might suffer organ failure. He also informed that the Annual day might be called off on this issue because students are very angry and the whole college is mourning. He also warned that anything could happen and told me not to go to college until the situation gets normal. I understood the criticality of the matter and assured him that I won't but the entire time my thought and well wishes were with that lone survivor. I couldn't bear the thought of the pain that he might have gone through. So I went to my father and asked him would he be ok? He said as a professional he had given his best effort and he believed the patient would recover well. Listening to this I got huge relief, because I knew that my father never lies to me. He always puts his best effort to his work and what can be bigger relief to me knowing him to be under my father's personal care? With coming days my father used to came up with good news on health recovery of the boy. He is recovering pretty fast; he would be able to walk soon with some help. News that my father was giving me was making me happy thinking that the guy will be ok soon and knowing that my father's hard work had paid off. One day I asked him if I could go to hospital with him. Without a hesitation he said why not! I had been to the hospital numerous times with my Dad since my childhood and I always bring flowers and this time it was no different."

Listening to her I felt lost, felt happy. I could exactly see how well her heart has been nurtured. How sensitive she has been made towards the feelings and emotion of others. That explained me the reason why she used to take care of me unconditionally even if I didn't care about her much and even though many a times I didn't deserve. My heart felt proud knowing that it has got such a caring friend to share moments with. By that time I had already let her hands go free without even realizing it when. I thought of hugging her but instead wanted her to complete. She continued…

"It was morning time when we reached at the Hospital. Dad finished his regular activities quickly and asked the attendant whether any patient needed emergency medical attention or not, to which reply came negative. He then asked me to follow him to the different room. That there I saw him for the first time, it was Sameer."

In between the narration I could guess that it was him only but I let her complete her talk, thinking that it would be inappropriate to interrupt her flow of emotion.

"I saw him for the very first time. A very decent and stylish looking Boy was lying on the white bed with one apple in his one hand and one magazine in the other. He tried to get up a little bit and greeted my Dad Good morning with a smile and Dad too greeted him the same. Dad then asked him how he was doing. To which he replied better.

Dad examined the report and instructed him to take healthy amount of food and fluid. After that Dad said ok, take care and looked at me and signalled me to offer him the flowers that I had brought. I looked at him, gave him a smile and he too gave a smile back to me. I handed over the flowers to him introducing myself, Neha...".

"Sameer here..." he responded very softly extending his hand.

By then it was lunch time and Swamy was approaching us. We could see this from distance. I was very angry at him since because of him only Neha won't finish her talk. However I could not avoid that as I too was hungry. Neha was quite silent, stable and serious during the lunch. It wasn't that talkative girl that I used to know, who would eat your brain cells even when you are happy, sad or mad. She always tries to make others happy even without any reason. For her the reason to happiness can be having lunch together. Today was the day when she needed the same help. So post lunch I tried to talk with Neha but every time I was getting up from my seat I found Neha to be occupied with some other work. So I thought better not to ruin her mood again forcing her to remember the entire incident once again. That day we returned home but she was silent in the bus, as wind before storm. I dropped her near her PG and returned back to my apartment. I was frequently looking at my phone whether any message of her popped up or not. I waited till dinner but nothing came. She did not ping me. It was terribly disturbing my mind. I tried to sleep but I could not. I turned my mobile data on again but still no message was there. I thought of calling her but I didn't. My roommate was noticing my behaviour so I kept silent for a while. But then again I decided to call her so I went outside and called her. It took some time but she picked it up. We talked casually for some time and when I asked her to continue what was incomplete; she said there was nothing left to say. Then I visited him frequently in hospital at least once in a week. The understanding grew stronger and we became good friends. That's all. Saying this much she concluded.

Listening to this I got angry. Not at Neha but at Swamy. Because I knew that when somebody interrupts and the matter is left incomplete. The teller loses its plot and mood. So when asked to narrate later they fast forward the entire matter just like what Neha did. So I requested her to tell me in details if possible. So she told me everything after that. Although she was brought up very affectionately she didn't have any much interaction with her friends. So when she met Sameer and saw him suffering her kind heart could not stop from getting emotionally involved with him. So she explained how they met time to time in hospital. How they became Facebook friend. How she had helped him with studies as well. Neha gradually felt that she has become a hope of mirage for happiness in the desert of someone's life. Although she liked Sameer very much, took great care of him and nobody even objected for that because he was recovering well. The fine day when Sameer was to be released from hospital Neha also went there to be a part of it. Sameer thanked Neha for her unconditional care and support that he had received both mentally and physically. He also expressed his feelings that, he wanted to take great care of her as well, just like her and just same as unconditional but for lifetime. To which she didn't give any particular answer then, but ended up giving a smile filled with sea of thoughts and saying she would love to be a part of his life.

What future holds for us is an area of uncertainty. We are a tiny boat on the Vast Ocean of life with huge tides. Everything lies on the mercy of the God. The very air that causes a boat to navigate when it breezes & sinks it when turns in to a storm. The very tide that helps sailing the boat may sink it when it's high. May be luck or God were not in the favour of Neha. Her father has felt her emotions, attachment and feelings for Sameer but he had no choice but to shut his feelings for one last time because of what the final test result came. Because no parents can give away their only daughter to someone who might suffer permanent organ failure in near future, because despite of their best effort Sameer's body's hormonal secretion was not responding well and was decreasing day by day. Which indicated the inevitable won't be any good.

What later on they discovered was restriction from home on several things for her. When tried to disagree to their decision both parents fought with each other over many trivial issues asking, whose child's fault it was. It came up to the point of standard of nurturing kid. So Neha tried to defend her parents from that of Sameer. But a clash was inevitable. Gradually it led to the misunderstanding between both and ultimately caused harm to their relationship. They started to part away but Sameer didn't want them to be like that because what they meant to each other and because of what they had received from each other. One day Sameer called Neha and sat beside her, Neha just saw him but could not utter a word fearing she would break down. Seeing this Sameer held both her hands and assured her not to be sad. Neha could not limit her emotions in her heart they came out as pears in the form of tears from her eyes. Everything was unbearable for Sameer starting from his own health to the tears of Neha. The one girl that meant so much, the girl who came magically from nowhere and gave a new meaning, a new beginning to his life was about to part away. Neha was crying like a child to which Sameer held her hands more firmly and told her that, 'Neha, with the utmost love and affection that I have for you, I want you to know that I can't put somebody's future at risk. Because I know that my health is uncertain. I do understand the concern of your parents and I respect that. I am truly grateful for the amount of good care that your father has taken of mine. I don't want his blessing to turn in to hatred. And I don't want both of us as well to be crying all the times for this. I want both of us happy. I want you to be happy lifelong. So my request to you would be to be with me as a good friend as long as possible, to be in contact as we are now, till the time you find someone in your life'.

After that day they used to talk less frequently knowing that it might affect their feelings. Although nothing was official but deep down they had made up their mind to part away gradually with time. A paper boat may sink in the ocean in a while but to kill feelings, it takes great courage. It takes unbearable pain.

'We haven't proposed each other till now; still we love each other, talk with each other, and care for each other'.

She seemed very upset. So I consoled her and requested her not to think much on that issue.

'It will be all right and I'll gift you JUNGLE BOOK in your marriage and in the background the title song will be there, just imagine...Good idea naa...'. She smiled back, saying, "Idiot!!".

Then we bade good night to each other.

Next day I was early to the office and was eagerly waiting for her. As soon as she came, I went near her and "Show me his pic…" I said. "No I won't", she tried to hide the pic, but I ignored her and tried to snatch the mobile from her hand. In the process of trying to forcibly take the phone from her, I was exerting all the pressure I could on her mobile screen. Suddenly she screamed, "Do you even know the cost of the screen? If it gets damaged, I am not going to leave you. If you don't know the price, just go and Google it. It's not in hundreds, it's in thousands.

I was shocked at the way she behaved; it was completely unexpected. I slowly freed my hands and walked out of the ODC. She sensed I was hurt, so she came after me. I went inside the pantry to have some tea; she came and stood beside me. Then she held my hands and asked –

"What happened?" she asked.

"Nothing"

"Please tell me"

"You made me realize where do I belong to. We don't belong to the same class; its better we maintain distance. I was not aware that the screen is so expensive and so I am sorry for the way I behaved. Please forgive me if possible and spare me", I said.

"Please yaar, I spat that out as I was not in a good frame of mind. Please try to understand", she said, repenting her own words.

"You differentiated me from you on monetary basis. I am really hurt. When I reach up to your level, I shall consider myself qualified to befriend with you again". Having said that, I walked my way back to my ODC.

"Sorry yaar", she said and started crying. She held my hands again and said, "Please Sid, you know I didn't mean all that. I am very disturbed since last week; please try to understand my situation".

I stood there, silent. After sometime, I took her hands in mine. This time, she handed over her phone to me, so I could see his pic. I chose to see his WhatsApp profile pic. He looked stylish and well-groomed, clearly reflecting the modern youth.

I tried to pacify her, but it proved to be of very little help to her. She was quite disturbed and was not able to perceive things clearly. Just then her mentor arrived and asked her about a script she was handling. Both of them walked back to her place. I came back to mine and got engaged in my work. After sometime I texted her in messenger –

What's up?

Checking a script. Some issues are there.

Carry on. Don't be upset, everything will sort out with time.

Hope so...

We left for lunch soon after. Post lunch I was to have a discussion with Varsha. She called me over to a conference room to discuss.

"Are you still angry with me...?" I asked.

"I was. I am not anymore", she replied.

"Look, scolding me and humiliating me in front of everyone won't do me good. People will just make fun of me and will consider me to be incompetent. I was really pissed off with the same kind of behaviour all these days, and that day I just lost my nerves. But I have immense respect for you; the credit for whatever I have learnt here till date goes all to you", I said.

"Don't lie to me", she said and smiled.

"Yes, it's true. I am not trying to impress you. You helped me to learn things sequentially. Mona and Sweety have helped me too, but they have always explained concepts assuming I knew the basics beforehand. Mugging stuffs won't help until I have my concepts clear about it".

"Yes, I agree with you. I also assumed all this while, that thing once told will be etched in your memory, but I understood that's absurd and impossible. I had no intention to humiliate you whatsoever. I have this habit of shouting at not just you, but at every other person, but no one complained about it till date. Your mail made me realize that I was wrong in my approach; people do get hurt when I say all that, and I should not behave in that way. I have no enmity with you; it's just that I want you to polish your skills, so i could proudly say that you have achieved a lot in a short span of time, that no one else had been able to do", she justified herself.

"I understand your concern for me, but you need to make me feel comfortable too. I need a viable and conducive environment to learn and grow", I put my thoughts across too.

"Yes I completely agree with you. Oh yes, now that you are familiar with the work here, I expect you to give KT to the juniors who will come over. I don't want them to face similar issues like you had", she said.

I nodded, and finally the discussion got over. I felt relieved. I came back to my place and tried to concentrate on my work. After I was done, I came over to Neha's cubicle. She looked at me and frowned.

"What's wrong? You spoke to Varsha?" she inquired.

"Yes"

"Is there any problem?" she asked again.

"Nope! All set"

'Good', Neha replied.

We were in a cab returning from office. Neha was eager to discuss our upcoming Kerala trip. She seemed excited and was constantly speaking about the itineraries of the trip; while my responses were limited to, "hmm... ya... yes, right..."

This went on until she asked my opinion on the list of hotels shortlisted.

'Hm...right', I said, my eyes transfixed on something interesting beside me...

<u>FOURTEEN</u>

She understood I was not attentive, and she followed the direction in which my eyes were fixed. A couple were seated next to me, and the guy was playing some x-rated video – which needless to say caught my attention. The girl was sitting on my right, and through the corner of my eyes, I could get a glimpse of her cleavage. I noticed she had an amazing figure. Neha felt irritated and she gave me a not-so-loving blow on my head with her cell phone.

'Ouchhh…', I squealed. Had that girl been alone, I would bet that she would have asked to swap seats with her. Left with no other choice, she got up from her seat and asked me to shift over to her place, so she could sit next to the girl. I looked at Neha and smiled; she smiled back at me too, feeling immensely relieved to have diverted my attention from the video and of courses the girl!

'So… Hilton Garden Inn… we will check with others too…', she said.

The smile broadened on her lips. Finally we got down the cab and walked towards our stop, hand in hand… I was feeling hungry and tired as well. On her suggestion we graced one nearby Dosa stall, offering variety of DOSA like Gobi Dosa, Masala Dosa, Paneer Dosa, Mushroom Dosa, etc. Being familiar with the shop, she took the charge of placing the order. "One plate Gobi Dosa" came out as order out of that single pamphlet with green and yellow background of banana leafs, printed both side, hard polythene laminated Menu.

'You are not taking anything?' I asked.

A big NO along with nodding head, saying "my stomach is paining, I will not eat" came out as answer.

"You are not eating that's why your stomach is paining. Take a sip of cold drinks at-least."

"No, I am not feeling well I will not take. Then she smiled, a sign that she was trying to hide something from me, which I came to know later.

After having Dosa, we were walking back to the bus stop. On the way, we stopped near a tree.

With a faint and quite unusual smile on her face, she was speaking to me – after going home you never ever think of me, you will always be busy with your roommates and Rajesh. In the weekend, also you don't come to meet me. You never ask me for a movie, you never ask me for anything.

"I am like that, by this time you should have come to know me… I don't deserve your care and love; you should reduce your love for me…"

"How many times, will you tell me this? Two days back, you told me the same, even Rajesh warned me not to love you, not to get attached to you to that extent. You don't understand. It's hard to tell your mind, stop loving someone, when your heart still does… I don't understand, you people will tell me how much should I love you…? Seriously, Sid you are my first friend, who is asking me to reduce my love, care towards you…"

"See I have lots of work to do after office hours; I have to cook myself. And being in PG you have not to bother for that. In addition, on weekends, I have to buy grocery and wash my clothes. Even after all that if I get some free time, I have to do my movie scripting. I have to think of my productions even and I don't have enough time. So how can I meet you? You don't have any work, that's why you are complaining.

She suddenly interrupted the discussion and asked me to leave. She kissed me on my left cheek and asked me to leave. I assumed that she was afraid, that we may fight again, in such type of discussion, so she was asking me to leave.

"No, I am not leaving today…" I uttered plainly with some anger.

She once again requested me to leave, "Please yaar, I have to go now within ten minutes".

I replied – "You always want me to be with you, so today I am not leaving. Tell me a proper reason for this urgency to leave within ten minutes, only then I'll leave."

"I can't stay more than ten minutes I have to go." She replied, fumbling.

"Why can't you stay back beyond that?"

"I cannot tell you the reason because you are a guy."

"You have to tell, I am telling you everything so you have to." I insisted.

"No I can't. Please don't force me. It's girls' talk, boys should not know all that", she justified.

"I am your best friend, so you can tell me. I have the right to know yaar."

"Chiiii...you are shameless, No, I can't tell", she laughed and after a while told me everything.

"Ok, today is my second date, that's why my stomach is paining and I have to change my sanitary pad."

At that time, her eyes were closed and she was smiling. It may be because for the first time, she was sharing the same with a guy. Once again, to have a clear picture I enquired – "Date? Means, you are going for date, with someone?"

Shyness took over her, and without looking at my face, she narrated. She told me that she had her period, which is common for every girl. In a month, it happens for 4-5 days, that's all, now please leave..."

I looked at her and smiled.

She requested me once again and offered – "Should I come with you till the stop?"

I said – "No, I am leaving..." Both of us started in an opposite direction.

"Still I have a doubt..." I asked turning back.

She interrupted and said, "Some other day Sid!"

"OK...bye bye, take care..."

She likes my company but that day she had to leave as she had no other option.

After reaching home, I had my dinner, checked my personal works, and was about to sleep, when my mobile glowed with alphabets "Dev Calling". It has been a month since we spoke. I answered the call, 'Hello...'

From the conversation, I came to know that he was disturbed. A lot of noise was coming on the call; maybe he was standing in some traffic area while talking with me.

'Still not returned to home...! You drank; right... Is someone there with you...?' I asked with concern.

'No one is there with me, I am alone yaar... Alone... I am happy... I don't need anyone... Can you come to Silkboard...' he told me.

'Why should I go to Silkboard now..., I am going to take rest...' I replied.

'Ok... sleep... You are also trying to avoid me, good... I can stay here, whole night... somewhere on the road...' from his words, I doubted whether he was really standing near Silkboard or he was making up a story. I asked him, 'Are you in Bangalore...?'

'Feeling very lonely yaar, want to hug you, want to come near you..., but...'

He cried and promised me that he was not lying. I asked him to come to my room, but out of guilty, he was not in a mood to come to my flat. I walked down to meet him near Silkboard. The road was almost silent, only big trucks, busses, and travels were passing one after the other. Dogs were quite energetic, howling, barking, and running aimlessly. I searched for him, for a while. Then I saw him standing near the over bridge, holding the cigarette and smoking. When I stepped near him, he started smiling and hugged me.

'Darling... your friend is alone now... he needs a partner, can you share cigarette with me, if you don't mind...' he started telling all nonsense, mute, I was listening to him.

He was quite broken up, from his delayed and unusual responses, I could make up that, he messed-up with his girlfriend, and disturbed mood prevailed. He drank a lot that night, and was crying and explaining me everything, demanding me to listen him completely. Though I was too tired, I tried to listen him. I felt very bad, once he finished.

It was obvious that I was unhappy with him, for an incident that happened two months back. Anyways, I liked him, he was one of my best friends, so when he demanded me to listen, I listened him carefully and tried to console him.

He told me, crying – "I am worth nothing to her, it seems I don't deserve any respect…, I did a lot for her, avoiding everyone, still…, I neglected my family, I neglected you for her yaar, I feel guilty now…."

'Leave it, you are a precious gift for me, my perception of you can never change for one wrong incident. Moreover, to be frank you deserve a lot more, so don't feel bad…, I am there with you. Your family is there, with you, we all love you and wish you leading a successful life. Your destination is not only "SHE"; your destination should be high enough to touch the sky. Please don't cry, I am there with you yaar…' I added the wishes of my heart.

"Forgive me yaar, once again sorry for that incident", he added.

"Forget about that, and please come with me, we will take rest… you had drunk so much, you will vomit, if you keep on crying, shouting…" I suggested him.

'Nothing is there in life yaar, don't know why I am feeling like a loser…' he added.

"Please don't think over that, if you would keep on thinking, you would get hurt…" I told him.

"Please come over to flat and take rest now, tomorrow morning we will talk" I told him.

It was almost 12 AM, night. The climate was not so pleasant. I was shivering due to cold. Still I was standing near him to listen to him until I saw a PCR van from a distance. I was sure that if they find him in this condition, unnecessarily we will have to pay for it. So, I forcefully dragged him to my room, and he couldn't resist. I asked him to take rest in my bed and then I lay down near him. He was changing his position frequently sometimes to left, sometimes to right and sometimes flat and straight. I was still, in one position. The lights were OFF, through the door, I could see the little stars, sky, partially covered-up by the clouds. I was silent for a while, thinking that he should take rest, only then he will be Ok, but he continued talking,

'Don't want to live in this world yaar, I loved her more than anyone, anything, but in return...'

'Life is like that, to whom we care for, we love; they don't bother about us, as they know, they would be loved unconditionally....They take it for granted...' I added.

"I had hurt you, so sorry for that..." he apologized.

"Leave it, and sleep now... Good night..." I quipped.

"Good night..."

Few people talk a lot, when they are broken up, deep inside. I felt very bad. Though I was angry with him, still it hurt me when I heard him crying. I prayed God, to give him strength to come out of the situation. I closed my eyes, but for a couple of minutes, I was alert of his state. Finally, he slept.

Next Day...

I was entering into my office campus, just then heard someone calling. I turned back to see, it was Neha. I went numb looking at her, whispering to myself, 'What The F!!!' Her look was totally strange, a completely new look indeed. I could see her beautiful bare legs; she wore Japanese folded cuff denim shorts, and a transparent white shirt covering her shoulder. Her hairstyle was different.

Neha – Hey! How do I look today?

"If you want to impress me, you should have tried it in a different way..., not by showing your legs or anything else...'

'Anything else means?' she enquired.

'I can see your black push-up inner inside your transparent white shirt, is it necessary to show me all this, in order to impress me', I asked in a soft voice.

'Stupid, why will I impress you, I can have a better choice than you...' she replied notoriously.

'Oh, is it...! Good... you are looking sexy', I replied.

'Sach!! Are you sure...?' she added.

"Yup, but one doubt..."

'What...?' she looked at my face.

'People say girls look hot in such sexy costumes..., will you allow me to check whether they really are..., I want to check by touching your... hottest part', while speaking my eyes gazed on her round curves. Suddenly I felt her left palm on my face, I mean she slapped me, saying – got it...? My hands are hotter than anything else, right...?'

'Hey, stupid girl, I won't leave you, you slapped me..., now it's my turn...' I ran behind her to slap her. Neha, was moving towards the campus. I was running, I mean walking very first behind her to take the revenge, just then, I saw one of my roommates, named Viren, whistling 'all eyes on me'. I texted her, that he was my roommate. Avoid looking at him. As I knew his nature very well, he used to suggest me that – impress the girls, and then offer her to sleep with you one night, so that you can enjoy her, after that leave her.

That was his rule, but my rule was different, never to hurt anyone in that way, respect girls. I never paid heed to such vague suggestions.

She walked upstairs; I followed her walking slowly. I could see people looking at her strangely. I came near her, and whispered slowly in her ears, 'everyone is looking at you…, you should be ashamed of yourself…'

'You don't need to feel ashamed when you know the consequence. C'mon Sid, it's quite a general rule, I am a girl, and whatever I do guys will keep looking at me…', she replied very casually and walked inside the ODC. Except me, everyone else admired her new look. Varsha blinked at me, trying to convey me that – carry on… I and Neha were target of playful teasing of Varsha, Sweety and other team members as they thought we were in a relation.

Sweety has been really helpful for me, as every Friday we start our weekend execution of scripts, after 6:30 PM, neither Neha wants to wait, nor do I, in that case Sweety comes up as a rescuer. She checks my execution, and for me, every Friday, she leaves late at around 9 PM.

That day, I started the execution and asked Sweety –

"Can I leave now, She and Swami, are waiting for me outside…?"

Sweety – "I told you to check the first run, and then only you can leave…"

She was gossiping with her friends, so I came back to my seat without requesting her anything. Just then, she pinged me –

"It's ok, you may leave, I will check it…"

Suddenly, a smile played on my face, I typed –

"Happy weekend. Bye Bye…"

FIFTEEN

It was Friday night, the weekend night. After one week of restless work, it was the day to celebrate for every IT engineer like me. I was standing in the balcony in shorts and earphones plugged in, thinking about the girl whom I consider, as my best friend.

If someone loves you more than you do…,

If someone cares for you, more than you do …,

If someone thinks of you, more than you do …

If someone wants you badly each and every moment to be beside her…

And just beside her….

Should you not doubt…? Is it love or friendship!!!

I used to ask the same to her, every time in different ways.

Whenever we fought with each other, I asked her—"What do you think, Am I your boyfriend?"

When she showed over possessive towards me, I asked her – "Why I can't talk with any other girl? Do you consider me as your bf?"

Whenever she cried for me, I used to ask – "Why are you crying for me, who Am I?"

"I am disturbing you a lot, I hurt you badly; I am not that good, as you think of me, still why you love me…? How much do you love your Sameer and me?"

For all those questions of mine, she used to answer:

"I don't care for others, and yes I am possessive for my friends and yaa I love you more than you love yourself. But I don't know why…, the day I will get to know the reason, I'll let you know…"

"Don't compare my love for you with him… Both of you are important for me in my life."

"But you don't care for me, you don't love me, why Sid….?"

"Because I don't know how to care. I am very selfish and bad. I don't deserve your love and care. You are simply wasting your time" came, my usual reply.

"Don't lie to me Sid, I have seen something in you, that's why I am expecting… and I can't be wrong. You know very well how to care, but the fact is you don't want to care for me, love me… You care for Rajesh, Dev and your other friends, but you don't care for me… Don't you think you are doing partialities…?"

"That's your misconception, I don't know how to show-up, but I do care for all of you equally… Still I remember the student pledge, that we used to recite after the prayer, in my school days –

'India is my country.

All Indians are my brothers and sisters.

Bla…bla…bla….

"Idiot, then you won't marry any girl…, all Indians are your brothers and sisters, right…?' she quipped.

In every 2 days, we used to fight for very vague things. One day, I was tired of all that stuff, I thought… Loving someone is not bad, if someone deserves. Frankly speaking, I care for her, as I care for rest of my friends. However, she used to complain; "This is not enough…. I WANT YOU… your attention, care, and love even more than you do for yourself".

That day, I was waiting for her call, as she was doing something. I messaged her on WhatsApp – "How much more should I wait for you… Tomorrow we will have to wake up early for Kerala trip, and now you are not allowing me to sleep."

"Just wait…love you" flashed on my mobile screen.

I - …..... too.

She – tell me properly.

I – letter will be over, so I am preserving the letters. In proper place, I will use.

She – "Today you didn't even kiss me properly"

I – Stock of my valuable kisses is very limited, and exhaustible.

She – Call me now…

Then, I called her, it was around 11:30 pm. The call began with a formal talk, and it continued with lot of stupid stuffs. She asked me, why I laughed at that time in the evening seeing a big white dog, while I was returning with her after dinner. At that time, she didn't get a chance to ask me as all her friends were there with her. And some were Odia also. I started narrating my stupid dream to her. The conversation or that topic ended with her stupid question,

"Where your hand was, when your dream got over?" She asked me and suddenly I started laughing. She was very clever, and her wild guess almost matched with the truth. She knows everything but sometimes behaves innocent, she wants to listen from me. She asked me that stupid question and answered the same, when I didn't. Her answer was somewhat like this – "chii… you were holding your costlier part in your hand….!!!"

I started laughing once again. Yaa… it's my weapon and my hand… what's wrong then…?

She – "Nonsense…"

"Yaa I am…"

After some stupid stuff, she reminded me of what we were talking about. After a while, I felt like enjoying with her the very moment. I was quite free with her. There were no limitations for me 'what to speak, and what not to…' She asked me then - do you like me, do you really care for me….?

I – Do you?? Then why every time you fight with me?

She –"Just Out of anger I tell you like that… However, I love you more. I can't bear to see you with others; I want you to be with me. Even If you want to be with someone, I should be present there. Moreover, that's my right as a good friend."

Then I replied that night in this way –

"ok… I am all yours…from now onwards. Keep me safely; else, this time if you hurt me, you would lose me forever."

she – I don't believe you…

I – "You have to; you don't have any choice… for the first time I am giving myself to someone. Hope this time you would not complain"

She – "Why suddenly…"

I – "Because, I have tried a lot. However, you are not satisfied. Now I am all yours. If sometime I do any wrong also, you can't complain. Because to whom, will you complain…, about your property…? To yourself….??"

'Finally you got changed for me…?' (I don't know in which sense) she replied.

"Still there are some limitations…"

She – What…?

"My genitals should be mine, apart from that everything is yours. You should not touch my precious part, I mean my weapon and my scrotum, that's exclusively for my wife".

She reacted to my statement, "Idiot, even I am not asking you for that trash…"

'Thanks… then I am all yours… Hmm, if you need those badly, my middle finger is exclusively there for you…' smartly I replied her back.

She – please stop all this nonsense darling…, I love you…

'Fuck you yaar…'

She – love you more…

I – love you too…

She – thanks a lot…, I will love you more than me. For me, first you, then me… first I would think of you, then about me…

I – "To that extent you love me…but see, still, selfishly I am asking you to return me, my weapon."

She – Listen Siddharth…

I – Please allow me to speak…

She – ok tell…

'My objective is very clear; I don't want to play with any girl. Loving someone as a friend is fine, but doing something

185

beyond that, is not good. If someday you ask me to fuck you, I won't. I can fuck, only the girl, to whom I would marry. So, except my dick, I am all yours…'

She – Please yaar, don't use slangs…

'Then what should I say…?'

'Your body's costlier part…' she replied.

I – I don't think, for me all my body parts are equal. For example, without hand, how I can write, how can I masturbate?

"Nonsense…you are…"

I – agree… I am…

She – By the way, do you really do…?

I – yup…

'By your own…?' she enquired.

Or what…? Should I call someone to do…?

She – chi chi… but how?

'Stimulate my own genitals using my right hand. It takes some time to come out…, after that it makes me feel relaxed. As if, we use to feel after a regular exercise. It's a kind of to and fro motion. My dick expands to the maximum size at that time', I told her.

She – You do it every day?

I – Nope… sometimes, when I watch those 18+ Warning stuff.

She – Is it necessary?

Then I started explaining her, the benefits of masturbation,

'Yup, if I don't do at-least once in a month, then it will reflect someday in my shorts, I mean if sometimes I see any bad dreams, white creamy liquid will be seen on my shorts, which is otherwise termed as "nightfall". My pipe will be full with urine, and pressed in-between my two legs. After a certain time, without my permission, because of bad dream it will leak out as nightfall. It's quite a normal process. My organ is in maximum size. The size will be small, when it is soft. Anxiety and cold weather causes contraction of smooth muscles, so the size looks small. If you want, I can show you'.

"Idiot, I don't want. By the way, I don't think this is a normal process. Sriti have not told me…"

'After marriage, you can have sex… right? And Sriti wouldn't have asked her husband about that and it's not mandatory that she would tell you everything. From my experience, as a guy I am telling you all this.'

Then I started explaining her once again, the need of masturbation, 'Doing it makes you feel good. It gets old sperm out of the way of fresh sperm. It relieves the tension that sexual yearning can bring about.'

In addition, some extra points I missed out, but it was there in the net, I researched for it in my engineering days. These are the other benefits of male masturbating, which I missed out –

It keeps us healthy. Cure Insomnia and we get good sleep after doing it. Research says masturbation may decrease incidence of prostate cancer. It stimulates our immune system. It releases sexual tension and stress. Masturbation can lower blood pressure in stressful situations. Masturbation releases the mood. It fights depression.

So, anytime, anywhere we feel like, we should do as…

It keeps our pipes clean. And it's a great way to kill time.

These are the points, which could have supported my ideas a little more, but she diverted the topic to something else.

She – Hey leave it… I understood, and it's very clear.

'Are you sure, your concept is clear or should I elaborate a little more…?'

She – No…

I – Ok… Some other day… good night, sleep well.

It was 1 AM. I came to my bed and tried to sleep. Suddenly my phone vibrated; a new message was there in whatsapp. When I checked, it was she.

She – My eyes closed, but I am thinking something…

'About what?' I typed back.

'About you… about whatever we discussed over phone. Promise me, you would never leave me alone'.

Yaa… Never, till the time I can feel your love for me…

28 Jun 1:10 AM - Neha: Hmmm…I will always love u, I will never get angry with you…

28 Jun 1:13 AM - Siddharth: K…, then I am all yours…

For some time, my eyes closed, and then she pinged me…

28 Jun 1:19 AM - Neha: I want to hug u now

28 Jun 1:20 AM - Siddharth: I want 2 show u my middle finger now…

28 Jun 1:20 AM - Neha: Nonsense.

28 Jun 1:21 AM - Siddharth: Or else, is it possible now?

28 Jun 1:21 AM - Neha: I want you… so I told you…

28 Jun 1:22 AM - Siddharth: I also want to show you my middle finger…

28 Jun 1:22 AM - Neha: Aaaaaa…

28 Jun 1:22 AM - Siddharth: At the time of fucking, girl makes this kind of sound.

28 Jun 1:23 AM - Neha: How do you know?

28 Jun 1:23 AM - Siddharth: Already I fucked…, that's why…

28 Jun 1:23 AM – Neha: to whom?

28 Jun 1:24 AM - Siddharth: after watching lot of porn, if you ask me then what should I reply…?

28 Jun 1:24 AM - Neha: From now onwards, you'll not see…

28 Jun 1:25 AM – Siddharth: Why?

28 Jun 1:25 AM – Neha: those are stupid stuffs…

28 Jun 1:26 AM – Siddharth: knowing or watching something is not bad, but we should act in a right way…

28 Jun 1:26 AM - Neha:k come I want to hug you…

28 Jun 1:27 AM - Siddharth: k feel me, I am there beside you…But be careful… I am only in my shorts, completely bare…

28 Jun 1:28 AM – Neha: then don't come, first wear everything…Inners at least you should wear…

28 Jun 1:30 AM - Siddharth: Whole day I am wearing…

28 Jun 1:30 AM - Neha: At the time of sleeping also…

28 Jun 1:30 AM – Siddharth: I want to free my organ at night, don't want to cover it with inners...

28 Jun 1:31 AM – Neha: then it will get more space and may increase…

28 Jun 1:32 AM - Siddharth: It gets increased when I Check in the morning… because my pipe is full of sushu(urine). If someone would touch at that time, then white liquid will come out…

28 Jun 1:33 AM - Neha: Nonsense, I will beat you, if you speak like this…

28 Jun 1:35 AM Siddharth: – but I didn't say anything wrong, you can check with my roommate also…

28 Jun 1:40 AM - Neha: come now…

28 Jun 1:47 AM - Siddharth: I am completely bare, still…

28 Jun 1:47 AM – Neha: Now you are mine, so I can see you completely nude

28 Jun 1:48 AM – Siddharth: then it's ok…

28 Jun 1:50 AM - Neha: Love u…

28 Jun 2:11 AM – Siddharth: never change your decision…

28 Jun 2:11 AM – Neha: I'll never…

28 Jun 2:12 AM - Siddharth: Don't ask me someday to fuck you…

28 Jun 2:13 AM - Neha: Plzz…I'll never ask you.

28 Jun 2:15 AM - Siddharth: Thnx a lot…

28 Jun 2:15 AM - Neha: I know my limitation

28 Jun 2:16 AM - Siddharth: Thanks yaar…Sleep now…

28 Jun 2:18 AM – Neha: come near me…

28 Jun 2:20 AM – Siddharth: I can't, so sorry…

28 Jun 2:20 AM - Neha: U can..trust me i won't touch u..

28 Jun 2:28 AM - Neha: Love u

28 Jun 2:28 AM – Siddharth: Wanna Kiss u…

28 Jun 2:29 AM - Neha: Where?

28 Jun 2:29 AM – Siddharth: anywhere, n everywhere…

28 Jun 2:30 AM - Neha: Love u…

28 Jun 2:49 AM - Siddharth: Me or mine…

28 Jun 2:49 AM - Neha: u… wait, let me do sushu…

28 Jun 2:55 AM - Siddharth: I am seeing…

28 Jun 2:56 AM – Neha: no problem

28 Jun 3:03 AM - Siddharth: Thnx 4 loving me n caring me

28 Jun 3:03 AM - Neha: Thnks for giving me such a nice gift...

28 Jun 3:12 AM - Siddharth: Bye

28 Jun 3:12 AM - Neha: Na...

I – It's too late, we should sleep now... Tomorrow we will have to wake up early for the Trip. Please do call me in the morning.

'No don't sleep, be with me like that...'

I – it's too cold even, and sushu is directly proportional to cold. And I am bare body, I am wearing just the shorts. If I don't sleep, I will have to go for sushu... all the time.

She – ok, good night sweetheart, love you...

Finally, I closed my eyes, put my bed sheet over me, and slept.

<u>SIXTEEN</u>

Saturday Morning, I woke up by the vibration of my phone. There were too many missed call from Neha, Swami and all they were standing outside my apartment gate waiting for me. I hastened up to make up for the delay due to my laziness.

We were going to Kerala, Boat house, In Cab we were sitting together as usual. She was sitting window side. I was holding her hand. She had put her head on my shoulder and was trying to rest. The fragrance from her body and hair were quite intimidating for me. But she was almost asleep as she had not had proper sleep last night. So I didn't think of waking her up. We reached there at dusk. When I opened my eyes, I realized that I was also sleeping leaning my head towards her.

Although everybody had had a quite fair amount of sleep in the bus, I was still tired. We drenched in the rain. We played, jumped to the water and forced other to get drenched. When night came we all were exhausted but decided not to sleep since one don't usually get such opportunities. Although unanimously it was decided nobody will sleep, I was having a bit of temperature and headache so I opted out saying I was not feeling ok and came back to our boys' room. Just then I heard Neha arguing with others.

Neha - ok, game over guys. I'm also not feeling good. Too much tired. Will rest now!

Swamy - What's this Neha, we all decided na! That we will play. You were the one who said that we should enjoy instead of sleeping.

Neha – Ok then, I am saying we will not enjoy tonight. Tomorrow we will.

Swamy – hmm, I know why you are leaving! Just because Sid left!

Neha – Say that again and I'll show you why.

Swamy - Don't try to scare me. Go if you want.

Neha left the place and directly came to my room. I was feverish. She saw me half asleep, sat beside me asked me if I was ok. When she came to know that I had temperature she got little worried and assured me not to panic since she had brought medicine.

"Just because you are a doctor's daughter, you will bring medicine even on holiday trip or what?" I said in a low and humorous tone.

"On trips, we should be really careful, because there will be people who will, out of over excitement, will end up doing stuffs that will get them into trouble. If it's raining, then some people, in the midst of their excitement will get drenched in the rain and will try to pull others too without realizing that the situation might turn out to be awkward specially for girls", she said sarcastically. Listening to this, I quickly bit my tongue, embarrassed. It brought a smile to me because I could know that she was referring to me only.

"Please have some food, so that you can take the medicine", Neha said empathetically, offering me a plate with food.

Though I was not in a mood to have anything yet I was touched by her concern for me, so I took the plate from her hand and slowly took little bites of food, reluctantly.

"How mean, you don't even offer me!" Neha said, mockingly.

I was more than eager to share my food with her, but one look at my plate and I became hesitant…

Before I could realize, I saw her taking a bite from my messed up plate.

'On any normal day, you usually refrain from sharing food with me, from the same plate. What made you behave differently today?'

'Yes…, I agree. But if I have chosen to accept you, then I should do it with your positives and shortcomings as well'

I remained silent; her statement brought a smile on my lips.

Finally after I was done with my food, she handed me a tablet 'Zero Dull'; I had no choice but to take it, and then tried to rest. She had held my hand with one hand and was playing with my hairs with the other. I was looking at her and I found something that I had experienced earlier. I could exactly see how my mother used to take care of me whenever I got sick. How she would put my head on her lap and play with my hairs until I fell asleep. It was the same 'true' and 'pure' affection that she had for me. Nobody had done that for me till the time I came to Bangalore. Although I became emotional in a low half slept voice I insisted her to rest. Unaware, when I slept that night; when I woke up the following morning; I was feeling warm and rejuvenated. I found myself properly organized on my bed. Somebody had put a blanket on me. In a matter of time I could guess that it was none other than her who had put her blanket on me and went to her room, because all other boys in my room were sleeping utterly disorganized and half naked. Only I was the odd one out who was looking organized and sophisticated.

The next day I was noticing her activities. Even though she was getting angry at times still I found a cuteness and affection in her each statement. Day went on to evening and we two were standing at the back face of the boat standing close to each other while the cool breeze was playing a romantic tone in my mind. "Do you want to go for the 'Titanic pose' here", I asked mischievously. "Idiot, Titanic pose was on the front end of the ship, not back. We will fall from here", she said after laughing a lot.

Those lines of her made me laugh too. We were having a lot of fun. As we were standing very closely to each other, the fragrance of her body was even more intimidating this time. Her open hairs were touching my cheeks. I could barely contain myself in that situation. It was the perfect evening with perfect amount of romanticism in the air. The sea water, the bright round moon, the cool breeze, the entire surrounding was asking me to hold her in my arms. I was no longer that rough Sid who used to say anything in front of her. I held her near her shoulders and made her turn towards me and then I moved close to her. I noticed she started to freeze a little may be because she was not expecting this move from me. I gazed directly into her eyes. She looked down but didn't try to break free. I then thanked her for the care she took last night. She said 'that's ok' with a low tone. I rubbed my right thumb on her cheek down to the left corner of her lips. She then looked up at me. My heart was pounding faster. I felt the restlessness of her breath and it was trying to say something to me. I could not help but open my heart and tell her that, 'I genuinely care for her and was happy the way she took care of me the other night. I felt as if it was my mother there. I felt the same affection in her shadow as well'.

Only god knows how badly I wanted to kiss her. So I said in a gentle tone "Neha please forgive me for what I am about to do next". She looked down without even saying anything. I pressed her tight against my chest; my left hand was on her waist and touched her lips with my right thumb. It felt so soft and that triggered a sensation in my body, never felt before. For a moment I lost myself. Failing to control myself I submerged in to her arm just like the tide was hitting the boat. That evening, I could not stop but falling in love with her lips.

Time went past and the next day we returned back. We all had taken leave for Monday, knowing that we would be late. Although we were dead tired, we planned not to waste that day also, agreed for a movie after having Lunch at Swami's place.

I helped them in cooking. By the time Simran arrived, I had prepared Gulabjamun. We had our lunch and then clicked a couple of pics, and then got ready for the movie. Swami and Simran took bus; Neha and I went on scooty, arranged by Neha.

I was sitting pillion to a girl for the very first time. I was quite close to her face, though her helmet was creating problem. I put my head over her shoulder and asked her –

I wanna kiss you…

Neha – everyone is seeing, and you are boy and I am a girl, what impression others would carry…?

I – you have stolen my dialogues; you should have something unique of yours, Miss Copy-Cat…

Having my head tilted over her shoulder, my lips were almost touching her neck but I was not able to kiss her, as the helmet was there, also my conscience didn't permit me to do so, publicly.

Neha – (notoriously) Control yourself man! It's sensitive there and I am feeling something…

I – sshh….., just concentrate on driving. First time I am pillion to a driver girl, so I shouldn't lose any chance to flirt.

Neha – you will flirt with me…, do you know the exact meaning of flirt?

I – No, I don't know, wait for some time, you will come to know…

Slowly I touched her stomach, and then I held her tightly, my hands circling her.

Neha – please yaar…, don't make me feel…

I – All the time, you complain me that I don't love you, now I am doing that. Trying to romance with you, you still have problem with me…

Neha – people are looking at us…

"I don't know, then stop somewhere I want to kiss you…" I demanded.

Neha – have you really started liking me…?

"Yaa, you shouldn't question me all the time, I told you that I am all yours. This time if you hurt me, I won't be there with you…" I told her.

Neha – I won't hurt you…

Neha – promise me that your love won't change with time…

I – promised, it should be limited to a friend. As you know, I can't fuck you…

Neha – even I don't want…

I – I ask you to stop the scooty, so that I can kiss you…

Neha – we are getting late Sid, they would have reached by this time. Within next 15 minutes, the movie will start, and we should reach there in time.

"Wanna show my middle finger to you…, you are very bad, not allowing me to kiss also", I replied.

Neha – agreed, I am bad, still I love you…

Finally, we reached the destination.

Simran and Swami were waiting there in front of the gate.

Simran – you should drive man…

I smiled, and whispered to myself – then how could I have earned a chance to flirt, though exactly I didn't do anything. We kept the vehicle in the parking and rushed in. Having Neha beside me, we all seated together. While watching the movie, we were in a pleasant tete-a-tete as if we were girlfriend and boyfriend.

An intimate scene was playing on the big screen, slowly I whispered in her ear - wanna FUCK U...

She - Yaa I am ready... by the way, do you know how to...

Yup, you want to examine me...

She - Give me your hand...

I – My hand or my finger...?

She – both

When she was holding my hand, I showed her my middle finger; if you love me then you should love my middle finger too...

My middle finger is exclusively yours....

She was losing my hand, and then at one point of time, she held my middle finger's top lightly.

I - oh you like my finger's top portion only, I mean you like my glans...

She – nonsense...

I – yaa I am..., still you love me, so you have to adjust with me. Now you can't complain yaar..., as I am all yours...

She – kiss me...

I – where??

She – nonsense... you promised me last night, so you should...

I – first you have to kiss my middle finger, then only I will...

The movie came to an end but not our conversation. We came out of the mall, and Simran's boyfriend was there waiting outside for her, seeing the scenario, Swami said –

Arey yaar main toh akela pad gaya..., you people got paired up...

Everyone laughed, Simran told – you can join us, if you want...

Swami – No no no..., you people go, your boyfriend will kill me...

Simran finally left, Swami took a bus for his stop. I bought some grocery items. With me, Neha was there. It took me another half an hour, after purchasing the items; we came outside to take her vehicle. It started raining heavily, so we had to wait there for some time. Then we moved in her scooty. This time, I was driving. She was sitting pillion. It was still drizzling. Since the distance was long, from our home, we got drenched in the rain, she and her shirt was completely wet. Soon it started raining heavily, she asked me to stop somewhere under the tree, for some time. I stopped the bike near a tree, a dim street light was there, but the road was very silent, of course, it was an off traffic area.

It was approximately 9:30 pm. I was standing under the tree, and trying to dry myself with the handkerchief, slowly she put her hand on my face. I was quite in mood, just waiting for her to give the signal – to kiss her. Just then, she hugged me quite tight, holding me in her arms. I could feel her in a very different way. Her top and hot body pressed on my chest, giving me feelings for the very first time. My hand was there behind her back. She gave me an exuberant hot kiss on my cheek, continuously pressing her lips, for a couple of seconds. I could feel her breath. For a moment, I forgot everything. My body was shivering in cold, but when her body touched mine, I could feel her body temperature and slowly I put my hands over her backside, to make her comfortable. Then I could feel her lips, covering my lips. I was untold quite, as I was also enjoying. Hardly could I resist then, I started kissing her. Therefore, I kissed her even more passionately. My lips were wide open, it was about to explore her face, her lips and many more. I kissed her and she allowed me to kiss her in my own way, perhaps she also desired me to kiss her. So, I did. It was the very first time; I kissed her without any hesitation. I loved the way she comforted me and held me.

However, I was afraid of something going wrong. She was allowing me to do, as she was very comfortable with me. She was the one, who kissed me on my lips. As a boy, I should have initiated that. However, often I kissed her, but not on the lips. It feels good when you come across a girl, that much closer. I was exploring her back in my hand, and she was putting her hands, in my front, starting from my chest to my lower abdomen. It was sensual and a kind of vibration was there in my body. For the first time, I felt like having a girl near me. All a man desires is to have a girl in his arm, all he desires is to feel the girl. The best part of girls are their eyes, legs, smile, lips, back includes lower back, and the chest. No longer had I felt like I was with my close friend. It was the moment, which disturbed me and attracted me towards a girl for the very first time.

It was real and natural feeling, there was nothing to imagine. Don't know how passionately it happened…, it took a couple of minutes to take in, what was transpiring and in no time, it went from innocent kisses to bold, hotter, more passionate ones. For the very first time, my mind was becoming dirty, and many stupid thoughts started running in my mind. May be because of watching porn, or because of my bodily desires, hidden inside, unknown to me, I longed for sleeping with her, explore her more, and wanted to see her in her inner beauty. Felt like kissing not only her cheeks, but also her tongue and lips, her body and many more. My body desired to have her with me in my bed, to see her merging in me without any hesitation. For a moment, I fell in love with her. To be frank, I forgot all my rules, and limitations. Rather, I imagined of sleeping with her someday. I longed to have sex with her, as our bodies were wet and in wet clothes, we could feel the silhouette of each other's body, at that time hardly our mind worked, all that I can say now is – our bodily desires dominated anything else. I never imagined of all this, but it happened that day. I allowed my body to touch hers. No one was there to restrict us, don't know, how passionate it was..., but I felt like giving myself to her in a moment, most probably so was the kind of feelings running in her mind.

It was already 10:00 PM, and still drizzling. I started the scooty, she was holding me from my back. I was quite happy, my stupid mind was telling me something, whereas my conscience telling me something else. And finally, we reached her destination. I bade her goodbye, as I had to take a bus from there to my place.

Everything was going well, till the time I reached my room. As soon as, I reached home, she called me to enquire, whether I reached or not. In between her call, I could see Rajesh's missed call. As soon as I disconnected her call, I received his call.

Rajesh – how many times, should I call..., doing romance with Neha or what?

I – yaa..., I kissed her.

Rajesh – so...

I – she kissed me...

Rajesh – and then...

I – she kissed me, and in no second, I could feel her lips covering my lips...

Rajesh remained silent for a couple of seconds.

I – what happened...

Rajesh – Finally, you have crossed your limit....

I – No..., but don't know how...

Rajesh – It's not fair Sid, you were not doing the right thing… Knowingly you are disturbing her relationship with Sameer. Instead of Sameer, imagine if I would have been there, who trusts you and feels that his girlfriend is safe with you. It's all about someone's trust. We shouldn't break that, and we should not replace the person. Sameer loves her, and she likes him, though from last one week, they were not talking to each other because of their family problems. Already there is a small gap in their relation, if you want to increase the gap, you can do that… But seriously, I never expected this from you…

I – Yaa, I could realize that I shouldn't have done, or shouldn't have allowed her… But what I did is that, I just kissed her…

Rajesh – As a friend, kissing someone on hand, or face is OK, but kissing someone on lips, is not fine. It indicates something else. Your bodily desire will increase day by day, and from a small mistake, you will not be able to stop yourself from sleeping with her. (Whatever limitations were there, slowly I could realize – It was already gone) Now don't cross one more step, I would say…, else you may be in problem. Think of Sameer, think of your mother, think of your family, will they allow you…

I – Feeling guilty yaar, feeling sorry for what I did… You are right. For a moment, I thought of taking the relationship forward…, but I was wrong. How can I forget, she is already in a relationship. There is her boyfriend who trusts me… How can I do this…, she should have stopped me, from doing all this…

Rajesh – you can't blame her, it's your mistake… From the day one, she likes you, so there were possibilities that she might get diverted. However, knowing that she is in a relationship, you shouldn't have crossed your limit...

I – Yaa... you are right, but what can I do now...?

Rajesh – It's already done, so leave it... you have just started, you can move a step back, that's it... Be particular to your destination, no matters how our mind gets diverted, but we should make sure that we are not hurting anyone...

After listening him, I could realize my mistake. I felt very bad. Rajesh is younger to me, but his suggestions were great enough to conceive, as I felt. We discussed for a couple of minutes more, and concluded that I should maintain a distance from her, then only I can move a step back from taking any further wrong decision.

I typed her in whatsapp –

Sorry yaar, wrongly my lip touched yours...

She – I liked it, in fact I did it knowingly.

I – are you sure...?

She called me and our conversation continued then after.

She – yaa, I love the way you kissed me..., it gave me a very good feeling....

I – So I know, how to kiss...?

She – Yaa... you know very well, I was wrong in my assumption that you can't kiss a girl, but you did it.... I love you... One thing I want to ask you...

I – Yaa tell

She – Finally you got changed for me Sid, I am very happy... if I don't return yourself back to you...?

I – means... ?

She – if I want you in my life completely...?

I remained silent for some time, and then she smiled –

I was joking yaar, now relax… Go and refresh yourself, I am going to bed…, fully tired.

Ok, Good Night, I replied before disconnecting the call. I closed my eyes for the day, but I was not able to sleep. All the things, that Rajesh told me, I started thinking about it, started asking my conscience – what I did, was it right…? Or I should not have done that, knowing that she is in a relationship. I should not have kissed her; I should not cross my limitations. I felt very sorry for Sameer. I felt guilty of betraying someone. I felt very bad, my conscience replied me – keep silence, with time you may get your answer. After some times of silence, once again I started thinking about it… Then I apologized to God for the mistake and slept.

SEVENTEEN

Next morning I felt swelling in my eyelids when I woke-up early. I was standing in the balcony, in my night suit. I saw two pigeons were making love; walking back and forth together, lock beaks and trying to kiss each other. Then I moved my face to the opposite direction, trying to avoid looking at them as the memory of last night's incident started disturbing me. I saw children playing in the ground, accompanied by their parents. Some were swimming with their dad, in the swimming pool. I could see parents looking at their children with immense care and love. It reminded me of my childhood days.

Whatever I surmise, whatever I trust, perhaps it's because of yesterday. I am talking about the evanescent shades of yesterday, in which my childhood swallowed up. Evanescent memories that disturb you, remind you of the past. The time's quintessential thing was trying to walk, conveying your message with a simple smile. Everyone was happy, when the little child in me spoke in dulcet voice.

In the stern daily routine of life, somehow the small child discovered his fondness for painting. Whenever he got time, he painted on a rough paper. Slowly the fondness for painting came in front of everyone and the schoolteachers encouraged him to participate in painting competitions.

I still remember, one Inter-school completion was there and the theme of the competition was – 'My Pet Animal'. Putting all my efforts, and with the help of my crayons, bottle paste colours and brush, I had drawn a parrot in the A4-size chart paper. After coming out of the competition hall, my dad enquired and I replied the same. All of a sudden, he shouted at me. He scolded me in front of my Mom – unnecessary wastage of time and money, he don't know the distinction between an animal and a bird. I am sure the painting will get rejected for the wrong choice of topic itself. I felt very bad cursing myself, "What have I done?" I confirmed with the senior persons in that competition hall, still… I didn't argue and remained silent.

Fortunately, after some days, my class teacher informed me that I won the second prize in that competition. I was very happy, waiting all the time to get the classes over. I ran to the front gate, seeing my dad standing in front of the gate. I took the back seat and all the way to my home, I was eagerly waiting for a perfect time to inform my parents about the good news. Just when I entered the gate of my home, I was not able to resist. I started saying, 'Mom, papa told that the painting will get rejected, but I won the second prize'.

'That's why he got the second prize, else he could have got the first prize', came out as my dad's instant response.

I always doubted whether my dad ever felt proud of me, when I received prizes for my achievements. Every time, he came up with suggestions – try to do better next time. Yeah,

I agree with him, maybe that was a very small achievement as compared to the achievements I was going to achieve in life, but still I believe – small achievements also count – a collection of such achievements of a child, makes a person 'UNIQUE' from the rest of the world. A word of praise, from your near and dear ones, actually counts; it helps a person to go ahead. Moreover, I believe success does not touch your feet if you follow the crowd, rather success is all yours if you can distinct yourself from the huge crowd.

With time, our basic needs, requirements change and grow. As a child, we want people's attention towards us, after that, we need a friend to share, to care, to fight, and to play with us.

I was not allowed to play, my childhood went in sufferings, when my classmates used to celebrate birthdays with their friends, I was not allowed to attend, not allowed to play with them. When everyone had a bike, I did not own one, had to wait all the time for my dad to allow to move in his bike. I cried literally. I did not had a choice to choose my favourite subject. I used to get scolding, when I produced the test paper copies to my father. I never scored well in social studies, as I hated the subject in which I had to mug-up like hell. My mother too got scolding because of me, sometimes in front of everyone – those days have been quite insulting.

Father – 'He is wasting my money and time; someday he will become a thief…, with your support. How many times, I will have to tell him to practice the things, but he won't listen me… Like a thief, he will hide from me. What can I do, if you don't want to study, just tell me, I will talk to the principal and ask her to discontinue your studies.

Mom – Please don't shout at him, he will do better next time...

Yeah, every time I promised to do better next time, the thing is that I loved mathematics, English and science, but I hated social sciences. So, I tried to manage getting somewhat more than the pass mark for the particular subject.

Giving the best effort to the rest of the subjects, I scored good marks and joined a good college. Now, again I was asked to prepare well for the engineering career. So, I did.

I got admission in an engineering college. But the situation became tough again, for me, to cope-up with it. Every day I had to travel for more than an hour in college bus to reach my college, the time, my college seniors utilized well to rag me like hell. I was unable to cope with the scenarios as it was the first time I was in contact with a number of unknown people. Being brought up at home since birth, hardly I conversed with my friends or relatives. My seniors asked me to do certain things that were shameful to do. They used to ask about sex stuff, porn stories, proposing seniors, etc. It was awkward for a child, like me.

I had no choice but to watch movie, to check filmfare magazines, I used to hide all this from my dad, knowing that he won't like all these. Recovery of any of these cost me the magazine and pocket money of two-three days, as a sign of punishment for my biggest crime i.e. giving time for my own passion. When all friends independently commuted on their bikes, I had to wait for my father to come, everyone used to tease me – 'are you a school going boy.' It was insulting for me, but hardly, I used to convey my feelings to him. If I ever asked him for a bike for me, scolding was the only thing I got back. He would start narrating his story of struggle – how he used to cross the river to attend the school, how he used to travel in cycle for 30-40kms or even more a day, bla bla bla…. How in a pair of pant and shirt, he completed his schooling. It was so pathetic, I was so disturbed but helpless.

I didn't had a choice to sleep according to my wish, time table was there prepared by dad. In morning, 6 am I was supposed to get-up and study. After a lot of fights, he concluded –

"Whatever you do, I don't care… I just want your CGPA above eight, mind it…"

I was not allowed to buy clothes of my choice. Shirts and pants including my inners, were chosen by my parents. And always they would come-up with the large-size, which looked very odd at me; all that I was asked to do is – adjust the bottom of your shirt inside your pant. Having no choice, I followed.

I lived a middle class life with just one hope that someday everything will turn out to be proper and "adjective" to life will change from "burden" to "pleasure".

Each and everything was to be shared with my parents, in order to have the things done. But there are things non-shareable with your parents or sisters; I used to keep them to myself. I wished if I had a brother, to understand me.

But in the whole process, trying to balance college life and home, I got to know what is life, how to get yourself exposed to certain situations.

Each situation, that I had undergone, may have been tough, but after that period, I got to know many things. Inside a home, are always safe and secure. Few things of your need, you get, even before you ask for them. Once you move out of your home, things are quite different. There are things to explore, many stories to capture, and a number of things to learn... You need to convey your message properly, else you may be among the left out ones, behind the crowd. Parents will never understand what type of exposure a child need, to explore the world ahead. You have to explore it all, yourself, you never know what you have to face... I remember the words of my school teacher, Mrs. Sisila Chaudhury, 'Tenth exam will be the easiest exam you will take in your life... You have not seen what life has ahead for you...'

It's cent percent right, I can feel it now.

Needs and hope keep on increasing, with passing years. For an adolescent, studies and getting good job, necessitates the life. Adding to the queue girlfriend, wife, child, and maintaining a luxurious life. All these are what we people fantasize about. There is no end to illusion. I also ask peoples to live their passion. The process of personified abstraction cannot be wholly different from existing people in the society, especially from middle class people's perception. As a human being, I also love to live my dreams independently...

Now no doubt I am independent, but once I had been disturbed, helpless one. I have all those rights to choose the things of my choice, as no longer my parents stop me from doing the things. They are confident in me that, I have started walking on the right track. But they are unaware of my vulnerabilities...

At that time, things were different; all I wished was to live my passion with full freedom. But now turning back to those days, and recollecting the things, it seems those days were worth-living. They used to choose everything for me, but the happiness of wearing a new dress was always unique in those days. Buying clothes from my salary never gave me that happiness which I used to get, when my parents bought oversized shirt for me in my childhood. There was struggle for small things, but at the end of the struggle, the destination was clearly visible. But now, neither the destination, nor the way to it, is clearly visible. There were restrictions, but there the chance of doing mistake was rare. With time, I got to know the things, no longer I named that as "restrictions", it was the love and affection, a fear of your near and dear ones for you of seeing you on wrong tracks.

To the Present...

I still remember the words of my mother. She used to tell me that, don't mess with girls. With time, we will provide you more than the best that you deserve. I felt like missing all of them, I felt guilty of last night's incident. Just then, my phone vibrated. It was my mom; I received. She was crying over the phone, telling that she saw a bad dream about me, last night. The dream was that I got married to someone, without their consent. I promised her once again, saying that – it's impossible! That day will never come, you don't worry.

'I know you won't, but still my mind is disturbing me... I am not there near you, that's why... I know my child is too innocent to face the world, if some day someone came in your life...' she replied.

I am not that innocent as you think, no one can take your child from you, and I promise you that. Now stop crying and smile at least. You should give me hope to go ahead in life, you shouldn't cry in front of me. Love you…, now go and take your breakfast. Do it quick…, else I won't talk with you…

She is the one, who comes to know the things even before I speak or convey it to her, myself. She is so attached to me that, whatever I do, she comes to know it beforehand. I have not told her anything of the last night's incident, but still she saw similar thing in her dream. Motherly love is just like that, they can feel the ups-and-downs of life of their child.

After the call, I received Neha's call. She called to wish me morning.

'Yaa Good Morning', replied in a casual voice.

She – what's up…

Nothing special, just now got up from the bed, standing in the balcony…

From my conversation itself, she sensed something wrong with me, as I was not talking in the way I used to, earlier.

She – It seems you are not interested to talk with me, what happened…?

I – nothing…

She – Are you fine?

Yaa…, how is Sameer, did u talk to him…?

She – he is fine, his final exams are there next month. He is not allowed to talk with me, till his exams are not over. This is the strict rule from his parent's side.

I could see Rajesh calling me, while I was talking with Neha.

I – Ok…, what about him, is he fine…, you wished him today morning….

She – Yaa, I messaged him, why you are asking about him today...

I – no nothing, I need to talk to my mother. Just before your call, I called her and the call went unanswered. Now I am getting miss call from her, so will catch you later on, bye...

She – Ok, bye...

I told her a lie, just to talk with Rajesh. I disconnected the call. Just then, Rajesh once again called me.

Rajesh – Good Morning, talked with her...?

I – yaa, she called me yesterday also. Just before your call, I was talking to her.

Rajesh – Make her clear that, you people were not doing right thing...

I – how can I tell yaar, if I react in this way, she may over-react...

Rajesh – Let her, but it's high time, you should close the topic here itself, else...

Yaa I understand, but I can't tell her all this, as I don't know how she would react...

'She might get disturbed a bit, but it's high time to make everything clear, else you will be in trouble bro', Rajesh replied.

After this, the whole day I did not reply to her messages. I felt like I was missing something, but my conscience didn't allow me to speak or message her, after doing such a mistake. I was not sure, whether I will be able to face her the next working day...

<u>EIGHTEEN</u>

Wednesday morning. Soon after reaching office, I started working, sitting in my cubicle. Wishing her good morning, was everyday practice while entering into the ODC. She understood that there was something wrong, and I was trying to avoid her. She was obvious in reading my behaviour and face. The whole day, I tried to avoid her putting work as an excuse. I continued this for the entire week without talking or discussing properly with her.

While returning to home on Friday, inside the bus she started asking me – What happened, you were acting strange today…

'Nothing like that', I replied.

Don't lie…, I know very well. From yesterday morning, I am observing you. You look disturbed and holding something from me. Will you please tell me?

'Nothing is there to hide from you, just I am feeling tired,' came out the reply from my side.

'Then kiss me…' she asked me casually.

'I won't kiss in public', I replied.

'You can kiss my hand at least', she demanded, showing me her hand.

No I won't…

'Why…, you have not kissed me even once in the whole day', she told me.

'In fact I don't feel like kissing you it's not right yaar…' I replied.

'Yaa… go ahead…', she encouraged me to vomit all those things, disturbing me from last few days, but I was unable to, as it may hurt her and above all I was not sure, how she may react, so I stopped.

'I am that much attached to you that I can read your mind very well, so don't try to outsmart…' she replied.

'Even I am not trying…'

'Then why that day, all of a sudden you enquired about Sameer, why you have not replied any of my messages? Why, today you were trying to keep a distance from me…? Do you have the answers to all my questions…? She argued.

May be I don't have a perfect answer to all of your questions…

'You have the right answers to all my questions, but the thing is you don't want to share with me, right…?' she demanded holding my hand tightly.

'I want some time alone to answer all of your questions. May be right now, I am disturbed and my conscience doesn't permit me to discuss all this right now. Try to understand, I'll tell you everything…' Slowly I pulled my hand from her grip and tried to maintain a bit of gap between us.

'Tell me now itself, I know very well that what's going on in your mind…' she spoke in a confident voice.

I remained silent for a while, then she continued her sentence, 'You are feeling guilty for that Saturday night…, right…?'

May be you are right to some extent…

'I am 100% right, I told you na that I am so attached to you that even if you utter a word, and stop speaking I can understand the rest all. All of a sudden, you asked me about Sameer, then talking with your mother, not pinging me the entire day, trying to maintain distance – all this indicates that you were feeling guilty after that incident', She talked in a confident voice.

'Yes you are right, I am feeling guilty… May be it was my mistake kissing you on that way… I shouldn't have done that. But believe me intentionally I have not done anything to hurt you, at that time don't know why I couldn't resist myself. I came to realize that I crossed my limit, when Rajesh told me that it was in no way right, what I did', I replied.

'You informed all this to Rajesh, are you crazy…? What are you thinking of yourself Sid, it's not the guy, all the time the girl will be blamed. How can you do this to me…?'

Some people standing in the bus were staring at us. It felt uneasy and I whispered very softly in her ear not to create any scene, as people were there, looking, and listening us.

She started crying, 'How can you tell all this to Rajesh? What impression would he be having about me…?'

'Sorry, I hurt you, but seriously it was not done intentionally', I tried to convince her but she was not in a mood to listen.

We got off the bus on the stop. Sky was full of clouds, and reddish in colour. Noise was so dominating, that we couldn't hear each other properly. It was a busy traffic area; bus, vehicles, and people were moving haphazardly. Few people gathered under the shed of a nearby tea stall, in order to elude the rain. I was standing with her in the drizzling rain. I was reticent to discuss the issue. She was holding my hands tightly. I wanted to request her to spare me, to allow me to bid good-bye for the day; tired of arguing with her.

"I am not going to leave you, you can't move away from my life just like this…" she said in a hushed voice.

C'mon, tell me, what the fuck, can you do? No longer you trust me, right…?

"Don't know, but I can't leave you just like this…" she replied in a rigid voice.

Then what the hell do you want from me…?

"Nothing much, but I don't want to move a step back. I want you in my life", she replied with a crying voice.

I can't…, move ahead with you…

'Why?'

'Because it was a mistake, and I don't want to repeat it once again,' was my reply.

"But it was not a mistake for me, it was love and I love you in all sense. Why do you play with my emotions? Am I your puppet…?" She was crying, holding my hands tightly.

I don't want to substantiate you, believe me, I am feeling guilty for that. So, I need some time, to get myself back to you.

"I also, feel guilty now. But, you can't leave me alone like this…" she said.

'Please leave me now, I have to move… please forgive me. Sorry, I can't be in your life anymore.'

We walked a little bit, towards the next stop, where she used to take bus to her stop.

"If you want, we can just be friends, that's it… nothing more than that", I replied after thinking a lot.

"No, I can't accept you as a friend anymore, I just can't…" she replied, to which I became furious. "Then, what do you want from me, be apparent… you want me to sleep with you, you want me to fuck you…, you want me to kiss you…, you want me to continue my mistake…?

'No…, I don't want all that, but I love you…' she replied softly.

It was exasperating, standing in the drizzling rain for complete one hour and arguing like this, to which there was no conclusion, it seemed. Neither she was clear in her objective, nor was she trying to accept my words. It may have been like, she knew what she was doing, but she was trying to hide the same from me. Don't know why, girls are obsessed to conceal their reality to the max, they can. Whatever it was, I was trying to convey her, to make her understand, she was not ready to perceive, or to listen. She was putting her points forward and crying as if only I was the culprit, in the act, which we both were part of. It made me feel guilty. I was helpless for a moment. Angry and exasperated, I asked her to leave my hand. It was raining. She was holding the umbrella in one hand, and her other hand was over my hand. I tried hard to free my hand from her. Though I was very angry, still I asked her in a soft voice – "please move now, and allow me to move. I am tired of these stupid stuffs. Leave me now; we can talk over the phone, late night". Even after hearing all this, she was not ready to budge. It annoyed me a lot, and finally I replied – "then go to hell, keep standing... I am leaving. She replied – 'you can't envision, what I can do today...!!!'

For an instant, I became vacuous. Spending time with someone, sharing your thoughts with someone, or being transparent to someone - is it a mistake?

I replied with a heavy voice – do whatever you like, I don't care..., Stand here, I am leaving. Bye...

She was still standing in the rain. I was completely drenched. I moved slowly away from her. Teardrops and raindrops were hardly distinguishable on my face. There is a great saying - "Memories warm you up from inside. But they also tear you apart". It's very true; I was able to correlate it with the previous memories. It was raining that day also, when we both went together to visit a temple. In the rain, we were sharing one umbrella. But feelings on these two occasions were diagonal corners of a room. That time I was not that close to her. There was an unsaid distance between us. We were returning from a journey. It was raining immensely.

She opened her umbrella and asked me to join. Usually, the umbrellas that women carry are small. So, it's difficult for two people to be under one umbrella. I was trying to maintain a little gap between us. She could feel that, by trying this, I got drenched in the rain. She tilted her umbrella to get me under; which exposed her right shoulder to rain. Finally, I came a bit closer. I was unsure what a girl may think of, when a guy accidently comes in bodily contact with a girl. A 'despo'...

Small children were returning from their school, wearing raincoats, reminding me of my school days. Some children were accompanied by their parents, while the others with their friends... Some were holding umbrellas also. They were holding each other's hand and were even walking together under the same umbrella. But in their case, situation was different.

They were a kind of "chotta-packet", two "chotta-packet" can easily share one umbrella in their case. And the most important fact- at that age, hardly anyone can feel the difference between a boy and a girl. There was no concept of boyfriend and girlfriend, when we were in school.

It started raining heavily; mud and water everywhere on the ground. Gradually, it became difficult to maintain the space. She insisted me to come a bit closer, and asked me to hold the umbrella. Now I was holding the umbrella, it now became a tougher job as it was her umbrella in my hand, it was my responsibility to protect her. I asked her – Do you trust me…, are you comfortable with me?

She smiled and nodded her head in apprehension.

She came closer, to me. In my left hand, I was holding the umbrella, and my right hand was free. It was creating hindrance, and she was unable to keep space with me, so, in order to make the situation more comfortable, I put my hand over her shoulder very gently. She was comfortable with me. Her wet hairs were touching my face. I was trying my best to make her feel comfortable in my presence. It was the first time. I was trying to protect a girl, who had entrusted me. I was very ecstatic and stayed tight-lipped. She was talking all the way. But I was thinking, whether I am doing anything wrong. I was questioning myself whether she would be carrying a negative impression of me. Whether people standing on the other side of road, would be thinking, something else and whether they would be commenting on her character. However, good you maybe, people will point a finger at your character if they see you with a girl. They wouldn't take the scenario fairly; rather they would have a misconception that something was going on between them. Truth was that we were just friends.

There was magic in the raindrops, a sense of uniqueness that you can't put it in words. Then we took a bus. She was not worried about herself. She was worried about me, how I would reach my PG safely. Her trust, respect, care towards me, was very cutely reflected in her activities. I was very happy, it was one of the best experiences to be in the rain, with a girl like her, under one umbrella, sharing your thoughts, doing mischief and talking nonsense, and caring for someone, protecting someone – it's a kind of esteem towards each other. When someone believes in you, it gives a very good feeling. Her impression towards me grew to some extent in this process, and vice-versa, which I could feel later. She is a very openhearted girl, and loves roaming, shopping and travelling. She needed someone – someone known to be next to her, so that she could do, all that she wanted, freely. I was the one, next to her that day. And as I said, I tried my best to protect her, to make her feel comfortable.

This was the first day, when I felt being with a girl is something different. It was raining all eve that day, and today as well, it's raining. The place was same and the set -up of the place as well. That day chaos did not let me hear her words; all I heard was that sweet voice. Today, the situation was different; I was tired of listening to her. I was trying to listen to my conscience, which did not allow me to stay furthermore, with her in the rain, talking under the same umbrella. I walked slowly across the road, turning behind a number of times to check whether she was still standing there or left for her PG. She was still standing. The situation was very tough, I was in a dilemma, whether to stop there or to leave the place. Finally, I left her and walked in opposite direction. I was in a disturbed mood; didn't feel like returning to my home. So, without thinking anything I boarded a bus to Mangalore. I was running away. I called Sanya - one of her best friend. She picked my call in the third attempt.

'Sanya, please ask Neha to move to her PG. It's raining and she is not ready to go back to her PG, still standing at the bus stop.'

'Why, what happened, all of a sudden?' Sanya enquired.

'We fought with each other, once again. And this time, I don't think I have done something wrong. Her attitudes, behaviour, expectations from me, are no longer the same I guess...Replying to message as – love you too...Caring for you, keeping promises, does not mean that ....'

I paid the ticket fare, holding the phone near my ear, pressed over my shoulder, I continued talking her, 'She asks me not to talk to any girl, in her absence, not to go anywhere with anyone, without informing her. She is creating a boundary for me, and instead of feeling comfortable with her, I feel uneasy. I can't keep myself restricted. I don't think she treats me as a friend anymore, I guess...'

Sanya listened to me silently and told me – No, she is like that. With us also, she behave in the same way. She expects from us also in the same manner. For her, her friends are everything.'

I replied – "your case may be entirely different from mine, as in my case I am a guy and she is a girl. Expecting something from the same sex may not look bad, but expecting something from the opposite sex might indicate something else, something different. I hope you understand me".

"Wait, I'll call you back, now let me check where she is right now", with a sense of care towards her friend, she asked me to hold my call for a moment.

I was not in a good mood. Feeling guilty, questioning myself - how can I hurt someone, how can I do such a blunder, how can I trifle with someone's emotion…? I was asking all those questions to myself, suddenly Rajesh called me. I asked him to call her and enquire about her condition, 'Feeling lonely and guilty yaar, can you please check with her if she is fine or not…'

'I knew that it will happen someday; anyway don't think too much…'

I am not thinking of myself yaar. I am really bothered about her. I don't want her to take any wrong step in life, which would make me feel guilty the entire life.

'Don't know how to tell you…She loves me more than her life, in return of that I can't afford her to lose herself in the darkest shed of yesterday.'

"Nothing like that will happen, think positive and don't feel that you are alone, I am there with you…", he was very much worried. He was the one, who was with me in that situation, who understood me more than myself. I thought of talking to my mom, but once again, thought came to my mind – not to disturb her. I felt disturbed, lonely, lost somewhere, and finally switched-off my phone and slept in the seat itself unconsciously, without having dinner. With me, my thought perhaps also took rest for the day.

NINETEEN

Just before dawn, when I opened eyes; I felt that I reached an unknown destination Surathkal beach, famous for its clean surrounding and light-house, is situated 20 Kms away from Mangalore. Travelling whole night after long working hours at office was tiring. I got off the bus, walked a bit towards the market to purchase at least a pair of clothes, as I did not carry any extra pair with me. Here I came to know a unique way of marketing and targeting customers. Hotels and guesthouses had tie-ups with shopkeepers, thus reaching out to each and every customer visiting a shop. I also reached one cheap guesthouse through the same tie-up.

After retiring for some time, I walked towards the beach; it was early dawn. Early morning sunrise was awesome to look at; the sunlight was adding colours in the water, reflecting and glittering all over the surface. Peace prevailed all over the place. I switched ON my mobile to capture the beauty and account of missed-calls popped up from Rajesh, Sanya, Neha and all others. I felt like calling Sanya first.

Sanya picked up the call and started shouting loudly, 'What happened, why you have switched-off your mobile, I tried many times, but...

'Tell me, how is she now...' I enquired.

'She is fine, no need to worry. By the way where are you...?' she enquired.

'In my world...' I replied plainly.

'Don't lie me, I called your roommate Sahil late last night, he told me you were not in the room', Sanya told.

'Don't know exactly where I am..., but yaa you can be sure that I am there in my world', I replied.

'Coming to office?'

'No..., sick leave...I'll apply sick leave...', I murmured.

'Will you please elaborate...? If you don't mind... what happened to both of you...' she demanded.

I took a deep breath, closed my eyes for a while; all the memories of the past flashed through my mind, some blurred with time and shock and some as real as the sand below my feet...

You never know...

When 'TIME PASS' becomes your 'PAST' time...

Few hour back I was a different person and now it was someone else standing in a different world. A world where no one recognized me; all alone I was trying to befriend with myself...

I could hear the surreal sound of the sea, where tides were playing on the surface of the tranquil water. It looked like as if they were staring at me. I wanted to divert my mind, but my inner conscience, reflecting in the clean water, seemed to speak volumes of the past.

I felt as if, along with Sanya over the call, the atmosphere also questioned me...

How and what all happened to me...?

How can I be so attached to someone, especially a girl...?

How everything got initiated...?

I closed my eyes, and words started flowing out of my mouth, with all emotions...

With no time, I could feel my emotions spread in bits of paper torn out of the diary of my life. I started writing down, sitting on a big rock, on the beach.

I was a guy, who believed that girls and guys can't be close friends. She proved me wrong. Now, once again I thought as if I was right in all aspects.

I told Sanya, earlier my life was completely different. I was a carefree bird, flying in my own world, with all my freedom. Suddenly, she came in my life and I felt like flying together was even better, rather than flying alone. Exploring the sky beyond you, exploring the new world ahead you, seemed more interesting, so I gave my life a new chance – and shared life with someone. This may have been one of the reason, I allowed her to enter in my life.

Sanya listened everything patiently and replied, 'I understand, but I want to see you both as good friends. For a small mistake, you both should not separate from each other.

I disconnected the call all of a sudden, tears rolled down my cheeks.

The dawn goes down to the dark dusk. The dark side of love and emotions were all around me, inflaming me. And the reddish sky seemed to be staring at me with questions...

I was feeling very guilty that day. Being friends with a girl, was my first mistake, asking her to be in the same project, was my second mistake, getting closer to her day by day was my third mistake, and treating her as my best friend was my fourth mistake, trusting or believing a girl was my fifth mistake – I was completely broken. I kept silent for some time. I was thinking from every angle. What to do?, How to do? – Questions juggling in my mind...

The dimness of the brightest star gave bluish sky a velvet violet look – a good number of stars along with the moon signalled the beginning of dusk. I started shambling on the beach. The trail of the double attacks of the cold breeze and disheartening thoughts was snapped with the jiggling and laughs; a couple was making while romancing. Don't know, why I kept staring at them for a while... May be because they were the only human beings present over there.

I was quite tensed, felt as if loving someone as waste of time, and life. Their juggling and laughs again drew my attention and revealed their drunken state. The man was holding a beer bottle and the girl was moving her hand on the man's body. They both were coloured people. They were making love, as a regular couple would do.

With time, I realized that they were devoid of the ability to speak but still they conveyed their feelings to each other very well. The girl was moving her fingers frequently; it appeared that she was trying to convey something to her partner and the guy was smart enough to capture the girl's thought and expressions. And, they kissed each other, lip locked, passionately. Their reflections over the clean bluish water, started romancing and dancing. However, the dance was not so professional in any way, but the sweetness of love, and emotions touched me deep inside.

That day I realized that inability to speak a word can't stop a person from conveying his or her inner feelings. We normal people are lucky enough to put our words forward in front of everyone. But we fail to do justice with the emotions and feelings we present through words. I felt as if it was not a curse, but it was good enough to be like that. As when a person is complete in all sense he or she needs more than that, expectation may not reach the tide of the sea. But when an incomplete person reaches another incomplete person, they love to share the incompleteness among each other. All other complicacy disappears in no time. They start living the dream of the partner as it completes the incompleteness of his or her.

I walked back to the guest room. Post dinner, I was about to close my eyes, lying in the bed. I was very disturbed that day. I was drenched from outside but inside, my heart burning. The stress of the entire day and the rain caused me headache.

I searched for the medicine so that I can have it and take rest. Although I decided not to think about her, when I found the medicine, it melted my heart again. It was the 'Zero Dull', medicine that she had given me. Because she knew that because of my hectic schedule and work, I often get mild fever and headache. So she had put it in my bag. Although I didn't try to think about her, I saw her presence everywhere around me. Although my body was free from her largest possible shadow, my mind was still occupied with her thoughts. Thoughts of the nights that had brought happiness into my life, thoughts that used to wake me up in the morning with an assurance that someone has already wished me good morning and waiting for my reply. Thoughts that made me feel special to her. Starting from the nonsense whatsapp talk throughout the night or the moments she was playing with my hairs or in the boat when I hugged her or the night I kissed her, every night was worth living thousand times. Those nights taught us the true nature of our relationship! I then knew that the dust had started to shine but the warmth and softness of the velvet that she had wrapped me in by her love, didn't allow me to free myself from her thoughts or even getting away from her.

You just can't evade the law of the nature, law of love. The amount and extent of love, trust, affection and care that she had given me was taking its toll. I knew, there had been way too many nights when we couldn't sleep properly. There were so many ways we fought with each other. But there were nights as well that made me memorize the love of my mother. A kiss that made me feel how deeply we were involved with each other's life! Although my mind was saying something but my heart failed to hate her. Just then I got a call from an unknown number. I picked up the call, after a long ring.

'Close the topic here. You won't talk with Neha from now onwards. Ok…?'

Is it Sameer…?

'Yup… now don't act innocent…' he told me.

Listen to me Sameer…

'Don't want to listen to your stupid story, just I want you to stay away from her, that's it…' came as a clear warning from Sameer. Before I could apologize, he disconnected the call.

I felt very bad; Sameer as I believed was not a guy who would doubt someone without reason. But...

Rajesh called me and informed me that he had a conference discussion with Sameer and Neha, just a couple of hours back. I was shocked listening to him.

TWENTY

'They wanted you as well to be in the conference but your phone was not reachable at that time.'

'Tell me what you people discussed…?' I asked him.

'She started crying all of a sudden and told that she kissed you and it was not a friendly kiss. It was more than a friendly kiss, covering your lip. When she told this, even I was shocked bro… I tried to convince Sameer that it was just an infatuation, it was just a kiss and she is too childish to make this an issue. After listening to her and me, he said - 'It can't be an infatuation, you know this better Rajesh. Even I knew that it would happen someday. You people were making me fool all these days… I can't trust you all anymore.' That's it, he disconnected the call. I felt humiliation and anger, so I too disconnected the call soon after Sameer.

Ohh…, taking a deep and a long breath, full of tiredness, I replied, 'Even I got a call from Sameer, he asked me not be in touch with Neha anymore.'

'Don't know what she is going to achieve by doing like this… Neither she will get your love, nor she will receive Sameer's concern', Rajesh told.

It's her madness to get me back in her life. But I can't do that Rajesh... For a year's love, I can't forget 25 year's affection and promise to my mom. I can't accept someone..., without her permission. My life is not only mine; I owe love and loyalty to my parents as well. I told her from the very beginning that I can't commit to any girl. She also agreed, so I was comfortable with her. I trusted her that she would never lean towards me... But now she wants me in her life. I am too sorry to tell her that I can't be a part of her life... Not only she, even I fell for her, it was just for friendship, but that night I was unconscious, I did it... I shouldn't have allowed her to kiss me, and I shouldn't have kissed her.

Rajesh – It was just a kiss, bro... not an irreversible blunder... it happens some time... Unnecessarily she is making an issue, let her do..., you just avoid her. It's good that before doing a big mistake, before entering into the circle of complicacy and confusion, you took your step back. Now don't think much, stick to your decision. Don't talk with her, as asked by Sameer. Let her realize that one-sided love can't succeed forcibly. Because of her madness, you shouldn't forget living your own dream.

'Feeling guilty yaar... I don't want to blame someone who loved me more than me. At the same time, I can't break the trust of my family also. It's good to have someone beside you who loves you...'

'It's good, but if that love of someone, makes the person feel that he or she is in jail, inside the boundaries of her love, then living is nothing but just hell ', Rajesh replied.

'What to do now, I don't know...'

'With time, everything will be OK… Just give some time to both of them. Till then stay away from her, it's my advice', his voice showed concerns for me.

Rajesh, Sameer's word, and my inner conscience – all of them repeated the same thing – I shouldn't keep any contact with her. I remembered last night's incident and her reactions and demand. I felt as if I don't have a choice, rather to love her…, to accept her.

She was holding my hand tightly, not allowing me to move, as if I slept with her. She blamed me, as if I had utilized her, though I never tried. I felt as if she was trying to show the power of having a boyfriend. Even if we did some mistake unconsciously, it should have been restricted to us. It shouldn't have reached Sameer's ears. She told her boyfriend, not to prove her right but to blame me and my love for her.

Thoughts and complicated scenarios of last two days, kept on irritating me – finally my inner conscience said aloud – I hate you Neha… I realized my love for her, was already dead by that time…

My hatred dominated over the love for her. I felt as if someone wanted to take me away from myself. I cried a lot, and then laughed aloud, thinking of the good and bad memories of the past.

Then I concluded – I hate her more than anyone in my life…

How could I trust a girl like her and why should Sameer warn me what to do, what not to…

I connected the mobile data and then blocked her in whatsapp. I blocked her in facebook too and changed my account name to an unusual one…

I blocked her number as well, as I decided not to keep any type of contact with her. I deleted all her snaps from my mobile and then shouted in the empty room – I hate you yaar... I will hate you throughout my life... I will try to erase you from my mind, and everything else... However, I am sure you will be there somewhere in my bad memories.

You were the first girl, whom I made friendship with...

You were the one, to whom I trusted the max...

Every time you proved me wrong...

Yesterday and today as well, you did the same...

I hate you yaar... I just hate you...

The cries and shouts hit the wall of the enclosed room and returned back to me, repeating my words of hatred.

TWENTY ONE

After 2 days…

Neha pinged me in the communicator Good morning, to which I didn't reply. She then came near me and with a smile on her face, wished me good morning. I neither wished her, nor looked at her face. She was about to hold my hand, just before that I moved my hand from her. She left back to her place. I continued doing my work. Varsha came near me to remind, regarding the previous discussion we had. According to the discussion, some fresher were joining; me and Swami were supposed to give KT (Knowledge Transfer) to the freshers.

Varsha – Hey Sid, they are coming today, please start from the very basic ideas about the products, and simultaneously do check their datacom skills.

I nodded my head, saying, "Yaa, I will do that…"

Then I got deep involved in my work. Suddenly, I felt like someone standing near me. One girl was standing near me in mute state. When I turned a bit towards my right, I saw a girl standing, she initiated, 'Hello, Is this Siddhath…?'

Yaa…

'Varsha asked me to take KT from you', she replied in a very soft voice.

'Ok, take one chair and please be seated…, give me a couple of minutes let me start the execution, and then I will get back to you…'

I did not look at her. I was just aware that a girl was standing near me, and was supposed to take KT from me. I checked my work, and then opened the manual documents to give her KT. Then I started describing about the project, 'We belong to Product Testing Department, under this department, we are having 5 different categories…'.

While narrating her, I glanced at her two-three times.

Then I felt like, I was getting diverted, so I promised myself not to look at her, as when I looked at her, the flow of explaining snapped, leading to deviation from topic or long pauses. I was not able to give my cent percent.

I explained her approximately for an hour, and then she left…, while I excused her for the day, I saw her once. I could get only left side's view, while she was walking towards her place. Her white kurta with ghee-coloured leggings suited her perfectly. Her hair were untied, and shining. The hair strand was bouncing on her cheeks while she was walking. I did not ask her name. Just then, I opened my mail to check Varsha's Mail about fresher's KT. A couple of names were there, I was unable to conclude on her name. For some time, I remained silent, asking to myself, 'Why, I was getting so distracted from my track, while giving her KT?

Why I was unable to look at her eyes…, what's wrong with me…?

It seemed to me that she was very beautiful, felt like seeing her, but my attitude didn't permit me to go near her. It may give a wrong impression of mine, and the thing is she would come near me a couple of times, to take KT… So better to wait…

I checked the timing on my system; it was 10:30 A.M, the time for the client meeting. The meeting was there because the project was going to ramp-down in the upcoming month. They planned to discuss about the transition phase and everything else. I noticed that some people had already deserted their cubicles for the meeting. So I moved out of the ODC. I was inside the elevator, just then received Swami's message – Hey…man, only billable guys are allowed to be a part of that meeting.

I thought, maybe he was joking, but the other thought was Swami never jokes in such things. I was just about to enter into the glass doors, where the meeting was going on. Varsha showed her hand, as a symbol asking me not to enter. Then she came out of the meeting room and very politely replied, 'See… Sid naam ke koi bandaa yahan kaam kar raha hain hamari project keliye, ye baat hamne client ko inform nahi kiya hai abhi tak, so tumahara andar jana sayaad thik nahi hoga' (See….customer don't know that someone named Sid is working in this project, so it's better that you don't join this meeting). I felt very bad, listening to her.

I walked away slowly, downstairs to my ODC. After the meeting, client and all team members went for the team-lunch, which was kept out of my knowledge. Then, a couple of questions started irritating me,

'Don't I deserve to attend the meeting…? As a team member, don't I deserve to take part in the team-lunch…?.

What's my recognition in the project, just a 'back-up'? how long will I have to starve for recognition?'

I was in my thoughts, trying to find the answers to my inner questions, just then heard Sweety offering me a bite from her tiffin, 'Sid… have it'. I looked at her face. 'Don't tell that only billable people should have it', she criticized in her way. I took a bite and left the place.

Swami and I had joined the project at the same time. Yet, all facilities were available for one, and no one cared for me – was that right?

Didn't know with whom to share all my dilemmas…

Meanwhile I had to handle the work as a backup. To avoid any hiccup, I looked at the work. I was tensed due to issues with Neha and at the same time, due to the work atmosphere around me. It appeared to me that everyone was taking pity on me, poor child…! I thought of taking release from the project. I was sure that I won't continue in that atmosphere anymore, but again the difficulty of getting a project came in my mind, which dragged me backward to devoid from concluding anything. I was sitting silently looking at the screen; the execution was going on. I could feel someone standing near my back, so I turned back. It was the girl, who took KT in the morning.

'Yaa Siddharth, I have some doubts, after checking the materials provided by you…'

'I can't tell you anything now, will discuss once I am free… You can go now…' in a shivering tone filled with aggression, I replied all of a sudden.

'Sorry… for disturbing you…' she said and was about to leave. I felt bad and guilty; I realized I should not have reacted so rudely. I turned back and shouted,' Oye Hello…'

She stopped. I asked her to pull a chair, and sit near me.

'Your name…?'

'Pooja'

'Don't feel bad, I was in a tensed mood, so…' tried to convey my feelings.

'It's Ok…' she replied.

'You can ask me…' I told.

Just then, the chat box turned blinking yellow. There was a new message. When I clicked on it, I saw it was Neha who pinged me. I minimized the chat box, and asked her to leave. As soon as she left with a smile on her face, I returned back to the chat conversation.

'I saw hatred in your eyes… How much do you hate me?'

'I hate you more than I loved you…' I replied.

'Can you please come near me…'

'No… I have some work, I can't…'

'Please…, just five minutes…' she requested, so I went to her desk.

She looked at my face and then put her hand over mine; I freed my hands from her with anger and hatred.

I was not willing even to look at her face, she was asking me a lot many things, but I stood there, mute.

Her system was logged-in and the execution was going on. I sat near her desk and opened a notepad on her system to convey my message.

I typed,' I don't want to talk with you… Feeling uncomfortable here…'

Then she typed sitting near me in the same note pad, just below – but I want to clear certain things...

'Then Carry on...' I typed.

'I want you to forgive me...' she typed.

'Don't think ever could I forgive you..., I hate you...' I typed.

'Please I can't face your hatred for me, I want you to break the silence between you and me..., can we sit and discuss face to face..., please...' she typed.

'No... I don't want to discuss anything with you anymore... Don't want to see your face... Don't ever dare to touch me; I will forget you were my friend...

'My mom wants to talk with you..., would you like to...' she typed.

'Yaa... to whom all you complained about me...? Since I have done a mistake, I don't have a choice but to tolerate everyone, your boyfriend warned me not to talk with you...; I think your mom will tell the same. So, don't worry, even if I am not ready to speak with her, I'll make sure that I won't keep any relation with you, further... I had trusted you as a best friend of mine, but you did not leave a chance to blame me, anyways do whatever you want to do, I don't care... Keep in mind, I hate you... Never in future, our path will coincide, as two parallel paths meet at infinity only... Bye forever..., Keep smiling always...' after typing this I just left the place, without waiting for her to type further as a reply to my lines. While moving from her place, on the way I met Simran, she wished me morning, I wished her too and then left, as I was not in a good mood. She then pinged me once I logged in into the system.

'What is the issue between you and Neha…, I could see you people, behaving very strangely now a days…'

'We fought with each other as usual…'

'What's the reason…' she demanded.

'Not now… will tell you later on…' I pinged her.

I informed Simran, over phone in the evening; she listened the whole scenario and then replied, 'it's quite understandable Sid, the way you both behave, indicates that you were in a relationship. Now if she demands something it's no way wrong… You should not have given her the scope to come up with all these stuffs…'

'I never thought of all that Simran… feeling helpless now…'

'Yaa… I understand. If she does something to her life now… then you would be responsible for that. See you can't stop people from falling for you, but you could have avoided her… Leave it, frankly tell, did you sleep with her…?' Simran asked me.

'No…'

'Then… did you kiss her…?' She enquired.

TWENTY TWO

'Yes, I kissed her...'

Good... Being a girl I know girls have a sixth sense about guys attached to them and it makes the girls want a guy even more. Now if she wants you in her life, she is no way wrong. You allowed her to enter your life... You kissed her, you cared for her, you did all that a boyfriend would have done, and then it's obvious that you have to face such things... Anyways, it's just a kiss, forget it and avoid her...

'I don't want to hurt her..., but at the same time, I hate her...' I replied.

'You can't please everyone, so it's advisable to avoid her... The more you will think about her, the more trouble you have to face in future, as a friend this is my sincere advice'.

I disconnected her call and then thought for a while, just then my mom called me. I felt like telling her everything, and so I did. She also advised me not to talk to her. Now, having no choice I tried to forget her. I tried hard to get myself engaged in certain stuffs, but in the meanwhile, if I got some free time, her thoughts irritated me.

The next day, I thought of applying for new project, but when I came to office and tried to login in the system, it failed. Again, I had to struggle for a system; I asked people to allow me some time to check my mails on their system. In that process, some people showed that they were too busy, indirectly they avoided me. I felt very bad. Pooja helped me that time and allowed to use her system for hours. With time, she created a very positive image in my heart. I felt like helping her to get the things done. I felt good and I started respecting her innocence, I responded her calmly even when she asked me silly doubts or something else.

Devoid of my system, I started sitting there at Pooja's desk, after checking my mails and project, I used to let her to do the execution. I guided her practically how to do the things, then leaving her to monitor, I kept myself out of the place. Once when I returned to my place, she was talking to one of her friend, in the next cubicle. She was speaking in a very low voice, but I marked her expressions and got to know that she was doing mimicry of mine, in front of her friend. When I saw her, accidently caught her looking at me, and then she silently took her seat. Then I went near her, 'Is everything alright…?'

She nodded her head, just then her friend chuckled and said, 'she was telling that you are boring kind of a guy, she has never seen a smile on your face…'

I was tensed that someone was preaching me on smile. I gave an angry look, and in return she asked me to sit on the desk.

'Yaa, it's fine now… pull that chair, and be seated'.

I seated myself, her friend was still staring at us. Don't know exactly what she was about to do. She pulled one

Xerox sheet from her drawer and started sketching my image over the sheet. I felt as if she was trying to make fun of me, I became angry at one point of time, but while seeing her face, I didn't feel like shouting at her. All the while, when she was sketching my image; I was looking at her. I felt the beauty of her, she was so beautiful and cute that no one can show his or her anger on her. Her activities were too childish; it seemed to me she was a recent college pass-out.

After sketching, she held the sketch in front of me. It was so amazing, that being an artist; I felt that no way can I do better than her. That stupid anger was clearly visible on my face in the sketch. Suddenly, a smile came on my face.

I could feel that she was the one, who brought my lost smile back after long seven days. Just then, I saw Neha passing through the way. I silently walked to my cubicle. I knew that Neha must have felt bad, seeing me smiling but that was beyond my control.

Spending 9 hours of loneliness every day in office was not that easy. Pooja helped me to kill my time, by asking me doubts and in the phase of knowledge sharing also, she helped me indirectly to revise the things and get myself updated. But I tried my best to distant myself from her, as my heart was empty, and I wished not to take any risk. She used to ask me about my friends and with whom I take lunch, bla bla bla...

I never answered her satisfactorily; rather I tried avoiding her questions.

I felt dearth of stories to tell... hard to believe that once I shared every minute detail with one of my best friend, starting from the size of inners I wear to watching porn and all private things that a guy do. It's of no use now... Nothing

I had nothing more to share with someone and I wished not to face the same once again.

I never thought that I will have to pay the price for caring for someone…

Time comes in everyone's life when people make their way out, when they no longer need you. Talking about Varsha, when I raised my voice for a proper position in the project, she reacted, 'you tell me what deliverables have you given to the client, so that we can place you in a proper position? I don't feel whatever you did is enough…'

'Then why you made me to stay so long, in this project. At times, I have asked for release but you were not ready for that as at that time you wanted someone to work for you… And now as the project is coming to an end, you don't need my help any more, in order to avoid the situation you are telling me all this…', I whispered to myself. I messaged her, coming back to my cubicle,

'Yaa Varsha you could have told me all these things four months back…'

'It's quite understandable that you no longer need me that's why you are behaving like this…'

'Do you remember in March I talked with you regarding some other project where I was about to get billability right from day one, and you asked me not to go…'

'Now I reckon that I shouldn't have listened to you. Anyways, history keeps repeating who knows -someday some other person may face the same. A person is not a leader by birth, whatever he/she achieves is because of the dedication, love, and affection of each member.'

Both Ram and Varsha made me fool and I was the real fool, as I hoped for good from them. They told me – 'if we give you billability, we will be in trouble. Client will question us, 'how can you do that Ram, is Sid that capable enough to be on board?'

'No Client is a fool, every person has a sense that a new guy can come up-to some percentage of your expectation. And if you people give me billability now, I don't think they would question you all of a sudden; they would accept me as a new joinee. Even if that is the case then how people are billable from day one in other projects, I whispered to myself.

I was all alone walking in the campus. People in the surrounding seemed to be staring at me. The guard even looked at my I-card to check whether I belonged to the company or not.

I was back to the past, unable to think of the present or future. "No one is there with whom I can share.... all that I am undergoing because of them. These characters have changed my life. They gave me a clear picture – how people may behave so selfishly at times, without allowing the other person to know the conspiracy. How people can utilize you to fulfill their needs... "This is what I learned from the so called "SELFISH ASSHOLES".

Varsha may appear rude, but her intentions were good for others – that was the impression I had after the first altercation in the beginning. But I was wrong. Actually, she was clever. She knew very well to handle any scenario and after that incident, she might have concluded that – it was not going to work, behaving rudely with Sid. So, she played a trick – she might have not behaved_rudely since then, rather utilize me in different ways. All the while, she behaved normally, to make me believe that everything was all right. But in between that she was trying to make me fool.

Everyone has some requirements from others. Their requirements from me, were–

a) There were lot many works to do, and Sweety had to move to some other works. So, she needed me as a 'back-up'.

b) She told me that before Sweety moves to some other module, "make sure that you can handle her work." I tried more or less successfully, but at the end I found, she lied to me. Sweety was not moving anywhere. She did it purposefully, giving me a false hope.

c) Day by day, I was asking about my billing, she lied to me repeatedly that soon she would talk with Ram and close it. But she was informed well in advance that the project is going to end after 4 months, so it's not possible to give billability to me.

d) I asked her numerous times, about creating my account in the project, she lied to me all the way that it is processing, and they need some time to do it, giving me a false hope that she was trying to help me out.

e) They had hidden me from client. I was working all this time only as a backup. Even if I solved the issues, even if I had to answer the client's mail, she asked me to put Sweety and Mona's name under 'Regards'. I should have doubted at that time...

Everything was kept unknown to me, I came to know just one month before the project was about to end. Feeling restless, tired of justifying myself, tired of the loneliness.

My mind was blocked, unable to come up with ideas, 'what would be the next step? What am I supposed to do now?'

Meanwhile, I studied hard and tried for new projects. I kept myself engaged, to avoid loneliness stopping me, from moving ahead.

A week after…

I asked Ram to release me, as I already had the choice to choose from the two projects offered to me, with billability from day one. Ram discussed with Varsha and replied me, 'You have to wait for some more months, immediately I can't release you… It may hamper the deliverable'.

'Everything has some process; we need to follow it…' he added.

I whispered to myself – yaa everything has some process, first when I joined your project, I should have been given the NDA forms to sign, then my account was supposed to be created. After that, I should have been tagged as a billable resource. Once I am done with my KT, I should have been asked to work…

You selfish assholes have not followed a single right step that you should have followed before asking me to work for your project. I remained silent instead of kicking hard on your balls; I have given all my efforts in the keyboard to make your work done… Now you asking me, 'why I have not kicked your ass earlier…!'

The only answer now I can give is, there was someone to give you a good blowjob, so I didn't bother disturbing you. Now don't ask me, who was that…

I remembered Swami says, 'there is a lady behind every successful man, and also there is lady behind every worst scenario that happens in day to day life'. I agree to it…

I walked away from him, with anger and just then, I called my HR, without a second thought and informed him everything. He promised me to give release within a day, so I felt relaxed. Ram was unable to bear the shock that he got from the HR, the scolding he got from him. He asked to meet him, and so I went near him once again. He started shouting at me in harsh words,

'For your nonsense, why should I get scolding from someone?'

I remained silent all the while, and finally he did it, he released me, with a warning that, 'I'll see, how you will get into other accounts…? Now get lost from my ODC…'

Though his language was quite insulting, it didn't hurt me in anyway, as from a person and personality like him, what more one can expect…!

Confidently, I stepped out of the ODC. I told this to all friends and they got shocked listening Ram's reaction from me. Instead of giving me support, they questioned me, 'why he is doing all this with you yaar, what will be your next step now…?'

'Don't know, but if I'll be in trouble I'll make sure that I will put all of them in trouble… I have sufficient evidence against them, I have recorded the conversation of him, I have the mail of Varsha's torture and behavior towards me… Let me see truth wins, or power of someone's designation wins…!'

More than a week passed, without meeting Neha, or even talking to her. It was a Saturday morning. I woke up, put my lappy over my chest and I was going through the mails. Just then, I saw a mail from Neha, entitled as 'My first letter'.

<u>TWENTY THREE</u>

My eyes were over the body of the mail that started with a formal salutation…

'Hi Siddharth,

I think this is the only way to communicate with you, as you have blocked me on whatsapp and facebook. I cannot talk to you directly as I don't have guts to see the abhorrence for me in your eyes. So I thought of writing a letter for you. My objective is very clear. You are my BEST FRIEND. Let me first tell you the meaning of Best Friend in my point of view. My Best Friend is everything for me. I can share each and every single moment with him/her.'

The letter continued with different aspects of her thought and care for someone, which was obviously no one else, but 'I'…

I heard my roommates, calling me to the common room. When I went there, I saw two of my roomies were checking the crackers that they bought from the market last night for the Diwali festival. They were calculating the total price and maintaining the common copy, so that at the end of the month, everyone had to contribute their share for the same. Viren was moving there in a towel wrapped across his waist, brushing his teeth. The tap of the washroom was left open; water flowing through the pipe was also adding noise to background. Sumit, laying flat over the mattresses, Sahil kept his face over Sumit's shoulder and both of them were busy checking offers and doing online shopping. The atmosphere was like, they were in the mood of celebrating the special holiday with full of crackers and light. My presence over there was mere physical, mentally I was lost somewhere, may it was because of the project, or maybe something that I was unaware of… or may be it because of the letter that I received a couple of minutes back…

'I want to tell you that, I am really missing you very badly (as a best friend). Today when I woke up, and switched ON my phone, I saw you have blocked me on whatsapp. When I was travelling, I saw your flat, on the way to office. I missed you when I saw a young couple sitting on the seat next to me, both whispering. After reaching office, when Sanya called me, I crossed your cubicle to meet her; I once again missed you… She asked me about you, I was helpless on answer to her question, remained silent. Then you came near Trupti but you didn't look at me even once, I was expecting at least once you would glance at me… I miss you every day in Lunchtime and tea break. After going to my PG, usually I discussed about you with my roommates. Since last week, I am not doing so… Yesterday they asked me whether everything was fine between you and me. I remained silent…'

'No… I shouldn't think of it much… I should engage myself in different things…' I whispered to myself.

I joined my roomies in the shopping mall; we were shopping for the week. As usual, Viren opened the refrigerator, took a 300ml energy drink, and closed the same. The intention is that while shopping, he will consume and give a sip to all of us. And while we were done with the shopping, he will open some other refrigerator and put the empty bottle there. So that, it won't get reflected in the grocery bill. We moved to the next store to check spices and other consumables. People moving here and there, along with young couples were also shopping. The young girls were selecting the items and the boys were following them with a plastic trolley bag. I recalled the previous incident with Neha, and so the letter that I read in the morning continued flashing in my mind, where she said…

'Actually you were right, you told me not to expect from you, still I was expecting… I forced you to be with me all time, though you don't bother to…

From the day one -

1) You were never listening to me, I forced you to make me your friend.

2) Airport day, you ignored me giving priority to Rajesh. I should have understood from that day itself that you never cared for me…

3) At the free pool time, for small things I used to fight with you.

4) When we went on vacation to our hometown, I forced you to come to my house, but never ever you asked me to visit your house…

5) I didn't allow you to talk with anyone; I wanted you to be next to me, all the time… I forced you to listen

to me… I wanted you to do everything according to my wish…

6) The fact is that you never wanted to be with me, I forced you to show to be with me….

7) At last I started blackmailing you, telling that I may do harm to my life, and you will be responsible for that…. Then having no choice, you sacrificed yourself for me. You kissed me; you touched me…, just because I wanted you to do so…

I am feeling guilty for my deeds; I blackmailed you, and played with your innocence. But believe me I can't see hatred in your eyes… As I loved you, and always will…'

We all roommates were stepping down the shopping mall, my left hand being occupied with a heavy polythene bag, which was shared by Sumit. I saw a small child holding small polythene, which was tightly wrapped with a rubber towards the neck. The small polythene was full of water and a small golden fish was floating back and forth in the water. A person was holding the small girl over his shoulder. I stopped for a while, thinking of Neha. She told me one of her childhood incident. The incident was like this – She used to catch the small fish, that swam through the canal beside her road, near to her home. She used to wash those fish and put them in a small plastic jar. Her hobby was to collect a number of small fishes every day. One day she noticed that the container size was not enough for the grown up fishes. In one side of her garden, she dug deep to make a hole, so that she could put those jar full of fish with water in it. She did so, but one rainy day, the fishes flowed away with the mud water. She cried all the day, went on hunger strike, asking her dad to replace those with a number of golden fish. She was too childish, but giving care, love and life to a living creature showed the true child in her, as a child loves and cares without any reason, a true love without looking for anything in return…

I was in my thoughts, but I was not aware that already I have crossed the road with my roommates. I got diverted from my thought, when I heard a chorus song, by a group of eunuchs.

'Mere angne mein tumhara kya kaam hai… Jo hai naam wala wahi to badnaam hai…'

They were dancing on the side of the road. Life passed on… The characters around me were moving in their life. I got a call from Elina, she wished me 'Happy Diwali' and I reciprocated.

'Your sketch is selected by the exhibition board, to display the same in the upcoming art gallery exhibition and you are invited to Mumbai man', she informed.

'Thanks for good news…, ll love to be there…'.

'I'll send you the official details to your mail', she replied.

'Yaa sure…'.

'How is everything going…', she asked.

'Seems I am OK'.

'No… you are not, your voice says you are not OK…, maybe you are not comfy to speak out what your heart says, it's OK…, But don't lie to yourself…', she told.

'Sorry I am not getting you…', I asked.

'Young man, Even if you don't want to share your problem, but I am sure, something is there that is disturbing you…, that is coming out in your voice, Am I right…?', she asked.

'Maybe… you are…'

'Your sketch is beyond the imagination, it's beyond the vast sea with full of emotion. A wide space is there between the two, a space of freedom, space of flexibility, though they were quite close to each other, but they are not restricted to anything. When you restrict your mind, your relation starts taking a reverse direction'. Once again, the letter reminded me of Neha's emotion, her attachments for me…

'All my life so far, everyone has cared for me but never had I cared for anyone. You were the first person, whom I loved to care for… I agree that I am too possessive for you, but it is no way my intension is to affect your lifestyle. One week back, I realized my love was not enough to make you mine… However, do not know why I reacted that day, and asked you to be a part of my life…

I was afraid that someday you might leave me behind, so I did like that. But my love was no way a fake one, and I don't feel I did a big mistake loving you more than you deserve…'

I was cutting the vegetables into small pieces, over the chopping board. My earphone plugged into my ears, listening music at the same time helping my roommate in kitchen. Rajesh called me all of a sudden. I received the call, 'Neha called me to wish happy Diwali, and she asked me to wish you the same from her side… It seems she was quite depressed, she felt like she doesn't have a right to even wish you'.

'It's Ok…, reply her thank you from my side…' was my reply.

'You can call her and wish her naa…' he told.

'I won't…'

'Your wish… So… are you ready to blast crackers tonight…' he asked me.

'Not interested, however I'll love to capture the moment with my roomies, what's your plan…'

'It's wastage of money. I feel crackers should be preferably used only by children for fun, we as a responsible citizen should avoid polluting the atmosphere, so I stopped burning crackers long back...', he convinced me why he was not going to fire the crackers.

'Ok Sir..., I respect your thought..., but we can't stop people from celebrating the same, right...'

He agreed and I wished him once again, before disconnecting the call. Then a pop-up message flashed on my mobile. It was Sameer, who wished me, 'Happy Diwali...'

I thought of wishing him back, but once again, that day's incident came to my mind. Sameer warned me not to talk with Neha. Then I recalled Neha's conference call with Rajesh and Sameer, blaming me in front of them.

Neha's mail continues with...

'I did a big mistake, telling everyone regarding the incident; we could have solved it ourselves.

I did one more mistake; I questioned you that you have feelings for me..., though you do not have any...

I asked you why you cried for me, why at times you replied me, 'miss you' and 'love you'. Having no feelings, one should not type all this... But I was not sure at that time; you did all this forcefully just to make me happy... Really, I am sorry Sid...'

I got a call from Swami, while taking rest on my bed, 'Hey man, tomorrow morning do you have any plan?'

'As such there is no plan' I replied.

'Then come to BTM side park naa... I and my roommate will be there. We will go for morning walk...' he told.

I gave him a word that I would be joining them the next day.

TWENTY FOUR

I messaged Swami and walked to the mentioned park. I reached there but I didn't find any of them. Then I felt like sitting on a long wooden chair. I called them to enquire their whereabouts; he received and replied, that they were going to take another ten minutes to reach there, expecting me to wait.

Then I saw Neha sitting alone, at a distance... She was sitting opposite to me, and the physical gap was too small than the mental gap... I felt like walking near her... Just then, the letter written by her, pulled me from taking a step forward..., 'I am not expecting you to forgive me for my mistake, but still I would wait for my Sid, to return to my life, at least as a friend... You have become a part of my life, I cannot live without you yaar...

With no time, I felt like I was sitting next to her. I felt as if not only the letter of hers, but she was whispering into my ears, 'Mu seiyi dina jaye wait karibi jou dina mate Mo Sid (I'll be waiting till the time, when my Sid...)

1) Asiki kahiba sshhh shhhh kana bhala, khusi?? Kana karuchu?? (...will come and whisper shh shhh... everything is fine, happy?? What are you doing?)

2) lunch re pachariba, kana khaibu..chiii kuti khdya guda, sepate dekhiba... (...will ask what I'm going to chose for lunch, horrible food is there..., let's check that side...)

3) Sid kahiba - e tu ete close aseni kahuchi...(will tell oye, don't try to flirt with me, maintain distance)

4) Jou dina asiki se mate kahiba ki mo place ta Swami nei jiba. (Someday Swami will take my place...)

5) Jiye asiki kahiba to bahaghara re mu tate jungle book debi(...will come near me and tell, in your marriage I'll present you the 'JUNGLE BOOK' series).

You were the best part of my life; I do not regret making friends with you...

I will wait for you till the end of my life...

This time I won't force you to come near me, take your own time.

If you feel you can return me my best friend, just type me a small – Hi... or GM or GN... I won't force you to type the complete words, as I don't want to waste your time for me...

I Love You (As a best friend).

Missing you very badly...

Waiting for my Sid...'

The letter was finished, but it seemed something was there left still unspoken...

When i saw her sitting sad with a hope that everything will be OK someday, I felt bad. I mean the girl who used to flourish my days with her cutest of smiles and naughtiest of activities was sitting there alone in despair. I decided to go and talk to her. This time my love and affection for her preceded over my ego and anger. 'Alone...! Sitting here alone or you came with someone...' I asked her.

'I don't have alternatives like you...' she replied very softly.

'Still you are blaming me..., I hate you...' I was about to move from the place, just then she replied, 'I am not blaming you, I am blaming Simran... She is trying to come in between us...'

I was surprised, 'what is she making up now...', but I remained silent to listen her this time.

'I saw you pinged her, but she minimized the chat box, seeing me. Don't know why...? Now days you people have become best friends, I shouldn't tell all this to you... The thing is I felt bad, when she was trying to hide your conversation. Maybe you people were discussing something secret...'

'You could have asked me, if you have any doubts. You should not try to know the things, checking someone's personal chat box. You should trust me that I can't hide anything from you...' I replied.

'I trust you the most, now tell me... to whom all you told about me and that night's incident...?'

'To all..., my parents, my friends...' I replied.

She got surprised for a while, felt very bad, it appeared on her face.

'I am serious Sid, are you sure...?' she asked to confirm.

'Yaa, they are parts of my life. I can't hide the things, at least when I face the trouble…., I felt that they should be informed about it, so I did it…' I added.

'Fine, Simran and Swami also know about this…?' she enquired.

'Yaa, Swami knows the things overly, but….'

'Simran…?'

'She knows everything…' I told her.

'You have created a nice image of mine, in front of others…, she cried. 'I became a joke in everyone's eyes… Nice gift you gave me in return of my love for you… Thanks yaar…'

'Thanks for informing Sameer and asking him to warn me not to come in your life… If you have felt so uneasy in my presence, you could have told me directly, was it necessary for you to inform him… So nicely, you blamed me… that I did injustice with you…' I replied.

'Sorry for that, but… how can you…' she was about to question me, just then I overlapped against her voice, saying, 'I can't answer injustice with justice… I am a very wrong person, so better forget me…'

I stepped one step forward, just then she told, 'I can't forget you…, want you in my life…'

'A 'WRONG' can't step parallel to a 'RIGHT'. And we individual always love to choose the person who is 'RIGHT' for us', I tried explaining her.

'I would love to choose 'WRONG', if the person is my best friend, who is 'WRONG In ALL SENSE'.

I could not stop myself from turning to her side, I looked at her. Maybe after two long weeks, we both were seeing each other. She kept staring at me. We both kept standing for a while, without speaking anything. Just then she raised her hand forward, asking my hand in return to get me back in her life. Emotions started flowing once again. I couldn't stop myself from accepting her offer of being a good friend to her. Immediately after shaking hands, I pulled my hand back, tears rolled down my cheek. She stood up and holding my hand tightly, she said 'Let's forget all that please..., I want you to return me my Sid please...'

'Can you trust me, once again...? Won't you feel guilty accepting me with my wrongs...?' I whispered.

'No... never...' she hugged me tight, I rubbed my hand on her hairs , pat on her shoulder and said sorry for making her cry.

"Not a problem, If you are there i can bear anything. And by the way if you have watched 'Rockstar' movie and not in a hurry, could you please hug me tightly" she said while sobbing.

That bought a smile on my face and the little left overs of anger also vanished completely. I could feel that its the same Neha who is naughty and always mad at me. Just then, she saw someone and smiled loudly. When I turned back, I saw Swami and his roommate Raj.

'Aise kyun dekh raha hain... (Why are you giving me such a strange look...?)', she asked Swami.

'Mujhe laga ki tu kiss karne jaa rahi thi...' (I felt that you were going to kiss him...)

We all burst out laughing... LOL...

Neha – kyun, KISS kyun karun, mein use KILL karne jaa rahi thi... (Why I will kiss him? I was going to kill him...)

Swami put his hand over my shoulder, and asked her, 'ruko ruko ab saadi karoge Sid se, yaa aapki family jahan shadi fix karegi wahan…? (Will you marry Sid, or will you marry according to your parent's choice….)

'Mein ek bahut rich person se saadi karungi, bahut sari dreams hain meri…. (I'll marry to a very rich person, as I have a lot of dreams…)', Neha told.

'Kyun ladkyian hamesa esa soochte hain ki rich wala admi se hi saadi karenge…! (Why girls used to think always that they should marry a very rich person…!), Swami commented and everyone laughed once again.

'Chalo dono esi bahane smile to kiye…' (Good, at least you both smiled now…)

It was quite understandable that, Swami had planned and called Neha and me to the same place, so that we could solve the issue and become friends once again. Swami, Sanya, Rajesh, and all other say the same: If she is there with me, her happiness is at the top level…

But my family members were a bit annoyed with her, at times they enquire about her and warn me, not to get close to her…

We gossiped for a couple of minutes; I saw smile on her face.

Then I got a call from Dev. I turned back to receive the call, they were busy gossiping among themselves. I received the call. Dev shouted over phone, 'Darling I am coming over to Bangalore. We will have fun…'

'Koi naya maal market me launch hua hai kya, milne aa raha hai tu…?'(Is there any new hot girl you are hooked up with now, and so you are coming…)

Swami was starring me, it seems he was listening to my conversation.

'Hmm... This time, I promised to myself to be with you... I have a good collection of adult stuff, we can check together. I am sure; you won't have checked those...'

He was confident that in exploring and downloading crazy stuffs, he was the one who would come first in the competition among us.

'From now onwards, I want three things in my life apart from my family, my friend Sid, cigarette, and wine', he added.

'So you won't marry...' I asked.

'Maybe NO...' he replied.

'Don't have the power to make someone happy...?' I criticized. Once again, Swami gave me a strange look, it seemed he was thinking that I am planning something crazy.

'I have the power, the desire... But No marriage, No girlfriend stuff... When I feel like doing something crazy, I can pay and get a girl in bed... No emotions, no argument, and no expectations, just I want to fuck and fulfil my desire, that's it...! Darling, there is nothing like 'LOVE', everything revolves around the four lettered word – 'FUCK', understood...?' he explained naughtily.

'Yeah bro... Such a nice concept! May I know the source?' I asked.

'It's my original thought... leave it, my interview is there next week. So, I am coming, plan to drink with me this time...' he told me.

I smiled and was about to reply him, just then I saw Neha near me. I remained silent; she snatched the phone and started talking with him. Given a chance, Swami asked me, "It seems you are planning to have a visit to that area once again". I understood immediately what he wanted to say, it seemed from our phone conversation, he was in a misconception that I was planning to join someone in the red light area.

'Have you forgotten that day's incident, it's our fate that Neha helped us…', Swami added.

'Hey you are telling something about me….', Neha enquired, hanging off the phone.

'Boys talk, we can't share yaar…', Swami replied.

'You have to, as a friend I deserve to know Swami. Now you should tell me…', Neha asked.

"I was reminding him about that eve's incident, he and MMS were standing on the road, bare foot, with banyan and jeans. It's our fate that you saved us", Swami replied.

She was too excited to know, as many times, though she enquired I had avoided answering her. Now she demanded and Swami started telling the whole story of the red light area. She looked at my face, and suddenly burst out laughing.

She was happy, chuckling, commenting, and feeling pity on me. But still she reacted in a positive way, as the fact was quite open now – even if she gets to know something bad about me, it would hardly matter. So I felt relaxed, as if I have given life to someone… I informed her about the invitation to Mumbai - that my sketch got selected by the exhibition board, and she wished me a good luck.

'Remember you fought with me, for that sketch...'

'Now too I want to fight with you. I have not told me all this, when you submitted, for whom you were doing, I was n't informed anything... that too when I am your best friend...', she demanded.

'Sorry yaar, you didn't gave a scope to speak about this...'

'It's OK... Now you give us treat...', she demanded.

With time, everything became fine. I got tagged in a new project and along with me two other freshers, named Smitha and Sashi joined me. Smitha, the short-tempered girl used to sit in front of the system all the time – it appeared that she loved the system more than anything else. That was her first impression on me. Soon, she made her way to get the things done in time. I found a bit difficulty to cope up with certain things. Then she helped me. Though she shouted at me sometimes, she said 'sorry' also. Everything and everyone's behavior in the new project was far better than the previous one.

As usual, Truth alone Triumphs, so was in my case... 'Satymeva Jayate'.

Yes, I believe that a man succeeds completely, when he is truthful. And we should have the guts to face the truth, even if we have to face maximum difficulties...

TWENTY FIVE

Few days later…

I, Neha, Sanya and Dev were invited for the birthday treat by Sameer. Two days back we celebrated his birthday with GPL and canvassing his face with all kind of wild art. Dev came to Bangalore two days back for an interview call.

We all met near Silk Board junction which was very crowded at that evening time. From there we were supposed to go to Bakasur Restaurant. One had to rush pretty fast in order to cross the road. We got small window of time in the traffic flow, so we all rushed towards the other end of the road; but then I noticed Neha stuck in the middle of the road. When I turned back I saw Sameer still standing at the other side of the road. Neha went back to him, concerned for the fear expressed on his face. I could see a hint of frustration on his face, a bit of anger. I thought may be Neha didn't hold his hand while crossing that's why he was angry. Then again I thought, 'Why would a man be so possessive about it?'

Neha stood with him until the signal came green. Then he came forward and I noticed that he was unable to walk properly. From there we took one auto to the restaurant. I felt guilty of pitying on his poor situation.

We all had our dinner there. We all wished him once again and gifted him.

After the dinner, we all danced but I saw Sameer was in pain while dancing. Neha was unaware of this. He then excused us and went back and sat on the sofa. We were still dancing. Everyone was happy except Sameer. May be he was thinking himself incompetent enough to make Neha happy. May be he was thinking he can't give all the things to her that she needed in her life. When we all came back exhausted, I realized that Sameer obviously felt humiliated for not been able to fit into the group because of his physical condition. He ordered some drinks that were eventually shared by Dev and Neha along with him. Sanya had a mouthful of it, but I strictly denied.

'What man, you can taste it, at least for me...' Sameer requested.

'He won't have it; even I failed to make him my drink partner, hehe...' Dev chuckled.

'Okies..., you are the odd one out of this group then, let's think something for you...', he thought for a while and then came up with the concept of Bottle shoot game, in which everyone agreed and I too, though forcibly.

'Guys, all you have to do is spin the bottle which involves either revealing the dreadful truth of your life or doing a dare – something stupid. Everyone will be given a choice to choose either of the option, if the mouth of the bottle faces towards him or her'. We were seated around a round circular table. The game started.

In the first spin, the bottle stopped spinning facing Dev. Given a choice, he chose 'Dare'.

Everyone remained silent for a while, then Sameer assigned him the task to make me drink, 'as a good friend of Sid, you can do this Dev, C'mon...do it'.

Dev knew very well that I won't like all this type of fun and so he refused to do the task, but Sameer and Neha forced him to do. With no choice left, he forced me to have it. I closed my eyes for a couple of second; he made me drink more than half of the bottle. At first, I didn't realize, but with time I could feel that I was not normal. The game continued...

In the second round, it was Sameer's turn and he opted for truth. I asked him, 'what if some day someone kisses your girlfriend, and you come to know later on...?'

'I won't resist, I would feel very bad. Especially when that someone comes out to be someone whom I trust very much. But in your case I trust you Sid... and I feel she is safe, if she is with you...,'replied Sameer.

Now once again the bottle moved and it was Neha. Dev asked her, 'if given a choice between Sid and Sameer, whom will you choose?

Neha's instant answer was – Of course Sameer...

Dev – Then why you kissed Sid...?

'Don't know what happened to me that day... Maybe on that moment I was wrong. But, I love Sid as a small baby of mine... It was the love for the baby in front of me. Also, Sid's lower lip attracted me to kiss him there. It was just a kiss; it was not a mistake. I would never consider that a mistake; never…, those three nights were as fancy as velvet, as smooth as a flower, and the smell fascinates me still; and the moments were worth living…

She cried and laughed, it appeared that the drink opened her up. Sameer was looking at me, with anger and hatred, at the same time; he was concentrating on the words of Neha, 'It's true that I can't see anyone with him, I feel it's me who has all the rights over him. For me, the first priority always has been Sid, but I could do nothing, I failed in the race of love, and everything else. As always, he is the one, who won at the end of every game, today also…'

She cried, a bit emotional. Dev was looking at me, I felt like speaking, 'I liked your presence; I will love to keep you as a friend in my life. A person will be definitely very lucky to have a girl like you in his life…'

Tears rolled down from my eyes, Sameer and everyone else were staring at me. Just then I laughed aloud and said, 'He he… nice acting I did, right… yeh… don't cry yaar(to Neha), I can't act anymore… I only knew all these days what difficulties; I faced to make you happy. Every time I have to think what kind of act, I have to perform in order to make you happy… Now spare me yaar, I cannot be a joker of the stage, all the time for you…'

'Thanks yaar, for tolerating my nonsense all these months… and yaa you didn't make me feel also, that you were acting with me, though you don't love me… You should get 'popular new comer award' for your live acting. Can you tell me, whether everything was scripted earlier…?' she cried.

'I am sorry, when a person knows his destination, he, or she do the things in a scripted way obviously. And it's true that you were not of my kind…, so we used to fight in a regular interval', reply came from me, consuming a sip of alcohol from the glass.

'So what… we used to fight with each other…, at the end of the day we were together, right?'

'No… I tried to pity you, but that was not love, why don't you believe… Sidharth is such a character that neither he can love someone, nor he deserves someone's love. He just know how to convince a girl to sleep with him, he never cares for emotions and all that nonsense. All he wants from a girl is sex. Body contact of a girl fascinates him as he is fond of porn videos…' I was telling in front of everyone with full of emotions, in me. Sanya pressed my hand in a sense of concern, asking me to stop vomiting all that crap.

'Please don't speak a word more, please yaar…', even Neha tried to stop me from speaking but I continued, 'I am a fluctuating asshole, who don't believe in love and emotions, all I want is a good count of girls around me. My mind frequently fluctuates, and if by chance, you get some guy like me, as your life partner, and then you are gone. Daily you will be crying and struggling to get his love, as it will be shared by a good number of girls…'

'How long can you do all this…. for max 4-5yrs, then you will be mine at the end of fifth year, when you will get bored of all these stuffs, certainly you would require someone's shoulder to rest on. Then I will be there, waiting all these years to get my love back'.

'By then I will be old, unable to satisfy your physical desires…' I replied stupidly.

'Even I don't long for it; I just want to love you as you were…'

'No…I know this very well if I would be there with you, you would change me entirely like you… Someday I will cry, longing for someone else's love… I don't want to get myself involved in all these stuffs yaar… Can you do a favor for me…? Can you just help me to return me my old Sid…?' I asked her.

'It took me a year's time to make a small place in your heart, but a small moment is enough for you to throw me out of your life… Every time it happened, I used to return to you, but never had you tried. So, Sid do you want me to insult you, to shout at you, to blame you… so that you can run away from me, so that you can inculcate hate for me… I don't think all this is necessary, you are free now… Look your hands are free now; no one is holding your hands…'

I turned back and just walked away, saying - I hate you yaar, don't ever try to flirt with me… If you do so, my middle finger is exclusively there for you…

I left the place, knowing that if I would be there she would inculcate more love for me, which was there for me in her heart, long back. Speaking to myself 'It's already a gap or misconception that has been created in Sameer's mind, I don't want to break his trust, I don't want to make my friendship being proved false.'

It's not just about you and your wish; you do not breathe in this world just for yourself. Your atmosphere, you background live with you; it should grin with you when you open your lips to give a wide smile… Everything may wind-up some day, but things, which will long when you are gone, are the trust, belief, the true love, and respect we had for our near and dear ones.

I heard someone calling from back, on the lonely road, the voice hit my ear, 'hai ruk...Bangalore ke ped rukha sukha hogaya hai yaar, chal paani deke ayenge, after all we are responsible citizen of our country naa....

Once again we were urinating near a tree, this time I realized he was slow, 'abe... tera pipe junk hogaya hai kya, itna slow kyun...?'

'kya kare, ab saath me ladki nahi hai to khud karna padta hai, aur frustration ke bajaye kabhi kabhi junk lagjaata hai... par awesome yaar tera pipe to frustration ke baad bhi bahut acha kaam kar raha hai be, rent pe lagayega...?', he chuckled.

I was still standing without replying to him, he added, 'don't worry... you are not alone, I am there with you and you know a competition can take place only with a minimum of two people in...'

'Competition...!', I stared at him.

'I have one idea. We can bed two girls and give a try... Let's see whose stamina is more...!'

Idiot he is...! I knew that he was trying to see smile on my face... He was trying to bring me those old days back..., where we used to compete but life was something else at that time. Even in the failure, life hopes for a better future..., which was no longer the same.

I know it's not that easy to breathe the life of the old Sid once again... It's not that easy to walk without her, it's not that easy to live without love... But I'll try to fly alone in my sky, I'll try to explore the new challenges ahead for me...

Friends... it was just a kiss... but it's hard to convince my heart, as it says - a kiss is always a kiss, you can't ignore it... It can be a 'feeling in the open air'. It can be a trust and hope for the future of every relationship. Neha was the one, who enlightened me how to live not for oneself, but for others.

She was the one, who loved this idiot, unconditionally. Definitely I would miss her in all small things – may it be while travelling in bus, may it be while having lunch, or shopping or while walking alone on the road, her fight, her anger, her affection, her hug, her kiss…

I'll try to love, even more than her… so that I will earn some day the love of my would-be, I'll try to fall for her, I'll cry for her… and hope I will prove myself strong enough to love someone and to be loved. I'll try my best to live the life that Neha has lived. I would love to step forward in the path, she has shown me…'

<u>EPILOGUE</u>

After a month…

Good processions of sick and scratched were coming in and stretchers were dragged every now and then. Nurses, doctors along with common people were running here and there in a hurry. Some were getting impatient and crying aloud and some were trying to make the others stand. The background itself was quite disturbing, with the seriousness and people's emotions, care and fear of losing their near and dear ones. I was standing in one corner of the Apollo hospital corridor, recalling the stories that I heard while the doctor was discussing with the surgeon, 'Disappointing! I don't want to discourage the guy but I am helpless… Blood clot in his brain has stopped the normal blood flow; it may lead to the death of the cells. His immune system has already weakened due to the large consumption of alcohol and the lower part is not responding to any kind of drugs… I am afraid, chances of his survival is dim… We can't risk an operation without his family member's consent'.

I was thinking about Neha, feeling bad for her, when she just stepped into the corridor. As soon as she saw me, she came running towards me. Holding me tight, she wept. She was quite broken, having seen the condition of the patient in the ICU.

I tried to soothe her. Gently tucking her strand of hair that fell on her face behind her ear, I was about to ask what had transpired. As if she sensed that, she started all by herself.

"After that round table day I don't know what happened to him but he started behaving weird. He must have thought that his physical unfitness might be a barrier in our relationship. He expressed his disgust when he said he was unable to cross the road like other normal people, when people were dancing and enjoying, while he watched them helplessly. He felt humiliated with the course of events that followed. Once he was back home, he got his medical check up done and was ready to risk any operation inspite of the doctors being against it; just to compete in a battle that he might never win. His parents tried their best to convince him too, but he was far from being convincible.

He fought with me everyday. He got addicted to alcohol since then. Yesterday he wanted me to accompany him for a long drive at 1 in the morning when the condition of his leg was far from worse; of course I refused. Later I learnt that he got drunk and drove his bike in the middle of the night. He was under the influence of alcohol, so he was far from being normal. Suddenly he lost control of his bike and hit a speeding truck that was approaching him from the opposite direction. The bike skid off the road, he fell at a distance and his cell phone got disconnected. It was only today morning that I got to know that the traffic police admitted him, and I informed you soon after. His family might be here any moment. Hope everything will be fine. Sameer....she said and let her thoughts wander.

I remembered the truck accident that Dev and I met with, in Cuttack.At that moment, I thought, I was going to breathe my last – I felt death so close to me. We both fell off his bike and were about to be crushed under the truck. I had closed my eyes… I felt the same here. A moment of carelessness may take your life…!

Sameer was resting in the hospital bed in the ICU. Occasionally he blinked his eyes, but that was very rare. Neha and I were waiting outside; I tried to pacify Neha as best as I could. I don't know if it was real concern for Sameer or it was just to soothe Neha.

The Nurse appeared in front of us with a doctor's prescription list, asking us to purchase the same from the nearest medicine store. I asked Neha to be in the waiting room, while I rushed to get the medicine. As soon as I came back, I didn't find her in the waiting room. I ran to the ICU room, through the glass window I saw three to four persons standing near the doctor and crying. I searched for Neha and entered inside the room, Neha turned to my side and started crying. From the conversation of doctor and the other persons standing there, I came to know that they were the relatives and parents of Sameer, and have arrived a couple of minutes back.

From the scenario, I realized Sameer was no more with us. He had left us. I knew that if they come to know that she is Neha, they may create a scene unnecessarily. I asked Neha to move out of the room, and we stepped towards the waiting room. She put her head on my shoulder and started crying like a baby, I was helpless. I was afraid that Neha is not that matured enough to take this in ease; I was sure she might do something bad to herself. So I tried to be with her...

Two incidents have brought a great turning point in my life: Accident and Kiss. The truck accident that Dev and me, faced couple of years back, made us closer to each other. And this accident of Sameer, forced me to get close to Neha emotionally.

The sky was reddish and I felt the wondrous effect of lightning striking the cloud with its huge roar, have torn the darkish sky to parts. We were walking towards the main gate of the hospital to take an auto. With no time, rain droplets started falling evenly all over. Still we were standing near the security room, next to the hospital gate as auto was not available there, maybe due to the bad weather condition. I got drenched in the rain, and the drops of rain made its way from my forehead to mouth, my lips trembling and mouth getting unacknowledged taste of salt.

The tears I had so long controlled finally rolled down my cheeks. I held her wet hands; the small droplets of water over her hand slipped through. She turned to look at me, her eyes wet. She tried to wipe my tears with her hand, wanting me to regain my composure – lest it might not be too much for her to bear, anymore.

"What was my fault, Sid?", she asked me, her tone filled with pain.

'To love someone, to live for someone, giving hope to someone or doing something unconditionally for someone, who means the world to you... Look at me now, where do I stand, I have lost everything. I presume this was my destiny after all...'

'You have not lost anything Neha, rather you gained so much...I never respected you equally even when I knew you were right and you rightfully deserved. Knowing that what you have done in this iniquity of life is what I could have never been able to do nor could have achieved. I respect your hope, your unconditional love and care for me and others'.

'Girl, I know it's not at all easy to live two different dreams for 2 different people at the same time. But you did it with all dedication and without any bias; a 'hope' for Sameer and a loving heart for me', I whispered to myself...

I was unable to contain myself. I wanted to apologize and say that I love her – but I was unsure, if I could do justice to her faith or not..., whether I could bring a new dawn in her life or not...! I was unsure of accepting her as my soul mate, but my heart yearned for it. At that moment I gave her a light hug out of love and kissed her forehead. 'Everything will be all right, Neha', I said slowly.

I wiped her tears and bid her goodbye. She turned around and started walking slowly, her half drenched dupatta was brushing the ground. I felt as if everything around me happened in a slow motion. I could literally see the droplets falling from the dark sky were hitting the ground and challenging it to hit back but everything was silent. The only sound I could here was the sound of the water drops.

Wind was blowing along with the dust of the rain
Though I can't cage the wind, I can cage the pain...
In my heart, or I can let it go along with the passing train

I felt numb; my eye movements began to wane
Nights of the velvet, for sure I want in life again....
And can't let this affair of heart to be in vain
So, with a broken heart I took her name...

"Neha, I have one...".

She turned back, interrupted in between and said,
"Some other day Sid!"

'But JUNGLE BOOK is out of stock yaar..., Sorry...', in
a very low tone, I murmured.

Listening to this she smiled, saying 'Idiot'.

I thanked God, for returning the cute smile on her face.

With a smile I cogitated 'Given a chance, I would like
to kiss the destiny for bringing me the unexpected journey
of love and relationship... Moments that I shared with Neha
were still afresh in my sweetest corner of memories. The
emotions that I used to consider as 'dusts' were the ones
to give me comfort of softness and warmth as the 'Velvet',
when I was drenched, cold and alone. The unpleasant and
pleasant of nights that I had with her were the ones which
showed me the new direction to the new dawn that was
about to be written in the horizon of my life'.

Acknowledgements

I would like to express my heartfelt thanks:

- God, for HIS warm blessings and making me capable enough to pen my words on paper.
- My family, for their never-ending support and belief they have on me.
- Sumit Mishra, the main editor of my book; whose untiring efforts made this book happen. Right from reading the draft full of errors to improvising it – his contribution is undoubtedly cherished and acknowledged.
- Poonam Gupta, my associate editor of this book, whose encouragement made me come up with my work…
- Rajesh Kumar, Devansh Gupta and Asit Kumar Mohanty – my creative editors and Preetisnigdha Mishra, my first reader and critic.
- My publishing Company Partridge India and my publishing consultant Nelson Cortez and Gemma Ramos, for providing me a platform to share my thoughts.

- My best friends, Avinandan, Liptakant, Rajesh, Manish, Sarada and my teammates Alok Patel, Yasmin, Radha Pavani – thank you for your support guys!
- Rohan Anurag, and Nitesh kumar for composing and directing a promotional song 'Zindegi meri samander koi'(Available in youtube: Zindegi meri samander koi)
- Shilpa N Vaddi for sketching out few of the key moments (placed in the book).
- Someone 'special' – the very reason the book has come into existence.

Last but not the least a big Thank you to all my wonderful readers out there. Your suggestions and feedback is highly appreciated.

I hope a long way to go with you people in future. Thank you all once again…

<u>About my editors:</u>

Sumit Mishra:

An Engineering graduate, worked in Wipro Technologies. A reader, always open for good discussions on social issues and literature, along with taking initiatives for social cause. Favourite past time is enjoying long long, sometimes non-sense discussions with friends in a dhaba/tea stall. Pursue painting, writing, and reading along with the professional endeavors. His own line on life: *"Hum jahan baithenge mehfil vahan jam jayegi, hum kisi mehfil ke mufliso-hairan nahin"*

Poonam Gupta:

An Engineer by profession, did her schooling from Auxilium Convent School, Dumdum and graduated from the Heritage Institute of Technology, Kolkata. Presently working with Wipro Technologies, Bangalore. Favorite pastime includes reading books, listening to music, and travelling.

Her views on the book:

A terrific read! This book has a perfect blend of emotions and drama. It primarily focusses on IT professionals, challenges at work place and their messed up lives. It also highlights the unsafe environment for children in, and as well as outside school premises. The book has many twists and turns which is sure to make the readers glued to it!

Photography by Asit Kumar

About the Author

A resident of Bhubaneswar (Odisha), after pursuing his Master degree, shifted to Bangalore starting his professional career in Wipro Technology. He spends his leisure time in photography, sketching, reading spiritual books, writing screenplay, dialogue, and creating storyboards.

Deepak's writings are inspired by real life characters and more focused on true incident/happenings. Here in this novel, it's focused on corporate atmosphere, friendship and the basic lifestyle of an IT professional, whose calendar month is comprised of 8 days (weekends) only, where he sees life inside the four walls of his room.

You can get in touch with Deepak via:

Facebook: www.facebook.com/Deepak Ranjan
Facebook Photography page: www.facebook.com/Dr's Photography
Promotional Song: www.youtube.com/Zindegi meri samander koi
Email: dmotionp@gmail.com/ dbehera548@gmail.com